A Graveyard
Visible

A Graveyard
Visible

Steve Conoboy

LODESTONE
BOOKS

Winchester, UK
Washington, USA

First published by Lodestone Books, 2018
Lodestone Books is an imprint of John Hunt Publishing Ltd., Laurel House, Station Approach,
Alresford, Hants, SO24 9JH, UK
office1@jhpbooks.net
www.johnhuntpublishing.com

For distributor details and how to order please visit the 'Ordering' section on our website.

Text copyright: Steve Conoboy 2017

ISBN: 978 1 78535 668 1
978 1 78535 669 8 (ebook)
Library of Congress Control Number: 2017931214

A CIP catalogue record for this book is available from the British Library.

Design: Stuart Davies

Printed and bound by CPI Group (UK) Ltd, Croydon, CR0 4YY, UK

We operate a distinctive and ethical publishing philosophy in
all areas of our business, from our global network of authors to
production and worldwide distribution.

For Karen, the one true love of my life, and brightest star in my sky.

For Erin and Lucy, my daughters, with a whole world ahead of them, a world that needs their light.

1

There's a graveyard visible from his bedroom window and it grows a little bigger every day. On the hillside it lurks, lurching over the rise and disappearing beyond it, bound by the iron ribs of rusting railings. This graveyard is drawing breath, and ribs are flexible. They expand. It's bigger today than it was yesterday. Not by much, but it's bigger.

Caleb hates it. He hates a lot of things, and he hates the graveyard most of all.

Sometimes he thinks the tombstones could be the teeth of some huge underground monster, biting through the tough ground with its slow, ancient mouth. He imagines its fat tongue, calloused with the passing of ages, licking the underside of the ground where mourners kneel with their flowers and tears, desperate to taste them, hungry for their misery. Other times those stones are the brittle fingernails of a surfacing demon, digging its way into our world, consumed by its lust for hot blood. On less imaginative days, those stones simply are what they are: markers of the dead. Here lies so-and-so, died of natural causes. Here lies another, killed in an unfortunate accident. And yet another, sinister circumstances. And another. Another.

Caleb's mother lies up there in her own cold hole, up there with all the other dead, up there amongst the flowers.

He watches a spot not far from her grave, a collection of blurry scratches smudged by thin, damp shards of rain. It's useless to squint through the watery slashes assaulting his window, but he does anyway, trying to count the living souls all the way over on Daisy Hill. There aren't many mourners. He would guess that there are fewer than ten. Weather does not normally keep the bereaved from a freshly dug grave, so Caleb assumes that the deceased was not widely liked, and not important enough for people to show their face for the sake of appearances. Maybe nine, maybe eight, maybe seven souls to remember and mark the passing of an existence. So few to signify something as great as the end of a life. Some of them might only be there out of a sense of duty. The rest? Will the memories they keep be good or bad? The bad ones hold tighter, Caleb knows.

But they all go eventually. Time sees to that.

It's not the first time he's seen such a pitiful turnout. It's the third time in a week. One is sad. Three is odd.

It shouldn't be too hard to find the new grave. Should be pretty obvious. A fresh mound of earth, a stone he hasn't seen before.

Caleb needs to go now. Rain won't harm him. He won't notice it much. And it'll be gone soon, pushed back by the ceaseless summer sun. Every day is the same routine: bright mornings warming quickly, then clouds bundle together for the downpour, then sunshine steams it all away. Every day. The same.

Except, perhaps, up there on Daisy Hill, something different is happening.

He'll stop in the garage on his way out to find a tape measure.

2

But first there is a sigh from his father. It is omnipresent, that sigh. It precedes everything his father says, it accompanies everything Caleb does. No mere exasperation, this. It is resignation that he must speak to the boy again. 'Are you really that dumb?'

Caleb can't remember the last time he referred to this man as 'Dad'. It's a word that seems to imply a closeness that lies cold and eaten by worms. A vague grunt is the most Caleb can muster – a sound that commits to nothing. It doesn't matter what his response is. It will always be wrong.

'If you hadn't noticed, it's pissing down,' says Father, granite-face ghastly in laptop-glow.

'I noticed,' says Caleb, pulling on first his coat, then his least-favourite baseball cap.

The keyboard taps sound hollow-flat in the quiet living room. 'So it doesn't matter to you that no normal person would go out in that?'

There's a whole bunch of people out there, is what Caleb can't be bothered to say. A whole bunch of not-normals. 'I've got stuff to do,' he mumbles, and it is a pain to him that between his bedroom and the outside world there exists this, the rest of the house. Passing through these rooms is nothing but a grey misery.

Father shakes his head like he's never heard anything so disappointing, and Caleb waits, but there's only another one of those sighs, and doesn't it pull at that place near the top of his lungs and the base of his throat, that pressure pocket where raw anger bubbles?

There's nothing more to be said here. As always. So Caleb goes out into the rain.

3

Drenched and breathy, he arrives too late. He's on the opposite side of the road as a pair of estate cars, one black, one blue, pull out of the northern gates, leaving brief thick tracks on the slick tarmac. Rain makes the windscreens hazy, obscuring details of the sombre suits within. One car turns left, the other goes right, and the rain washes the tracks away. He feigns nonchalance, not certain why, feeling only that he should. He acts like he was walking up this path all along, past the graveyard with no interest in it, until both cars are gone from sight Then his heels squeak in a slippery about-turn, and he jogs into the graveyard. There's an urgent blip to his pulse, a thrum of anxiety, like he knows he's doing something wrong, like the mourners might decide to come back.

'Shut up, stupid,' he spits at himself. Past the wrought-iron gates he goes. Between the twin chapels that face dawn and dusk respectively. Along the central avenue, then up the steadily rising hill. He flits along pathways he's followed a hundred times and more, going off-gravel for short cuts, kicking up mud and never once setting foot on a grave, never disturbing a flower. The rain paints the world in greys, and he cuts through it all, a blaze in his orange raincoat.

Mum's grave is up there, over towards the oak trees. The mourners were more to the west, and Caleb slows down, scanning the lanes for anything new. He doesn't worry about looking a little suspicious. There are no other visitors in this weather, no one to look up from their quiet rituals and frown at his presence.

Just a boy and the dead.

Three minutes of trudging along the alleys of the interred, and he doubts himself. This isn't the spot. This is nowhere near the spot. He might as well close his eyes, spin round, then walk in a random direction. That's how high he feels his chances are. A sigh. It sounds nothing like his father's. Nothing. It is irritation. It is wishing that ideas worked out in real life the way they did in his head.

Near the top of Daisy Hill he looks back and out towards the town he's lived in for nine years, sees his house that was once a home, the window into a bedroom that is sanctuary from this cold, grey world. In that small space he is in control. Small, but it is his. It changes only when he changes it.

He should give this dumb hunt up, take his measurements, get back to his room. It was a burial with a small cloud, third in a week. So what? And if he's heard nothing of deaths in the area… Again, so what? He never listens to anything anyone says, and Father has no care for conversation.

There was nothing to be suspicious of.

But still.

Still.

It comes to him then. He's not quite high enough up the hill. There's an elevated area with older graves that needs checking. He trudges up, socks squishy, left trainer squeaking. His momentary loss of conviction is forgotten.

He finds the spot quickly. There aren't many plots here, and they're dotted about, no regimental lines of the deceased. No vases of lilies for these fellows. The weeds keep them company.

This grave stands apart. Recently dug and filled in. He's not sure why it's odd. He moves a shuffle closer to read the inscription, chewed as it is by Time.

EASTON
UNTIL THE DAY DAWN

The sparseness, that's what's odd. Five words. No first name. No dates. The appearance, that's also weird. This headstone has been here for a while. The recently turned soil indicates that the buried has not. Why bury someone in what is clearly an old plot?

5

Odd.

Prickles run through the hair-wisps on his neck. Someone is near. His stomach plummets. He really has been followed. One or more of the mourners has come back for him.

His crazy-foolish boy mind screams of horror to come: he is next for someone else's old grave, and no one will ever know what became of him.

He's ready to run. He's ready to try to escape.

He tenses. He looks.

The girl. Halfway down the hill, framed by the distant twin chapels. She holds a busted grey umbrella over her head in one hand, a black ball in the other. Her hair is bundled up in midnight clumps, held by pins. She is as colourless as the world around him, but her dress is layers of green and blue. The hem is soaked and muddy. She shakes the ball, lifts it, peers into it for a moment, almost drops the cumbersome thing; it doesn't sit comfortably in her small palm. One last look at Caleb. Not a hard stare, but a lingering gaze. Perhaps she is making a decision.

She walks away, disappearing behind well-tended hedges, and Caleb releases his breath.

A lot of kids have a lot of names for her. The ghoul. The crypt-creeper. Zombie-girl. Queen of the dead. Other stuff. Worse stuff. A real freak. This isn't the first time Caleb's been in such close proximity to her. A handful of times he's spied her, watching him from afar. Always she stands there until he's about to squirm in discomfort, until he fears that the worst of all possible things will happen, that she will come over and speak.

He suspects that one day she will do exactly that, and he's not equipped to deal with it.

That's a worry for another day. As is this whole headstone business. The only way to find out anything more would be to dig up whoever is down there, and he'd never ever even think about doing that.

He trudges back down Daisy Hill, a head full of questions.

4

Measuring a graveyard is a longer job than he expected, but Caleb is patient and diligent and there's little else to do in the summer holidays. It's six weeks of trying to find ways to fill in the time. Forty-two days. He sleeps for eight hours usually, leaving sixteen hours per day to fill. Sixteen times forty-two. In the face of such numbers, graveyard measuring and mystery solving strike Caleb as excellent ways of using up time.

The tape measure is not endless. It stretches three metres. Another problem: his arm-span does not have a width of three metres. He has to hold the measure against the railings in stages. Pin it there, in the middle, against a railing. Hold it steady. Bring his left hand along to take over from the right. Keep a finger on that spot. Right hand to the end. Add three metres to the tally. Pull the tape measure over, and start again. Keep count. Three. Six. Nine. He's grateful for his baseball cap. It keeps his eyes clear in the continuing downpour. He works on. Steady, not wanting to mess up. Accuracy is important.

Being busy is good.

Twenty-four. Twenty-seven. Thirty.

'Morning, Caleb,' says Mr Sebastian, the old feller from the bottom of his street, a newspaper tucked under his arm. 'Should I ask what you're up to?' He twirls his brolly, spraying out a spin of droplets.

'I'm doing important research,' says Caleb, flashing a small, polite smile.

Mr Sebastian nods like he already knows that. 'You'll catch your death out here, young man.' He continues walking, whistling an optimistic tune.

Was thirty-six or thirty-nine next? A guess won't do. Back to the beginning.

It rains on.

5

After he finishes the measuring, there is the hateful business of returning home. Father berates him at length; a monotone drone from the living room, starting from the moment Caleb opens the back door. He struggles with his waterlogged trainers, his soggy socks cling to skin as the voice reminds him that he's dumb and he'd better put everything straight in the washer and all the while Caleb holds numbers in his head. He's down to T-shirt and underpants while hearing all about immaturity and growing up. He's putting powder and conditioner in the drawer as he listens to Father warn against big messes in the kitchen and threats about what will happen if colds are spread, because he's a busy man and doesn't have time for all this nonsense.

Neither does Caleb.

He goes up to his room as the lecture carries on, fading to the faintest rumble as he closes his door. He has repeated the numbers rhythmically in his loudest thoughts since the moment he rolled up the tape measure, blocking out everything, including monotone drones. He writes them on the back page of an old jotter.

313.15m x 341.6m

There's great relief in seeing it written down, a peculiar but welcome sense of achievement. A big chunk of time and effort for those two measurements. A base he can work from. It will prove one way or another if he's going mad. If he actually *is* going doolally…well, he'll keep that to himself. But if he can prove his suspicions are right…

In that instance, he has no idea what he'll do.

For now, Caleb waits for the weather to clear.

6

The bruise from this morning aches. It's a pressure pushing out from her flesh. It reminds her constantly of its presence, enough to be uncomfortable, an annoyance. Her threshold for pain is high, physical pain, that is. The memory of the incident itself is close to insufferable. Heat flares up in her face. Embarrassment turns her stomach as she remembers the laughter, the name-calling, her own uselessness.

Why couldn't she stay on her feet? Just once. And if they all hated her so much, why did they come looking for her? For six weeks they could rest their eyes from the misery of seeing her in class. They could stay away, instead of cornering her over by the bins, pushing her around and shouting 'pass the ghoul' and calling her Chicken Peck. Her temper had stepped up. She'd shouted in Vic Sweet's face, right up in that pockmarked face, and in that moment she took control, she shocked them into silence, and she was walking away and her stupid lame foot gave out and she hit the ground hard. They had loved that, laughing like there was something dangerously wrong with them. There was a weight on her back and she thought this time it would be really bad, she wouldn't get out of it in one piece. Then there was a kick to her backside, and they were gone.

The tears were the worst thing. The burning shame of them. Those boys had got to her. She'd let them catch her out.

It was her own stupid fault.

They'd got her here. The graveyard. Her own territory. School is one thing, but here? Of all places, here?

The world hates her, and she can't figure out why.

She'd spent the rest of the morning in her secret places, some of which not even Grandfather knew, although he thought he knew them all. Hollow tree trunks and old sheds and more provided shelter from rain and people.

Then she'd seen that boy again. Caleb. Funny-looking kid. Indie type. Scraggy hair and baggy jeans. Always stood in a schlump, like standing up was a drag. He turns up in the graveyard often, and it isn't always to visit his mother. Sometimes he wanders around aimlessly. Sometimes he stops to read random headstones. Today he went snooping.

Caleb's lucky her grandfather didn't catch him. The old man doesn't like people sniffing around ceremonies. Respect is Grandfather's favourite word. He says it's the only thing that matters on these grounds.

She doesn't know Caleb. She's never spoken to him. He's just the only kid who's never called her a name.

Eight doesn't like him, though. Eight told her stay away.

Maybe one day Eight will change her mind. Maybe the time isn't right yet. Or maybe he's as bad as Vic and those other bastards. Yes. That's probably it. A vaguely pleasant face does not mean there's a decent person underneath. It usually means the exact opposite. They come at you with a smile, then ask you how many coffins you've slept in lately. Then they really stick the boot in.

She must accept that she's an outsider. But outsiders survive. They don't get caught by the bins.

Grandfather calls through the bathroom door. 'Misha, don't use all the hot water!'

'I'll be out in a minute,' she shouts. It's the third time she's shouted this, but she doesn't realise it. She remains sitting in the tub, skin doused in the warm downpour of the shower, long hair clinging to her body.

Eight is silent in her room.

7

313.15m x 341.6m

Caleb wishes he hadn't done such a good job of remembering those numbers. They're now laser-burned into the meat of his brain. He tries to think of stupidly catchy songs to overwrite the data, but nothing comes. He still hasn't got rid of it when the rain eventually stops early evening, fat cloud-clumps roving off to wring themselves out further west. He's been stuck in the house all day. There has been nothing to do but stay in his room, staring out of the window. It's the only place in the house where he isn't likely to cross paths with Father. He has to get out there, into the freshly lit outdoors. To do what? Anything. Nothing in particular. Look around. Be somewhere other than the house.

As he pulls his trainers back on, Father calls to him, 'Your grandfather's been on the phone. He's after a hammer. Take one from the toolbox. Tell him I want it back tomorrow. The old goat should have one of his own.' He follows this by droning about how useless Gramps is and why does he have to keep ringing at the worst possible times, and Caleb blocks it out. None of it is of any use to him. He's heard a thousand variations before, and each time makes him feel a little worse.

He hates it.

He also kind of hates visiting Gramps. It's not as fun as it used to be. He's getting a little strange. Tells odd stories. Asks weird questions. Says things from the middle of non-existent conversations. He's still nice. He's still Gramps.

Sort of.

He lives a few streets over, a very short walk. Father hasn't ventured near in four years.

Caleb tries the door. It's unlocked as usual, so he lets himself in. 'It's just me, Gramps.'

The answer comes from the kitchen at the far end of the hall.

'Why do you say that every time? Just. It's just me. Like you're nothing to be excited about.' All of his trains and carriages are lined up on the dining table. He picks one up, sprays it with polish. 'Make people think that maybe you *are* exciting. It's me. I'm here. Strong, like that. You use the word just, you allow people to adopt the position of disappointment. Oh, it's just him, they say to each other. We'll forget about him and see who comes in next.' He sets to rubbing the model train carriage with a dirty tea towel.

The smell of polish is more prevalent than oxygen in the room. It burns Caleb's nostrils. 'I didn't mean it the way you're saying it. I just meant…'

'Doesn't matter what you meant, it matters what it sounds like. Sound is more important than meaning.'

Caleb frowns. This sounds like a normal conversation, but Caleb's only been in the house for about a minute and feels that he's wandered into slightly wobbly territory. 'I brought the hammer,' he says. It sounds like a normal thing to say. 'He wants it back tomorrow.'

'I suppose I should thank him for his generosity.' Gramps picks up another carriage, gives it a hefty spray. 'I'll have the trap finished by morning.'

'Still haven't caught him?'

Gramps almost drops the carriage. 'Don't call it him! It's it! You'll start with calling it a him, then you'll be giving the filthy vermin a name, and then we've got real problems!' Caleb makes an effort not to roll his eyes. The subject of the mouse is a particularly strong agitator for Gramps. 'Never give it a name! That would make it feel at home. And if one of them feels at home, the others will follow.' He's eyeballing the skirting boards, looks ready to swing train segments round like clubs. 'I keep him on his toes so he never feels settled. Won't touch poison, the little bugger. But I'll get him. This trap will be foolproof.'

'Him.

'What?'

'You told me not to say "him", but you just did. You said, "I'll keep him on his toes".'

The confusion pushes Gramps's wrinkles all together. 'Did I? Blast! How did he...it. It! How did it get under my defences? This is exactly what I've been talking about, Caleb. Even I can slip up.' He selects the carriage he was dealing with when Caleb arrived, starts polishing it again. 'You must always think about what's coming out of your mouth, and what it means. Get yourself some cream soda. It's in the fridge. You'll be doing me a favour if you drink it. It's turned against me in recent years. Gives me tremendous wind power.'

Caleb opens the fridge. There's cherryade, and no cream soda. He hates cherryade. He doesn't really want a drink anyway. 'You're running out of milk, Gramps. You want me to get some from the corner shop?'

'Hmm? No, no, I'll do it myself later, gives me an excuse to get out of the house.' He sprays more polish. It's looking like a very good idea for Gramps to get air, and get it soon. He'll be off his head if he stays in this atmosphere too much longer. Even with a window open, Caleb feels woozy. 'I spotted you earlier, sunshine, going into that graveyard.'

That fluttering tickle of guilt again. Not like he's been trespassing or breaking some law; it's like he's been seen doing something private, something that's his and his alone. 'Uh-huh,' he says, because it doesn't commit to anything.

'I wasn't spying on you, kiddo,' says Gramps, without realising how much worse that makes Caleb feel. 'Just happened to be passing by the front room window, looking out at the rain. Saw you down the road, running through the gates. That's our Caleb, I said, there he goes again.'

It's hard to know what to say, so Caleb doesn't say anything.

'Happen to see you going in there quite a lot. I'm not a spy; this is only what I see. Some of the grannies around here, they see you sometimes too. You know how it is with old people and graveyards.'

'Uh-huh,' said Caleb, although he doesn't know at all. He chews the corner of his bottom lip, wonders when it will be polite to leave.

'Don't suppose your dad knows anything about how often you're going up there?' A shrug is an honest answer. 'I can't imagine he's changed his mind about you hanging around there. He won't be happy, will he?' It would be easy to tell Gramps that the man is never happy, so what difference would anything make? 'Don't worry, I'm not one for running around telling tales out of school. But do me a favour. Come with me a moment, will you?' He leads Caleb to the front room, putting the highly polished train carriage into his pocket.

In all of Caleb's life, there's only been one change to this room. It's the same two sofas with the same bobble-fluffed throws he sat on when Grandma listened to him read aloud so slowly, so haltingly. The same pictures of places so old they're out of time, in the same flowery frames. Same smiles, same wrinkles, only deeper as time moves on. Ornamental cats that have never moved, always stretching, rumps in the air. Same smell that always reminds him of Grandma, a small old woman who looked like she'd last forever and who faded and died once Mum was gone. It is preserved, this room. Caleb's memories may well wait here forever. That is both warming and sad. It pulls at him, and confuses him.

'Come on, Caleb, I want you to look out here. Lovely day now, wouldn't believe it was tipping down earlier. It's turned into the perfect summer's day, hasn't it? All the kids are out again. Look at them, down at the park there, swinging about like bloody monkeys.' The park is at the end of the road farthest from the graveyard. There's a metal climbing frame, spider-shaped. A fort that spits out children down its gleaming slide. A thing that spins. A thing that rocks. A thing that rocks and spins. 'Look at all the fun they're having. It's full of life that place. And where is it you go? Up there, with the dead. In the rain. Do you see what I'm saying? Can you see the difference?' The graveyard is at one end of the road, the park is at the other. That is the difference to Caleb. Opposites. Gramps's voice goes into soft and caring mode. 'I know your mum's up there. I know that better than anybody. That's my girl. And it's alright to visit sometimes. It's healthy and normal to do that. Sometimes. But death isn't for the young, Caleb. That's not healthy, that's not normal. You've got to spend some time in the park. The air's fresher there, my boy. You get what I mean?'

Caleb gives his smile, the one that reassures people, makes them think he's listening.

'Good. Now, you don't want to be wasting your summer holiday on a crotchety old devil like me. Off you go. Just live!'

There's that word 'just' again.

8

He sits on the very top of the fort, back against the spire, while some girl screams at him to get down, it's her turn. He blanks the grubby little nutter, figuring she'll give up soon and find someone else to annoy. There are plenty of other kids around here for her to scream at. They whirl around in dervish swarms, hunting each other in swirling packs that disband every two minutes, and the noise is a senseless squawking mess. He hates it. The meaninglessness of it all. He wonders how they don't give themselves headaches.

And that's all he thinks of them because, through the trees at the edge of the park, over the roofs of the houses behind the trees at the edge of the park, there is the hill with the graveyard sprawled across it, and he's watching it carefully, watching it like he might catch it out, might see it flex or stretch.

He knows he won't see a sudden moment of expansion. It must be a constant, gradual thing. Tiny increments. The universe does this. Forever expanding. Moving on and on. Such things can only be proved by measurements.

313.15m x 341.6m

If he gets the same numbers, or close (he'll allow for errors), then Caleb will let it go. He will. But he must go back this evening, because he won't rest.

He has an alibi. Anyone asks what he's up to, he'll say it's part of an art project for school. He's going to try to make a scale model, that's what he'll say.

And if Father doesn't like any of it, that's just tough.

9

'Do you see what I mean?' the old man asks Misha, and he's tapping parts of the diagram with a stubby finger. He lost the ends of each digit, up to the first knuckle, on his right hand. He tells people it was in an accident with a chainsaw, his own fault for letting his concentration drift. This story is exactly that: a tall tale. A lie. The truth is, as Misha knows, is very far from and much more dangerous than chainsaws. Granddad physically has to turn her head with his hand to get her looking in the correct place. 'Please, Misha, focus. Here, at West Nine, everything is higgledy-piggledy. It creates an imbalance that's hard to address, given current layout and numbers, but look closely here...' The stub thumps an area halfway up the hill, not far from where she saw that Caleb earlier today. He'd be tiny seen from this angle, high above the large map, which spills over the table's edges. Miniature Caleb stares at the miniature map-version of her. He doesn't call her a name, doesn't tell her to piss off, doesn't demand anything of her. What he does is look puzzled. She feels an urge to push the mini-Misha closer to him. Mini might dig in her heels, but what chance would she have of resisting God-Misha's will? An enormous hand will descend from the heavens and force her forwards, digging two thin ditches as she goes. Then she'll be face-to-face with the funny little indie boy, and she'll say...what? Should she tell him to stop snooping around? Should she ask what he's looking for? Should she tell him to get on with it, do what everyone else does, call her Ghoul Girl or the Corpser or whatever else he needs to? Yes, call mini-Misha something horrible, give her a shove so that she falls and lands on someone's flowers, then God-Misha can shake the land itself with her thunderous anger, and smoosh him under the heel of her palm.

'Well?' says Granddad. Misha's gut squirms a little, because she can't think of a fake answer. 'You haven't heard a word I said,'

'That's not true,' she says, confident now that she doesn't need to lie. 'You said about layouts and numbers and the imbalance of it all.'

Granddad shakes his head, rubbing at the deep wrinkles over his brow. Worry lines, Misha calls them. The more furrows there are, and the more they scrunch together, the more worried he is. And before he hides it all away, before he smooths his lines as best he can, before he puts on a thin smile that can't hope to fool the way it's meant to, Misha wishes she could be less of a disappointment to him. He'd never say it, but she's not what he wants, expects or deserves.

This knowledge is a long, slender needle of pain that eases a little further in every day, too slippery to pull back out.

'I'm pushing too hard, I know. All these extra lessons...'

'It's a little bit like getting triple homework,' she says, looking up at him through her swathe of lashes. It's one of the looks she practices in the mirror. It works, filling out his smile.

'No school, and I'm making you work harder than ever, eh? What a horrible old man I am.'

'You are, Granddad. A real horror.'

He rolls up the map. The large sheet of paper needs nimble work from both hands. 'I bang on a lot, I know. But it's important, my girl. You have to learn this, all of this, and we have to do all the boring bits like layouts and arrays before we can bring it all together...'

'I know,' she says, and she really does know, and even talking about how boring this stuff is makes her feel bored. 'It's just... nothing more's going in, it's like my head's all full up.'

'No more tonight, then,' says Granddad as he slips the map back into a cardboard tube and puts the tube back with the stack on the sideboard. 'Let's have supper. There's still some stew left in the pan.' He shuffles away in his tatty slippers, looking for all the world like just another doddery old chap with his head partly in the clouds and partly in his memories.

Misha trails off to flop onto her bed. She should be pleased. The torture is over for the evening. No more thinking about things that shouldn't happen. But her eyes feel hot, and her lungs are clenching together. She saw it in Granddad's face. She's let him down again. All he wants is her attention, and she can't even give him that. There is so much that is wrong with her. That's why boys corner her by the bins. She is life's mistake, and they sense it even if they don't know it, and they know in their knuckles and toes that they must get rid of her. She's so wrong that, even in her fantasy at the map, it was Caleb she smooshed before those boys. Caleb, who is yet to do her wrong.

When Granddad calls for her to come get stew, she doesn't hear, and he forgets, and she spends the rest of the night on her bed in her big, dark, dusty room, and her thoughts turn into dreams and her dreams are bad.

10

Before he climbs out of the window, Caleb takes one more look at the recordings he's written down. The first

313.15m x 341.6m

has a time and date beside it: 3.15pm, August 2. The second set of results were recorded at 6.30pm.

314.05m x 342.1m

Even now that it's getting late, when it's easy to doubt himself, to believe that he made a mistake, he remains convinced that he was careful. He really was. He took his time, didn't rush. No slips, no fumbles, not even any interruptions. His concentration had been absolute. According to these results, the graveyard has grown ninety centimetres in one direction, fifty in another, and has done so within three-and-a-quarter hours.

He doesn't realise how deep he frowns, how his face folds slightly in at brow and chin.

He returns the jotter to the bottom of a pile of exercise books and papers in the bottom drawer of his desk. It's not as if Father ever comes in here to root around, but Caleb feels protective of his odd and disturbing discovery. He not ready share it yet. He needs more. Not that he'd bother to share it with Father. Who knows what kind of withering abuse that would bring? There would be the classic sigh, then anything from a selection of possible verbal attacks. A bit of grief for bothering him with something so ridiculous, perhaps. Or accusations that Caleb must be up to no good, hanging around that graveyard again. A load of senseless shouting about acting dumb, about shameful behaviour, about this, about that. A combination of any or all of these responses is what Caleb could expect. Words like 'honest' and 'really' and 'truth' only ever serve to rile Father up.

Time for some fresh air. And a whole lot of space.

Out of his bedroom window he goes, dragging his quilt and pillow with him. Across the slope of the roof he creeps, until he reaches the garage roof, and here he makes himself comfortable, using the quilt like a cocoon. He wriggles his head deep into the pillow.

Straight up there's one hell of a view.

It's another clear night. The stars are all sitting way, way back in the sky, and he hates it. Hates the way he's drawn to this. Hates that he can't stop looking, despite what it does to his insides. It aches him. It's a dull thrum, a craving he struggles to understand.

Look at it all. There's so much in the darkness. It goes too far to think about.

He's one kid on one roof, in one town, in one country, on one planet, in one solar system. One. The stars don't care about his sorrow, because they know nothing of it. All the way out there, so, so far, it wouldn't matter to them. To them, or anyone else.

They glitter at him, jewels at the bottom of oceans upon oceans, and he tries to feel the distance, get a sense of what endless actually means.

Why is there so much of it, so much that it makes this planet tiny, a blade of grass in a swooping field? This one little ball with life smeared across it. Life that makes choices it thinks are important will have an impact on the grand scheme of things. The grand scheme is too, too big. People's worries and miseries are all pointless because one day they'll all be dead and gone and gone is forever and the universe will keep on going until it stretches itself into nothing and then that will be gone too.

This single insignificant boy looks up into forever and knows those stars are not big burning eyes staring down at him. The stars are looking to where they are going. They're leaving him more alone with every passing second.

Look at me, he thinks. *Look at me, just once.*

Just.

11

Beneath those soaring stars, each concerned only with its own bright journey, a boy slips into a sleep of twisting dreams, and a girl wakes in a tangled sweat, and a graveyard gets a little bit bigger. All the way out here, however, no one is looking.

12

He wakes, head-heavy, like his dreams had too much weight for his brain. The stars are gone, replaced by a mushy cloud soup that has spread across the sky. A revving engine: that's what woke him. Father's car pulls away. He's got ready and left the house for work without bothering to check in on his son. Caleb has another day to himself, another day in which it will rain hard, like it does every day.

Caleb struggles out of his cocoon, wondering how many of the neighbours across the street have spotted him sleeping on the garage roof, wondering why none of them care enough to say anything to Father. Perhaps they have, and have walked away baffled by his indifference. Perhaps.

He drags himself and quilt back through the bedroom window, changes PJs for slack jeans and an Alkaline Trio hoodie, and heads straight out before the rains fall. That graveyard has had a whole night to grow, and he's going to find out how much.

What Caleb doesn't realise is how much things are about to change.

13

She scrubs, elbow aching, willing the words to disappear. The paint is smudging, but putting up one hell of a resistance. It wants to stay on the headstone. It wants everyone to read what it says.

MISHA THE CREEPER GOES WITH THE DEAD

At least Granddad hasn't seen it yet. This one, or the other two. It would upset him a lot. Anger is a hard rock in her heart, jagged and sore. Vic did this. Him, or one of his mates. Which is the same thing. Twice in twenty-four hours they've invaded. Her summer of peace is over, it seems. Vic has her squarely in his sights, and if doesn't let up? She'll have to do something about it.

Eight says so.

Her arm refuses to do any more without a break, and she relents. A couple of minutes won't harm. Granddad's off out to the supermarket doing the weekly shop. He'll be gone a while. He finds the amount of choice overwhelming, and fascinating.

She sits, looks to the sky from this vantage point halfway up the hill. Clouds are piling up on top of themselves, layer upon plump layer of dark grey bundles. It'll come down in torrents today, muddy streams weaving through the graves. It means the day's practical lesson will be even more of a chore, because Granddad won't allow the elements to cause any delays. He always says the timetable is too tight to change, and her poor attention span over the last few nights isn't helping. She refuses to use the phrase 'it's not fair' because that's the kind of whiney phrase she hears the other kids say, but the refusal doesn't alter how she feels.

It just isn't fair.

She shouldn't have to clean this up. That arsehole Vic should. 'I'll bury you, Vic Sweet. One day I'll bury you, and I'll laugh while I'm doing it.'

It's a soothing thought.

That boy again. He's moving slowly along the southern railings. He's stretching something. What is he up to? Misha's feeling fiery, so today's the day. She makes her way down the hill. The graffiti can wait a little while longer.

14

He has a rhythm going, a rocking version of a side-step that almost makes a game of counting the metres. A couple of cars have gone past, and he must have looked seriously weird to the drivers and passengers, but that doesn't bother Caleb. People don't tend to approach him anyway. They know they won't get much in return.

One hundred and five, one hundred and eight, one hundred… and the count stops. The girl is opposite him, staring at him through the railings.

'You planning on decorating?' she asks, and the next breath he catches is the wrong one, hitches raggedly in his pipes, so instead of answering her, Caleb gapes.

He was right. He's not equipped to deal with this. And she's staring at him. She isn't filling the silence. She's letting it stretch out, pull itself thin, until it threatens to snap loudly. He has to say something. She's got to speak, surely? But she's not. She's waiting and waiting for him to speak. Oh God, this is worse than he ever imagined it being! Why won't anything happen? It's not the silence that's stretched and snapped, it's the universe, and it's done it at this hideous point, and this is all he will feel, this savage burn in his face, and it will never end because Time just broke along with all of everything. Burning up under the gaze of polished green eyes. What had she said to him? Something about decorating? His head's all scrambled eggs. That doesn't mean anything. Answer her! 'No, I'm not decorating.'

Cale's own coolness amazes him. It is amazing that the ground doesn't freeze beneath his feet.

'Okay,' says Misha, dragging the word out for longer than is necessary. 'So you've got plenty to say for yourself.'

If Caleb had ever bothered to imagine how this first conversation would play out, this would not have been one of the outcomes. He shrugs. She tilts her head forward. Only the slightest of tilts, but there's something about it that asks, 'Well?' Words are required. 'I'm busy,' he says, using Father's tone, the one that says no interruptions will be tolerated.

Her dress is a mass of red pleats that swish as she takes two steps forward. 'I know you're busy not decorating. So what are you measuring up for?'

He means to say, 'School project'. That's why he invented the cover story: to use it. Instead he says, 'What do you care?'

'I live here.' It comes out like a challenge, and doesn't it look like she's egging him on?

'And I'm not doing any harm.'

'You're always around here, Caleb.'

Her use of his name is like an electro bolt down his veins. She uses it softly, despite the hard consonants. 'Look, you've made me lose count. I've got to start again.'

'So start again.' Swish, swish, and she is up at the railings, and she's very close for a girl who's always watched him from a distance. 'I could help you keep count.'

'But you don't even know what for.'

She pushes a scrunch of hair from her vision. 'You're going to tell me what for.' She turns and heads towards the gates. She's coming out. The quick swish of her ruffles. The lively bounce of her hair.

Caleb knows it would be rude to run away, but that definitely isn't what stops him. He has a measurement to finish. He's done one side, and needs to get this one done too, otherwise it's time wasted and he'll only have half a piece of evidence. But what's he meant to tell the girl from the graveyard? Because it's clear she's not going to shut up and leave him alone.

He could tell her to get stuffed. Simple. He could tell her that Vic Sweet plus two are metres away and locked in on her. Too late.

She steps out onto the pavement and Vic catches her by the elbow-crook and spins her a half-turn backwards, spins hard. The railings clang as she bounces off them. Vic pins her upright before she drops, pushes his sneer close to her face. His two buddies stand at either shoulder, going into shield-mode automatically. The buddies laugh like they can't believe their luck, but Vic says nothing. It looks like he's squeezing her shoulders.

They're not big lads. But Vic has a reputation. And the three combined are bigger than Caleb.

He didn't ask her to come over.

Vic pulls back a fist. He's going to punch her in the face. A girl, in the face.

Caleb's voice is trapped at the bottom of his throat.

The fist powers forward. It unfurls at the last instant, palm slapping into the railing by Misha's ear. She flinches, couldn't stop herself. The metallic shrill of the blow resonates down the road and up the hill and deep into the graveyard.

The echo stretches.

Vic's laugh is a harsh hyena-bark. The other two copy the vicious noise and high-five each other.

Caleb's heart thunders so hard he might be sick.

'I'd love to smash your face in, ghoul,' sneers Vic. Then he leans in, whispers something Caleb can't hear, and it must be pure poison instead of mere words, because Misha pulls as far away from him as she can.

Why does he have to be here watching this? Why didn't he wait until it rained before he came out?

He's not the right boy for this place and time.

And great, now Vic's looking directly at him. This is what it's like under the bridge, in the shadows, with the troll. 'You want to knock me out? You want to save the little ghoul? Come on over. Come on and take a shot.'

Silence. Even the clouds have gathered to watch.

Vic lets Misha go at last. At long, long last. 'You've got nothing, have you? No balls. Didn't think so. You just keep on looking;

it's all you're good for.' More hyena laughs. 'You want to watch what we do to her next time? It'll make your eyes bleed.' There's a desperation to the laughter now, a need to be heard enjoying the joke louder than the other boy. Vic starts walking, the other two fall in behind him. Caleb's in their path. He steps to one side. The wrong side. Dipping a shoulder, Vic alters his course to bump solidly into Caleb. It's Caleb's turn to slam into the railings. 'Out the way, hard man,' growls Vic, and the trio bark and snark as they bundle away from the graveyard.

Caleb closes his eyes, wishing his blazing cheeks would cool, telling himself to breathe normally. The first rain-flecks hit his face. He's sure they hiss and steam on contact. It's not only the rain he feels on his skin. It's her eyes. The accusation. The expectation of an explanation. He'll have to say something.

Something. There must be something.

Why should there be something? None of this is his fault. He hasn't done anything.

He hasn't.

He can't look at her, and he's got to see, so he looks.

Misha is already back within the graveyard boundaries, away up the hill, swish, swish, swish. She's gone, and Caleb's on his own again.

It was a short but unpleasant interruption that's over now, that's all. Just a little blip.

He heads back to the beginning of this stretch of railing, and starts measuring again, counting the numbers loud in his head, loud and clear. The rhythm has gone.

15

The third set of results are recorded carefully in the jotter.

316.4m x 343.8m

This piece of evidence looks very convincing to Caleb. With only two sets in place, it had appeared that the only reason the measurements didn't match was human error. Caleb thinks, though, that it is unlikely he'd make another error, one in which both sides were longer yet again.

More measurements will back this conclusion up, he's certain.

It does mean he'll have to return to the graveyard, though. The graveyard. Where she lives.

Sinking into the sofa, staring at the conservatory roof as it is lashed with rain, he wonders why he's bothered. So what if she lives there? Is that a good reason for him to stay away? They've barely shared a conversation. He doesn't know her. He doesn't owe her anything. He's got an important project to complete. There is definitely something incredibly odd happening up there, and someone should be doing something about it.

Caleb took the job, and he'll see it through to the end. No matter what.

Is the rain harder today than it was yesterday? He's surrounded by noise like lentils pouring into tin cans. It's good to listen to whilst warm and snug on cushions.

Just because she lives there doesn't give her any say on whether or not he can turn up. It's a public place. And it's not Caleb's fault that she's rubbed Vic Sweet up the wrong way. She did that all on her own. That girl has no right to give him accusing looks. That's if she gave him any looks at all. It's not as if he'd been able to turn his face towards her until she was already gone.

No. Whether he saw it or not, she looked. It was a look that wondered how he'd been able to stand there and let it all happen.

'If it'd been serious, I would've stepped in,' he says. He intends his voice to sound low and meaningful, like an action hero, but instead it comes out small.

The hard waves of rain distort the glass into folded plastic sheets. The world has blurred. This must be the last day of this weather. The clouds must be empty after this, wrung dry.

His comics lie on the coffee table, sprawled and ignored. Caleb's taste for adventure has been suppressed. He tosses the jotter to land on top of the pile, leaves his arm to swing off the side of the sofa.

He doesn't care what that Misha thinks. He's spending a lot of time thinking that he doesn't care what that Misha thinks. This is stupid. She'll probably stay away from him now. No more awkward approaches, no more squirmy conversations. She hates him. She'll stay away. So it's kind of worked out for the best.

This is like being inside of a giant's eye, looking out while the tears fall.

16

Inside the hollow of the tree trunk, she is away from everything except the musty smell and the stream of drips, and neither of those bothers her much. The left arm of her dress is soaked, which doesn't really matter. Her hem and ruffles are mud-clagged, and her dresses always end up like this before the day is done. It's what washing machines were invented for.

She sits within the emptied-out guts of the ancient oak and sucks a single strand of her hair, freshly plucked from her head. How sad that this is the best place for her on Planet Earth. Going home would mean listening to Granddad's anger and pity, and it's difficult to choose which is worse. The rants are long and circular. The pity reminds her that she's a figure of hate. The rants are caused by her, whether indirectly or not. The pity says that her life will be like this forever.

Can it really all be anger and misery from here onwards?

The tree's innards are cool and damp against her back. Her head taps a slow rhythm on the rotting wood. She's been doing this for half an hour, and it's starting to hurt.

It's hard to know what she was expecting of Caleb. She wasn't stupid enough to think he was some kind of hero, was she? Then again, perhaps he *is* a hero, but no one ever said that heroes would help a creature like her.

That draws a dry, sharp laugh from Misha. The boy's no hero. Her misery had been nothing more than an unwelcome interruption for him. He'd stood by and waited for the business with Vic to end so he could get on with his strange and stupid task. Whether or not she'd been in danger didn't matter. She'd been in the way. That's why he never called her a name. Complete cold indifference. No interest at all. It's almost as cruel as Vic's threats of physical violence.

Why does she care? He's a stranger. Eight had been right as always. She wonders what Eight will make of today's events.

She'll ask later.

That's if she ever decides to leave the shelter of this tree.

17

Up on the second highest of her bookshelves, at the end and resting against the wall, sits Eight. The small window, which is the only blemish on Eight's smooth, spherical surface, fogs over as if it has been shook. When the fog clears, there is an answer to a question distantly asked.

BURY HIM

18

Perched on the backrest of the park bench, which is still damp after the early departure of the rain, Caleb asks a question of Mickey Dee, one of three Mickeys that he knows, all in the same year at school. 'You heard about anyone dying lately?'

Scrawny Mickey Dee, doing keepy-ups, shrugs before an answer comes to him. 'My granny did, like a month ago or two months ago, or something. She always had a ton of sweets in the kitchen drawer and I could help myself.'

Caleb nods, although he's sure that this isn't the information he wants. 'Anyone else? In the last few weeks maybe?'

'Dunno,' mumbles Mickey Dee. Then he brightens. 'Someone been murdered?'

'No. Well, maybe, but I don't know about it if they have.'

'What you asking for then?'

'Because it's weird. There's been three burials up on Daisy Hill in the last week, but no one round here's got any idea who they were.' It's frustrating him. A little too much, perhaps. He wants to growl and bark and shake his fists at someone. Mickey Dee is the fifth kid he's asked about this at the park. Kids are usually all ears when grown-ups talk about the big stuff like death, and kids love talking about grown-up secrets, but so far he's turned up nothing. The forever-snotty Sam over on the swings has also lost a relative in the last few months, and one girl broke down in tears about her cat Jupiter, and that's all.

Mickey Dee drops the ball on the forty-third keepy-up. 'Old people die all the time,' he explains. 'They get old, they die. You coming for a game?'

He's lost interest in Mickey Dee. 'Not my kind of thing.'

'Football's everyone's kind of thing,' says the confused boy before running off to find someone with more sensible tastes.

Caleb wonders if it's worth asking anyone else. One or two kids are glancing at him warily. Word must be getting round that he's asking weird stuff. Might as well knock it on the head. Perhaps he'll ask Gramps about it next time he's there, although there's a chance that the old man will forward such discussions to Father. The only time Father ever listens to Gramps is when they talk about Caleb, graveyards and the dead.

If Gramps is looking out of his window today he won't see Caleb lurking near the graveyard. He's giving this evening's measurements a miss. He'll do another one in the morning. No need to be so full-on about it.

He clutches the tape measure in his pocket. The plastic is making his hand sweat.

That crazy girl's claimed the top of the fort as her own again, and she's showing no sign of budging. He won't be getting up there any time soon, so he jumps down off the bench and leaves the park.

He steers clear of the graveyard.

19

Granddad is not happy. 'I've been looking for you all afternoon! You know fine well how important it is to be on time!' They're going from North Six where he found her towards Daisy Hill. He's stomping, she's dragging her heels, getting further and further behind. He turns on her, all bristles. 'Do you think maybe now's the time for you to hurry up, Misha?' She skips a few steps to catch up, but she's soon lagging again. She can't help it. His strides are huge, and unlike Misha he's filled with urgency. 'Don't think we're skipping the theory just because you're late. We'll do it after the practical, so I hope you're ready for some hard concentration.' She wonders if he's seen the graffiti that she failed to get back to and remove. It would explain why that scowl carves his brow so severely. Then again, the fact that she hid from him for a full afternoon is plenty provocation to turn Granddad sour like week-old milk.

She's got something she'd like to say to him. It's about how much she doesn't care. It's about how all his efforts to teach her are pointless. She can't take it all in, so why try. Everything is a waste of time. Everything. Time itself is a waste. It's just a measurement, a distance between miseries, and who really wants any of it?

She can't say anything like that to Granddad, though. It's too personal. Too real.

'Please keep up, Misha! Everyone's due at any minute!'

This has the undesired effect of stopping her in her tracks. 'Everyone? What do you mean?'

Granddad takes another four huge strides before realising the girl has halted. Exasperated hands wave frantically for her to come. 'Misha, you are trying my patience! Can you please move?'

Her only movement is a tilt of the head. 'Who is everyone? I thought you said we're doing practical.'

'We are. You're taking part in today's convocation.'

It seems to Misha that this day's sole purpose is to find out what makes her suffer most. 'I can't. I'm not ready.'

'You'll be fine.'

'You've got to be joking. I don't even know anything! You tell me all the time not to mess around with stuff I don't understand…'

'I meant on your own. Don't mess around on your own, without supervision. We won't be messing around today. This is the real thing.'

Granddad doesn't do jokes, so this must really be happening. But it can't be, it can't. 'Granddad, no. Please. All that will happen is I'll look stupid and I'll do something horrible…'

'You won't be in any danger.' He's trying to be nice and gently encouraging, but his foot's tapping wildly in a puddle. 'You'll be with people who know what they're doing, who've done this dozens of times…'

'And I've never done it at all!' Her voice is reaching a shout and she can't help it. 'I haven't got it. You know that, I know that.'

'Nobody "has" it, Misha. Nobody is born with it. It's a skill to be learned, and we all learn differently. We've been on the wrong track with you, that's all. If we bring you in on the real thing, I think it will all come together for you.'

Why did she come out of her stupid tree? 'Crosswell is there, isn't he? He hates me.'

'What on earth…'

'I overheard him telling you I'm a waste of time. I heard him! And he doesn't even keep it secret that he hates me. He looks at me like I just got scraped off a shoe. And there's that woman who laughs at everything he says, even when it isn't funny…'

Granddad goes back to collect her, pulling her along by the wrist. Not rough, but firm. 'Being involved in the process will teach you more than you think. The more you do, the better you get. And I don't know why you worry about Crosswell. He's a stern man, but that's only because he knows how serious a situation this is. Listen to him, learn from him, instead of treating him like an enemy. We're all on the same side. Now please, let's get a move on, they'll finish digging before we even get there…'

20

He's half into his coat and hopping into his other trainer as he tumbles out of the front door. Father's pulling up in the driveway, frowning at him, like he's sure the boy is fleeing from some crime. It occurs to Caleb that Father will be proven right: the dishes aren't done, and he'll catch hell for it when he gets home. He's running now, though, and can only spare a brief moment for regret, because they're up there again. Those people.

They're burying another one. Already.

He has to see.

21

It's that look.

She's told Granddad over and again about it. She wasn't making it up. She wasn't. There it is right there on that big ugly face. How can Granddad not see it? Crosswell is scowling at her. Scowling.

The rest of them are no better. All looking at her like she's crashed the party and ruined the fun. Misha wants to yell at them. *'I didn't ask to come here!'* she'd shout. *'I've been dragged here, I want nothing to do with any of you, so you've got no right to look at me like that!'* The shout sits as an iron ball in her chest, too heavy to move.

Other voices are rising. Granddad took Crosswell to one side for a quiet chat. They're not quiet now. 'This is not the time,' says Crosswell in a deep vibrating monotone. 'You want to play games with the child, do it later. Right now we have—'

Granddad is red and flustered and in no mood to wait for sentences to end. 'You said yourself that the training isn't working, so we'll try it this way instead.' He'll deny it, but Crosswell is upsetting him. Crosswell is always upsetting him.

'We'll try? Try? We don't get another go at this. If anyone messes this up, we can't reset and try again like it's a computer game. The damage that could be done…'

'What damage? You make it sound like we're a bunch of kids who'll let something Other come through. Why do you have to be so dramatic? Every one of us…' Granddad halts, realising how loud he's become. When he speaks again it is in low tones, but they still reach Misha's ears, like they want to be heard. 'Every one of us knows what we're doing. Unless you consider yourself to be an unskilled novice, Crosswell?' The bigger man doesn't like that, not one bit. And he's a good deal bigger than Granddad. Six inches taller, broader shoulders, thicker neck. Crosswell might not be a young man, but he's certainly younger than Granddad, perhaps by twenty years. If he wanted a fight, he would have it and win.

His big shoulders bunch up as if he really is about to let loose with his fists. If he dares, then Misha will jump on him. She's not scared. 'Clearly you've forgotten the importance of what we're doing. This isn't some little side-project. It's not some lesser task. What we're doing—'

'I know exactly what we're doing! There are no side-projects! There are no lesser tasks! This is it; this is all. If Misha is to learn, this is where and how.'

They stare at each other, immoveable forces.

If Misha's nerves were bad before, they are now out of control.

The woman, Morgan, the one who laughs at all of Crosswell's jokes, breaks the silence. 'Can we get on with this please, gents? The day marches on and a bottle of vino awaits my return.' Her voice is stagey, like she expects everyone to be watching her performance. She smiles and rolls her eyes whenever she says something she thinks is particularly interesting.

Misha hates that.

Crosswell laughs even though nothing at all funny is happening, at least as far as Misha can tell. 'You've got no idea what you're doing, old man. You're spending all your time playing at schools, silly games for silly girls. I don't think you're capable of—'

'Of what?' Misha has never heard Granddad's voice like this before, not even when she's at her worst. The words are shards of slate, cold and brittle. 'What am I not capable of, Crosswell? Leading? Being in charge? Shall I step down and hand it to you? Shall I hand you all of this?' He sweeps his twisty hands around to encompass the whole graveyard, and suddenly it feels as if the inside of Misha's chest is infinite and filled with rushing space. Such an urge within her! She'll give up every wish to have this one fulfilled: take it, Crosswell. Take it!

He's laughing again. Softer this time, like the whole thing was a joke all along. Like everyone's having fun together. 'Nobody wants to take your place. Nobody could, could they? I'm just expressing concerns the whole group has, that's all.'

'Hug it out, boys,' calls Morgan. 'We've got to show this girl how to turn the bones.' The phrase gives Misha the shivers. It sounds a lot like something that no one should do.

Granddad clearly wants to say a lot more to Crosswell, but he's very aware of everyone looking at him, especially his granddaughter. Now is not the time. He gives her that anaemic smile, the worst of all his masks. 'Yes, we should really get started. The revenant won't wait.'

'I thoroughly agree,' says Crosswell. He never can resist getting one last shot in. It's ignored by Granddad. It's stored away by Misha. Stored with all the rest.

'Everyone into positions,' Granddad says in a brisk officer voice. 'Misha, you're at sextus.' She looks at him blankly. 'Between Morgan and Grayson. There. Right there.' She shuffles over as slow as she can. Impatience pulsates from him, but he tries to hold his smile. 'Come on, Misha, no need to be shy, we're all friends here.'

An outrageous lie.

Morgan reaches out and strokes her arm. An ice cube against the skin would be less chilly. 'Us gals together, huh?' Misha nods as speaking seems pointless. 'You listen to me, hun, I'll keep you right.' With that ever-present smirk and cold plastic eyes, there's little right about Morgan. Misha's had bad dreams about this woman. Eight's had grimy things to say about this woman. The unwanted touch is lingering. She steps back, almost falls into the pile of dugout dirt.

Granddad thinks she's messing around and snaps. 'Misha! Take this seriously! Do you know what's at stake here?'

'Yes. You've only told me about a million times.'

'Damn right I have.' A deep breath. Composure recovered. 'This is where we prove ourselves, understand? Here and now.'

He jumps down into the open grave, lands with a thump on the coffin.

Misha doesn't want to prove herself. She wants to leave the graveyard and this miserable rainy town and all these horrible people. So many awful people.

22

Sneaking is hard when the very ground under your feet is against you. He can't stick to the paths and the roads, as they will see him. If it is a simple burial, and they see him, they will wonder what business he has crashing the gathering, and word will race back to Father and that would be unbearable. If they are up to no good and see him, he will be chased away, or worse, and worse is working some terrible tricks on his mind. As he slips and slides across an unplanted flowerbed, worse tells him that those dark-suited people near the top of the hill will teach nosey boys hard lessons. As he weaves around the rough trunks of trees, worse tells him of open graves and how easy they are to fill.

Would Father still be worried about the dishes?

Halfway up the hill his heel skids through a mud puddle, shooting too far forward. He flails, snatching out for a branch to catch hold of. But there is no branch, so Caleb slides into the splits, and he's no good at the splits, so he lands on his backside with a loud splatty splash. Very loud. Dive-bombing into a swimming pool would be quieter.

Surely they heard that.

They'll be coming for him. A pack of them, running pell-mell down the hill, accelerating. Spades and shovels and worse will be in their hands.

He should run away. Get back home where there's no suited strangers and no open graves. Watching from behind glass and distance, anyone can be choked and stoked with bravery. Out here, there could be very real danger. Irreversible danger.

He's a boy who's only ever played videogames. But he's also the only person who knows something bad is going on up here. He has to find out more.

Wet and mud-clagged, he peers around a tree, convinced a hideous face will glare at him from the other side. Nobody's coming. They're all still graveside. Six...no, seven people, a mound of mud behind them. One of them jumps into the grave. He needs to get moving. Quietly.

23

Gramps stands at his living room window, folding his ironing. He blames himself. His talks with the boy have done nothing. Clearly he's been too subtle. He'll have to be a lot more direct.

He hopes it's not too late.

Once he's done with these clothes, he'll go over his trains. They're long overdue a clean.

24

Misha's guts roll like ocean waves as Granddad prises open the coffin. Talking about these convocations, seeing them from far off, it's all so different to being right here on the precipice, here at the mouth of the grave, here in this moment when the dance is about to begin.

Grayson, he who never speaks, is first to start humming, holding a single steady note, like he's testing it. He holds it a long time, draining the air from his lungs. It seems impossible to Misha that he can carry on so long. She feels as if she can't catch enough breath for herself. Then he drops down through the octave, hitting each note hard and low, holding each for a few moments. There's the tiniest pause for breath, then back to the top of the octave, then he starts back down. Two notes down, the man standing beside Grayson joins in, but from the top note. Harris keeps rhythm with Grayson. He looks nervous. Misha wishes she hadn't seen that worry in his flitting eyes. The buzzing under her skin refuses to subside.

At the foot of the grave stands Esme, her face crinkled with folds, her eyes always behind sunglasses. She adds her rasping voice to the round, again two notes into Harris's scale. Misha has heard the Scales before, but from outside the group. It's a lot different, a lot scarier, being within the circle as the Scales approach her position. There are moments of discord as the trio go through the octave, staying in perfect time, each person two notes adrift from the last.

There's a dreadful creak from down in the hole, and Misha has always thought herself brave, but whatever's happening in the grave is something she never wants to see.

So she takes a quick glimpse, the most fleeting of glances. Granddad, feet braced against muddy walls, heaving open the coffin to look inside. The leather of his skin, the wire of his neck muscles; a vampire desperate to return to its slumber.

Morgan's humming now, hands flourishing along the Scale, and she taps Misha hard on the shoulder to get her attention, as it will be the girl's turn in mere seconds, and Misha can't do this, it's a mess of noise, she can't even do the Scales for more than ten seconds when it's just her and Granddad, and she'll mess it up and break the chain and leave an opening

and

Morgan points

and

she's humming, and she's going to cry because she will get this wrong even though she's concentrating so hard. There are five voices – six now – that are all hitting different notes in each moment, and her ears keep training in on each voice in turn, and she wants to sing the same note as them, not something out of tune. It's an unending, always fluctuating buzzing vibration. She's convinced she's not hitting the notes right. She can't. Her throat hurts already.

The lurkers at the edge of the circle, the ones that Granddad says are real, really real, they'll be on the group in a heartbeat if the Scales fall. Something, reaching for her, for all of them. Pushing. Pressing.

She must stick to her Scale.

The others are humming strong and loud. And, Misha realises, so is she. It thrums in her chest. It feels good, and powerful. It comes easy. It wants to *be*, it wants to exist. Round and round go the Scales, and the pressure at her back fades. Their voices have woven into one, become a force. She's no longer scared of upsetting the Scales. She's scared that it will simply stop.

The volume swells, and she isn't yet aware of the watching boy in the bushes. She's aware of just one thing: she's succeeding.

25

It's her. That Misha girl, with all these suits. Whatever's going on, she's a part of it. She actually spoke to him this morning, and yet she's up there. With them.

He stands absolutely still, and every muscle in his body is aching to move.

Why is she there? And what is that noise about?

Caleb thinks of things he's heard in school. About people in things called cults. None of them are good. A lot of them involve devils, and blood. He's heard stuff about Misha too, but nothing like this. He wants to be still, but he can't stop trembling.

26

They're here. The revenants.

It's not imagination. It isn't a case of the creeps. The disturbance has stirred them, drawn them in as bloody meat will pull in sharks. They come because they smell the chance to feed.

Granddad has never said where they come from, and she's never wanted to ask. But now she wishes she'd asked more and listened more.

Because they're here.

Misha doesn't know when she shut her eyes. Perhaps when she sensed them coming. Perhaps when she couldn't bear to see anything more of Granddad in the open grave with the dried-up old corpse.

That thought sends her skin crawling up her back.

Concentrate! The Scales!

The noise of their humming is a hypnotic sound-wall. It brings the revenants up short. It holds them, confuses them. She senses them prickling, struggling to understand, to find a way through. Misha's guts tell her that they must never, ever get through. It's exactly what Granddad's told her dozens of times, yes, but her guts are far more convincing.

Her innards tell her something else. These things can't exist. The world can't be like this.

She falters.

27

That noise, the wrongness of it, the pulsating cycles of it. It makes Caleb want to cry. And the old man in the grave, he's shouting, his voice coarse and panicky.

Of course the man's panicky. They're burying him.

These people have ordered him into the hole and they'll bury him alive. Caleb is about to witness a murder. A horrible, grisly murder. What could the old man have done to deserve it? Caleb can't imagine the horror of such a death. Doesn't want to. Can't bear to think about being down there begging for his life, shouting for help that isn't coming, pelted with shovel after shovel of mud, dirt landing in his mouth and eyes, and the mud getting higher around his legs, and higher, and higher, and then his legs can't move at all, and then his arms are trapped under the weight of soil, and then it's up around his neck, and cutting off his air

and Caleb feels himself choking and gasping to breathe

and why can't he keep quiet when he's this close to murderers and he's got to go and help.

He can't believe that the girl is up there, a part of this, on the side of the sick killers in suits. *No, can't think about her! Someone's in real actual danger, and I'm the only one here to see it and I need to go and get help, before they start shovelling!*

But would help come too late? He's near the top of Daisy Hill. There's a lot of running back to do. Then he's got to get in the house. Then Father won't believe him. Or Caleb could go to Gramps. But the old man might be having a bad day and not understand what he says. Perhaps a stranger would help. But there might not be any strangers. He might go running down to the street to find someone and no one's there to be found.

How much time is he wasting?

Seconds. His mind is racing so fast. But there's no time to run. He's no hero. He can't go striding up there and beat them all up, including the girl, the girl, what's the girl doing here? Caleb can't run, can't fight. He'll shout.

28

Her brain forgets the Scales, wants to scream at Granddad, because none of this is meant to be real. Why couldn't he and his horrible friends do this without her?

He's down there, slowly turning over the crumbling remains of a woman long dead, and he's chanting instructions, and he's so lost in what he's doing, they're all so lost, so far into the Scales, that none of them has a hope of seeing that she's losing control. Sextus has fallen.

In seconds a revenant will be on her. On them all.

Where is she in the Scale?

A rasping whisper, rushing around from the other side of the grave.

A note, any note!

She starts humming again. She's a split-second off the beat and she's started at the wrong time for sure, but it's okay because at least she's humming.

A boy's voice shouts from somewhere distant, 'Leave him alone!', and before there's enough time for that to confuse Misha, she's shoved in the back, jolts forward a step to the very edge of the grave, and the soil gives out under her foot, and she's falling.

29

He'd expected to be shouted at, or chased. What he hadn't expected was that Misha girl throwing herself into the grave. Some of the suits are looking into the grave after her. Some of them are staring at Caleb.

One thing: that God-awful noise has stopped.

He suspects he should run, but his legs are rigid. She could be hurt. She could be trying to get the man out. They'll bury her as well.

'I'm going to get help!' he shouts. They'll come running to stop him now. There'll be no murders done tonight. Unless they catch him.

Caleb regains control of his legs. He turns, ready to sprint for home. And as he turns, there's a phosphorous flash by the graveside, and a suit, a woman, is launched backwards into the air.

30

Granddad reaches out to catch her. Fumbles. She lands flat on her back. Something crumbles beneath her. Air whuffs out of her lungs. A firework bursts at the base of her skull, shooting sparks across her eyes, sparks that glitter like stars fleeing the darkening sky. Her lungs forget how to work, lie flat in her chest. Granddad's saying a lot of words quickly, but they come to her scrambled. She's sinking. Or the mud walls are stretching up. And narrowing. It feels like they're sliding inwards, and the remaining light is retracting. That boy's voice again, louder yet further away: 'I'm going to get help!' She likes the sound of that. Help should come quickly, Misha thinks. There's movement beneath her, like the ground or whatever she's lying on wants to roll her over. Granddad's reaching down for her, and he's taking a long time about it, like she's shrinking away from him, and none of this is quite right and she might be sick. A searing white flash blinds the sky and floods the grave with heavy light. A woman screams. She wonders if it's Morgan. Something's rolling her over. It's got a solid grip for something that's been buried for so long.

Buried. So long.

It's a dead hand that holds her.

Misha hasn't screamed since she was a toddler. She's screaming now. Fear, tearing through her throat. More hands have her. She thrashes, lashing out.

'Misha! I've got you, I've got you!' Granddad's voice is sharp, like she's come up for air after too long underwater. Time runs normal up in reality.

Granddad hauls her upright, kicking out at something. She won't look at the hand; she won't look at what the hand belongs to. She can't. Her mind might snap.

Now that she's started screaming, she cannot stop.

'Keep off her!' bellows Granddad, swinging another kick. It

lands with a dry crunch. 'Misha. Misha! Listen. I'll boost you out.' He laces the fingers of his hands together, leans back against the mud wall of the open grave. 'Come on!' She places her foot in the cradle of his hands. 'You head straight home. You don't wait for me. You don't wait for anyone. Go!' He heaves her up towards the sky, and she gets hold of solid ground, and scrambles out of that awful hole, and then wonders whether or not she should jump back in.

There's a lot of shouting, and running, and a pair of torches swinging around. She can't remember anyone bringing torches. Crosswell, Morgan, Grayson, the others are thirty yards downhill, their motions lively, frantic. Waving his arms in big sweeping gestures, Crosswell pushes his people out and around to surround one of their own, the one with the torches.

They aren't torches.

As the beams slice from one person to the next, Misha sees that they are blazing out of Miss Neuman's face, out of her eyes. They're as bright as twin lasers. Neuman's mouth unhinges. From it belts a crackling wail, an animal warning. The message is crystal clear: come near and die.

Misha wants to be nowhere near a thing like that. She'll run back to the house like Granddad said and lock all the doors and windows. And that will be her marked forever as a coward. Crosswell and the others already hate her. They'll blame her for this, even though she wanted nothing to do with them in the first place, even though none of this was her idea.

She won't let them call her a coward. She won't. Not even Vic Sweet gets to call her that.

She runs towards Torchhead Neuman and the others. She has no idea what she can possibly do. Crosswell shouts at her to get away, and he has a round mirror in his hand, they all have a mirror, and Neuman is whirling and spinning those two beams like a broken disco ball. When the lights hit the mirrors they fragment, they bounce off at crazy angles, and one beam flashes across her eyes

through her eyes

and she sees Oh God she *sees*

the world stripped bare, blasted by some terrible weapon, all flesh and prettiness torn away, all pasted in icy blues and steely whites that scorched to the very back of her head, to the very core of herself, and the trees no longer have leaves or bark and they lean in her direction, and the grass has seared away from the hard jagged ground, and the gravestones burn white hot like metal too long in the fire, and the occupants of those graves seethe with fluorescence, and Crosswell and Morgan and the others are without suits or skins or flesh

and Neuman is monstrous, a grinning, glowering invention of a mad god

and the beam is gone. The trees are dressed. Everyone has their skin on. The ranks of the dead are all hidden from view by six feet of earth. Neuman's still a demented Halloween lantern.

Misha sinks to her knees on the rain-soft ground. She's overly aware of the flesh on her bones and it's all turned to rubber. Two voices shout at her at once. 'Get away, you stupid girl,' bellows Crosswell

and 'I told you to get home!' hollers Granddad, emerging from the grave.

She wants to tell them that she can help, she really can, but her jaw feels slack. Neuman's going off like a lightning storm, jagging at anyone it thinks might lower their guard, flickering back when it can't find an opening.

Neuman, hunting for weakness, spins towards her. She turns away so fast her neck hurts: that cyanotic version of the world is a place she never wants to be again (see not be – never wants to *see* again, because she was never really there, not really, was she?). Misha turns, and see the boy fleeing.

He's been spying.

The rubber leaves her legs. She runs after him. No shouting at him to stop, no yelling at him to come back. All her energy goes into running.

And she's fast. A hunted lifetime keeps her fleet-footed, and she *knows* this graveyard, know the very ground. Her feet remember where every bump and ditch lies. Only slippery mud can slow her down. Caleb is all spinning limbs. He can barely keep his balance. Hearing footsteps behind him, Caleb speeds up. He doesn't look back to see who it is, doesn't know it's her, just wants to go, go, go.

He veers off to the left, darting behind a hedge, trying to shake off his tail. A mistake. He should have held a straight line for the gates. There's a slim chance that he might have got away from her. She doesn't take the same left, keeps running alongside the next hedge. He's weaving through trees now, which slows him a little. Misha's getting faster. She feels like she could take off, soar off the side of Daisy Hill and keep accelerating. Her elbows pump, her legs blur.

Caleb shoots out from behind a tree, crashes into a bush he didn't see until too late. The dense foliage tangles around his ankles, pulls him down. He hits the ground hard, one arm at full stretch to protect his head. Misha leaps on him, lands squarely on his back. She pins his shoulders, leans close to his ear. 'Couldn't stay away, could you? You're in big trouble now, and it's your own stupid fault.'

Her turn for a mistake.

Leaning forward leaves her off balance. Caleb bucks and rolls, throwing her off. She tumbles, but is quickly upright, and grabs Caleb even as he's finding his feet. 'Get off!' he shouts, shoving her away. 'Just leave me alone!'

'Leave you alone? You're the one who came looking for us!'

'Us! You said us! I was right, you *are* one of them!' He's angry, like he's been tricked.

'One of them who? What are you talking about?' Misha suddenly feels like she's the one who's been caught, not the other way round. It's uncomfortable. It's weird. She's done nothing wrong.

There's a lot of shouting further up the hill.

'I knew there was something going on up here, I knew it, and I'm right, and I saw it all, I saw everything they've been up to, and you're a part of it.'

Her fingers flex rapidly, her shoulders hunch, her head tilts forward, she glares at him from under the hoods of her eyelids. 'Like you've got any idea what's going on. Like you've got any clue what you're talking about.'

Even though her voice dropped really low, and despite the escalating noise of whatever's going on behind the trees, Caleb heard Misha clearly, and he heard the threat within the words, and he doesn't like her broad, ready stance, and he takes a step back. 'I know enough,' he says. 'I've heard about cults, I've heard what they get up to.' He tries to put the threat in his own words, his stance.

She laughs. Genuine, musical, delighted. A girl who's heard a wonderful joke so good she can ignore the howling madness that's tearing through the graveyard. 'Oh my God, you think I'm in a cult! Oh my God! What did you think we were doing, drinking the blood of virgins, summoning Satan and all of his minions?'

Caleb's not quite sure what virgins are, but he's not about to admit that. She's already laughing at him. 'If you're not in a cult…' All those noises seem far, far closer than can be safe. 'If you're not in a cult, then what were you doing up there? Because it didn't look like anything normal.'

'You don't need to know.' She steps right up to him, intensely serious, the seriousness of a teacher telling someone their exam result might ruin their life. 'It's not for ordinary people like you. If any of them saw you, if they find out who you are, they'll come after you, you better believe it, and no one will stop them.' A loud crack. Loud enough to be a tree trunk splitting down the middle. Blazing eye-lights chopping and whirling. The unholy air-ripping of its screams.

Neuman comes screeching out of the trees.

The children run.

Misha peels away at incredible speed. Caleb, needing to be far from the mad monster with light bulbs where eyes should be, automatically follows her. She yells something at him. He can't make it out. The monster's screeching too much for him to hear anything else. She waves. Points. Shouts again. 'Get out of the graveyard!'

He looks to where she pointed. The gates. The way out. He'll have to double-back on himself to get there. His gut tells him no turns. Keep going straight. Get as far from it as possible. It's only a few paces behind. Thump, thump, thumping after him. His back is cold, like he's being chased by a glacier. Relentless, inhuman, hungry. Caleb runs harder, the world bounces frantically. He can't catch Misha. She's a sprinting machine. All pistons. Those lightbeams. Everything they touch changes for a heartbeat. A glimpse of wasted blue grass burning away from the ground's steel layers. Misha becomes a flashing x-ray. Fences appear made of enormous bent claws. And what are those shapes he can see underground, through the ground, right through the very ground itself?

A thump. It's tripped. He does a quick look over his shoulder. There it is, ten yards back, face-first on the ground. He might get away! It looks up. Its beams flash across his eyes

through his eyes

and he sees Oh God he sees

A slap across the side of the head snaps him out of it, sets his right ear ringing. It's Misha. She came back. 'Run, you idiot!' She shoves him in the direction of the gates.

The torchhead monster is getting up.

Behind it, the suits emerge from the trees.

Caleb runs. He slips again and again but doesn't fall and doesn't stop running until he's home.

31

It's all about those few dishes.

Father is relentless about them. 'I don't ask you to do much, Caleb. It's a simple little job, it's five minutes of your time, but you're still too lazy to get off your backside and do it. I mean, what is it that you think, Caleb? That it doesn't need doing? That I should go to work all day long then come home and tidy up after you?'

Caleb washes them as fast as he can with a heart in his mouth and his nerves on fire. He nods along with everything Father says, gives out some 'sorrys' and 'I knows' in all the relevant places. Wings flutter against his lungs. The doorbell will ring at any moment, and Father will answer because he'd never listen to Caleb telling him not to, and the suits will be there asking for him, and Misha will be behind them, glaring at him with her head tilted forward that way she does, looking at him like he's something monstrous.

No knock at the door. Yet.

But it's coming. It is.

He pulls the plug from the sink, gets a tea towel to dry the dishes, and still Father is ranting. 'It's the same thing every day. I ask you to do something, then you don't bother, then you apologise, then you promise it'll be different tomorrow, then it's exactly the same. It's not like I'm asking a lot from you. It's basic cleanliness. It's learning how to live like a human instead of like a pig. It's a little bit of your time. I know it must be a wrench to pull yourself away from such important things like computer games and comics and...'

It's tempting for Caleb to place the glass he's drying back on the drainer for a moment, look Father calmly in the eye and tell him a truth like, 'I watched some people try to bury a man alive and I was chased by a monster with lights for eyes and I saw the stuff that's underneath the world we see, and you're going mad because I didn't do a few dishes? Which of these things do you think is more important? You tell me.' He'll never say that. Not even as a grown-up. He finishes drying that last glass, and puts it away in the glasses cupboard, and stands with his back against the fridge, and waits for Father to finish telling him what a disappointment he is and how ignorance is the least of his crimes.

Caleb's heart hammers because people are out looking for him, they are, and they'll come here and they'll get him.

Or that thing will come. That thing with the lighty-up head. The lights that peel back the skin of the world.

Father's walking away, shaking his head. It's possible that he asked a question that Caleb didn't answer. Too busy thinking about x-rays and the steel layers of the ground and the buried shapes six feet below. And the sky.

He can't think about the sky.

To his room he runs, taking the stairs two at a time. He almost doesn't dare to approach his window for fear of what he might see. Almost. Curiosity remains resistant to all efforts to squash it. He steps across his room, and he feels the blood drop out of his head and upper body and arms and flood into his feet, making them lumpen and draggy. The thinness of his veins, the dry heave of his pumping heart makes him feel pasty and faint, and he flops onto the windowsill, propping himself up with jelly elbows. He looks out into an evening grown dusky, casts his eyes over the graveyard and up the hill.

There's no one to be seen.

It's hard to tell from this distance, but he thinks the grave's been filled in. There's no way they've done that so quickly.

No dirt-pile. No suits. No Misha. No torchhead monsters.

Movement, bottom right.

False alarm. Just an old man walking an old dog slowly. The same scene he's stared at a gazillion times before. Except he's seen what's underneath. He's seen the world with life blasted from it, with nothing left upon it but the cold hungers of dead things.

His ear still rings from when Misha slapped him on it. If the slap's real, then the rest is real, including that insane monster that shouldn't exist, that burning sun wearing a human costume.

Was that other world real? When those lights fired into his eyes, was everything he saw just in his mind?

The old man with the old dog disappears out of view. There's nothing but the breeze moving. Caleb sinks down to make a lower profile, and watches for the enemy, and wishes he'd never measured the graveyard.

32

Gramps watches his step and eases his way across the attic. There's only a partial flooring up here. A foot in the wrong place will mean an awkward DIY job at the very least.

The suitcase is up here somewhere, amongst all the other luggage, boxes, bags, and knick-knacks. When he finds it, he'll have to be careful taking it down the ladder. He's far from being a nimble young man. These days he's just an old man with bad memories and worse enemies. But, as he roots around in dust and the stark light from a bare bulb, he remembers this much – it's not merely old age that scrambles his recollections at inconvenient times. It's not merely old age that's eating at him.

33

He'll give sleeping outside a miss tonight.

But Caleb knows he won't be able to get to sleep. And on those nights when he can't sleep, his only hoped usually is to take his quilt out under the stars.

Those stars, in that sky. How can he sleep under it ever again?

He feels hunted, a rabbit cowering in its burrow. Nobody's knocked at the door. The phone hasn't rung. The enemy hasn't come for him. He hasn't seen them roaming the streets for clues. That doesn't mean they won't turn up. They must be asking Misha about him. She's bound to tell them where he lives. She hates him.

But if that's so, then why haven't they come for him by now?

He's been within these walls too long, breathing the same air over and over. It's an evening that's gone on for days. He's sure the ceiling's coming down on him.

Out of the window he goes, dragging his quilt along with him. The base of his throat clenches to hold down the panic. He doesn't want to be out here; he has to be out here. But he's skittish, looking out for ambushes. He creates his quilt cocoon and lies down quickly, vulnerability driving him to snuggle down low. He thinks himself mad to be out here.

It's a little bit thrilling.

This is how he imagines it would feel to feature on a Wanted: Dead or Alive poster, his face sketched in an evil distortion, a price underneath it. Going through every day wondering when the baddies will catch up with him or when someone will shop him to the baddies must make all the nerve-endings buzz...a lot like his are right now.

The monster in a human suit. That doesn't give him a buzz. That makes him want to cry. Up until now, life's been a dull and occasionally awful experience in plodding through the hours, but at least there's been no actual monsters.

Until today.

It can't really exist. It can't really be a monster. There must be another explanation. The sight of a man being buried had already scared him. Perhaps the fear had sent him briefly loopy. But if that was true, then why had Misha run away from the same thing? All his thoughts about that girl start with why. *Like why am I thinking about her again?*

There's a sound approaching, a rhythmic sound amongst the usual sighing of the deepening night. It's a call. Someone calling out. Caleb lifts his head a few inches off the pillow, concentrates on the sound. It's a single syllable, repeated at intervals. He counts, like he's calculating the distance of an incoming storm. Ten seconds. Every ten seconds someone calls out the same thing.

'Kay.'

His throat is no longer flesh and saliva; it is dust and lava. He's heard this voice already today, booming and crackling like an aged speaker, turned up too loud.

'Kay.'

Caleb's been outside barely five minutes. He imagines the monster lying low all day, only coming out when it caught his scent in the air.

'Kay.'

Sinking down into the quilt, willing himself to be flat, Caleb tries to quiet his breathing. It's far too loud. The rise and fall of his chest causes the quilt to whisper. Too loud.

'Kay.'

People must be able to hear that in their houses over their TVs. He knows it's getting closer, but how close is it now? Around the corner? In the street? A few doors away?

'Kay.'

To Caleb's ears that single word is booming. Hot tears bleed down the sides of his face.

He's desperate to take a look. The monster's either far enough away that he can sneak a quick peek, or it's so close (and it sounds like it's at the end of the drive) that he needs to run and never stop.

'Kay.'

He rolls very slowly onto his belly, slides forward to the edge of the garage roof. Sliiiiiiiides, and what a thin, rasping noise the quilt makes on the coarse roof, the smallest of indistinct sounds that could give him away to the horrible thing in the street.

'Kay.'

A pair of searchlights sweep the road. They rove at random like beacons on a lighthouse gone mad, swooshing across the sea of tarmac. They are beacons that search for him. He should push back away from the roof's edge, push away, keep flat and pray. But then he won't know exactly where it is. And the movement might catch its…lights. (*What happened to its eyes, where are its eyes?*)

The monster is five or six doors away, stops every few steps to scan around, and Caleb is rigid with fear.

'Kay.'

The loud monotone intonation never changes. It is insistent, yet patient. It will search onwards and forever. It is ceaseless. It is an engine for hunting. It's almost at the end of next door's drive, and its lights scour everything: pavement, cars, tarmac, walls, and gardens. All of these things, when the light hits them, are painted cold and stark. Flowers are withered and sharp. Vehicles are torture mechanisms made of cogs and needles. There are no bricks in the walls, only bones. Caleb hates looking at all of this, at the hidden dead world beneath the one he inhabits, yet it's fascinating. It's incredible. He bets no one's ever seen anything like it.

His mouth is dry like stone.

The monster is outside his house. A demon summoned in a graveyard, loose in the streets. It stops, turns its beams on the front door.

Does it know he lives here? It can't, it can't possibly. Unless one of the suits sent it. Or Misha did. (*She didn't she didn't she didn't.*)

'Kay.'

It's calling him out. It knows he's here. It knows.

It moves on. Left to right it searches, left to right.

Caleb's chest burns hot from holding his breath so long. He lets it out in a long tight stream, watching the monster walk away. It stops again two doors down, casting that phosphorous gaze over the neighbour's house.

'Kay.'

Gradually it tromps away. Hunting.

Caleb has no idea what he's going to do about this. He doesn't know who he can tell that will believe it. The only people who have actually seen it are the suits and Misha, and they're all enemies, so he can't turn to them for help. Well, the suits are definitely enemies. Misha is…difficult. He doesn't know about her. Not at all.

He doesn't know about a lot of things lately.

He really hates that.

So Caleb lies incredibly still, telling himself to get up and get back inside before that thing returns, get inside and stay there for good, but he's too scared to move quite yet, too outright jelly-bones terrified to twitch even a pinky. *I'll go inside in a minute,* he tells himself, *when it feels safe.*

But it doesn't feel safe, and he doesn't go inside, and sleep refuses to come.

34

There's a packed bag tucked under her bed. It's right at the back behind a box of books, where it's unlikely to be seen and found. It's not a big bag and there's not a lot in it. A change of clothes. Some snacks. A notepad and pen. A book for long journeys and quiet nights. A small purse containing the small amount of money she's saved or found. It's more a short-term survival kit for getting through the first couple of days out in the big wide world, after which she should have a long-term plan in place. She organised it in case of emergencies, or if the urge to see whether or not the world has better things to offer became too great to resist.

This might be an emergency.

Surely Granddad will give up on her after this. From the sounds of things, Crosswell wants her head mounted on the spikes of the front gates.

'You wouldn't listen, would you?' Crosswell bellows. As far as Misha's concerned, it was pointless Granddad sending her to her room out of the way. She can hear everything, especially with that big idiot shouting like he's dishing out orders on a battlefield. 'Stupid old man! You can't see the truth when it's right in front of your face! The girl is an idiot. She's never had a hope of being able to handle it. We've told you this over and over again and now this, now Neuman's gone, and you still won't listen!'

Misha hates him. Really hates him. The kind of hate where, if he disappeared forever because something bad happened to him, that would be absolutely fine by her.

'It's you that doesn't listen!' Granddad this time, his temper lost. A tremor in his voice. Is it fear of Crosswell, or fear of his own temper? 'It has to be her! *It has to be her!* How else can I say it before it gets through your thick skull?'

Morgan next, purring like a cat, but still perfectly audible to Misha. 'Now, now, let's not get too heated. Crosswell makes a good point, if somewhat poorly. The girl clearly has no aptitude…'

'She has a name! Use it!'

A moment of silence. Opposing sides weighing each other up. Misha takes Eight down off the shelf, holds it close. Her only friend, blunt and true.

Morgan continues, but with a bitter edge. She thinks men should only ever flirt with her, not shout at her. 'Misha doesn't possess the necessary skills. It's not her fault, or yours. Look, a lot of people can't paint, and a lot of people are no good at maths, see? Our Misha…'

'*My* Misha was under extreme stress. It's no wonder she couldn't perform! She knows none of you has one little bit of faith in her. I asked you all for your co-operation, for your help, your trust, and you couldn't do it. No, shut up; just shut your mouth, Crosswell. You are worse than a child. All of you, less than children. You bully a twelve-year-old rather than do what has to be done.'

Misha snorts. If they are bullies, then they are not less than children. They are the same. Vic Sweets will always be Vic Sweets, and people don't change, and life has no hope of getting any better. It's all a big joke, and someone somewhere must be laughing, because if no one's laughing, then what's the point?

Crosswell fumes. Morgan shushes him. 'It's not bullying, it's trying to make a point. You're wrong about her; it's never going to work. You're refusing to look at it from anyone else's angle. What if you're wrong?'

'What if I'm right? What if I'm right and you lot have destroyed her confidence? Have any of you taken a second to think about that?'

Misha shakes the ball. 'Well, Eight? Have they taken a second to think about that?'

An answer resolves itself in the window. *Don't be silly.* Eight shakes itself in her hands, and three more words appear. *Ask proper questions.*

'That was proper, you horrible old thing. There was a question mark at the end and everything.' She understands what it really means, though. Eight knows her well. It's hard for her to ask what she wants to ask. The question has caught its hook in her throat. It's a very final question. It's a path-changer, a bridge-burner. Difficult. She wants to and she doesn't.

Eight hears the question anyway. *Not yet,* it says, and the answer is both a relief and a disappointment for her. Running away would be easy, and hard. She trusts Eight like she's never trusted anyone.

'How long?' she asks. 'How long do we wait?'

A while longer. Eight won't be pinned down any more than that. She's had it almost a year, and knows that pressing for more accuracy will only agitate Eight and lead to it going silent. It doesn't like to talk in hours or days or weeks. So, while the shouting continues outside her bedroom, while Granddad, Crosswell and Morgan fail to agree on who's most wrong, she decides to head out and hassle Grayson. The window slides up without a squeak, and she takes Eight with her. She likes the oddness of carrying Eight around, likes the way it confuses people. It's heavy too. Good for hitting people. Not that she would. But she might.

In pyjamas and slippers she tromps through the midnight graveyard, over dirt paths and muddy puddles, and very quickly her footsteps become squishy. Her autopilot almost takes her through the copse of trees, the one Neuman burst out of. Might not be the best idea at this time of night. There won't be anyone there, but still.

Still.

She walks around. It only adds another thirty seconds to her journey. There's Grayson sitting approximately where Neuman landed after being blasted back from the graveside. Misha considers the distance that Neuman flew. 'You know,' she says good and loud, making him jump, 'the grave's right up there, and Neuman hit the deck all the way down here, right?'

'We're busy,' growls Grayson. He's not a fan of surprises. Or Misha. Just like all the others.

She acts like she didn't hear him. 'Wouldn't you think that some bones would be broken? A lot of bones, maybe even the neck.'

He doesn't turn away from the Weave. 'It's late. Little girls should be in bed.'

'You wouldn't think it would be able to walk around, would you? Not with all those different bits of itself all snapped and busted.'

He turns to glare at her. 'She's not an it. She's called Neuman. She's a person.'

Misha shrugs like it doesn't matter. 'Is she? I mean right now. When she's possessed. Because you can call it what you want, but that's what it is. Do you think she's still in there? If she isn't, what will happen when you get her back? If you get her back. Don't suppose you thought of that.

Grayson hums a note but drops a loop, and snarls in frustration, and the whole construction shudders. 'You've done enough damage for one night,' he snaps. 'Be somewhere else.'

Eight says there's nowhere else for me to be yet, she thinks, as she caresses the ball cradled in her left elbow crook. 'Is that thing going to work?' she asks, pointing at the complex weave of the light-map.

'Yes, because you're not involved in it, now shut up.'

'By the time you've made it, you probably could've found Neuman the normal way. You know, walking around and asking if anyone's seen anyone who's possessed and had torches for eyes.' She knows what he's really doing. When it's complete, the map should lock onto Newman's position and help draw her back to the graveyard, no need to go hunting the streets and risking a dangerous showdown. Misha likes winding Grayson up, though. His shoulders are so tense they might rip out of his suit. She knows he'd love to slap her about, because she asked Eight, and Eight told her blunt and true.

She's got this urge to keep pushing until he does it.

But she's bored. All the grown-ups are very busy doing not much. Three in the house arguing, two out here weaving, none of them wanting her around. So she'll go for a little lookey-about herself. And perhaps things will get exciting. Perhaps she'll find Neuman and prove to the grown-ups how much better than them this stupid little kid is.

Besides, she's never actually seen someone spirit-locked. Heard about it, all about it, but never seen before tonight. It's fascinating.

She walks off down Daisy Hill. Grayson doesn't care enough to notice.

35

He is about to get the fright of his life.

Two minutes before his nervous system jolts him with iced electricity, Caleb has his plan of action all sorted out. Of course he's not going to tell Father, and of course he's not going to approach Gramps about it. He'll make an anonymous call to the police; say there's a vicious crazy woman called Neuman walking the streets. Then he'll stay away from the graveyard forever. He will. Even if that means never visiting Mum again. Then he'll let Father answer the door at all times, no matter how much he shouts at Caleb to do it. Father already hates him, so a little bit of extra disobedience won't make a difference. And if the suits do come knocking and convince Father he's done something terrible, Caleb will take the punishment. Should Father insist that he talks to the suits or apologises, then Caleb will lock himself in his room and let the punishments mount up. Father already hates him. It won't make a difference.

That's the plan. It's all he can come up with. Not particularly heroic. Frustrated tears tremble behind his eyes. He won't let them out.

He'll go to the nearest phone-box and make the call. Soon. He'll go soon. He keeps catching the faintest hint of that repeated syllable, *'Kay.'* It's far off, and he doesn't hear it often…but he doesn't want to bump into that thing in the street. It runs. It wants to do something unpleasant to him.

'What are you doing up here?' booms the voice of the face looming over him. He cries out, tries to jump out of his quilt, head-butts the looming face, which lets out a girlish cry of its own. Caleb's legs have quilt twisted between them, and he falls, falls towards the edge, the drop.

His dizzy guts flip to the floor a split-second before the rest of him.

A hand catches hold of the neck of his T-shirt, yanks him back to safety. Yanks hard. His feet are still a-tangle, and Caleb falls on top of his rescuer, flattens the girl. Air whuffs out of lungs. Caleb finds himself staring into Misha's eyes.

His breath won't start, and her eyes are deep, and he's only vaguely aware of the eight-ball on the pillow beside her, and it's not until later that the three words in its smoky window will come to him.

'You in the habit of squashing people you meet?' she wheezes, and he leaps to his feet as if hauled up on violent strings.

'What you on about?' he flusters, sure his face is glowing in the dark, a fierce hotness. 'You in the habit of giving people heart attacks and making them fall off the roof?'

'You didn't fall.' She stands, giving him that weird unwavering look. 'I saved you. That's what happened just then. Right now. Where I grabbed hold of you and stopped you breaking your neck. And after that you said, "Thank you for saving me," didn't you? Oh, that's right, you didn't.'

Caleb's in a fuddle. He'd been busy lying under his quilt in fear, harming no one, bothering nobody, and now, seconds later, he's upset this strange girl with no idea about how he managed to.

His mum warned him in one of her letters that girls are trouble.

'It's gone midnight. Why aren't you in bed?' And why won't his face cool down?

That expression doesn't leave her face. They're in the same year at school, so how come he feels like he's younger than her? 'Been a bit of an exciting night and everyone in the graveyard is a tad agitated. Hey, in fact, I think you were there. You know, that whole thing you caused?'

'I didn't cause anything, you lot were the idiots digging up graves and throwing people in, and stop doing that sarcasm thing, it's so annoying.'

'Forgive me if I've hurt your feelings.' She clearly doesn't mean it. The curtsey is really, really doubly annoying.

He runs a shivery hand through his hair, grabbing a little, pulling a little. His scalp prickles. 'Just go home. Kids aren't meant to roam the streets at night. It's weird.'

She's whip-quick. 'Just go indoors. Kids aren't meant to sleep on garage roofs. It's weird.'

He wants to tear his hair out completely. Big clumps, rip and tear. 'It's not weird. It's…'

'It's what?'

'It's what I do, okay? So drop it.'

She shifts conversations like they're building bricks she can click together any way she chooses. 'You're going to help me find Neuman.'

'Who?'

'Lights for eyes.'

'No. No I'm not. I'm not doing anything with you. I'm going in, you're going away.' He starts gathering up his quilt. She snatches it away from him. 'Hey, what—'

'Listen, before I push you off the roof for real. Whatever you think, you were a part of what happened up there.' She points to Daisy Hill. He can make out a small, flickering glow. 'That thing wandering the streets is crazy. Bad crazy. Someone innocent could get hurt before my granddad and those idiots get their act together. We need to lead it back to the graveyard where we can deal with it properly.' She picks up the eight-ball, shakes it. 'Is this boy a coward?' She stares expectantly at its small window. The only thing weirder than what Misha's doing is the fact that Caleb finds himself eager to know the answer. It's foolish. An eight-ball's answers are random and have no bearing on reality.

But still.

Misha raises an eyebrow at the answer, then looks at him as if making a decision. 'Hmm. I suppose I should have seen that coming.'

'What? What did it say?'

'Why? What do you care? I thought I was the weirdo who's meant to go home.'

It's fortunate that the night's air is cool, or his head might explode. 'Why can't you give me a straight answer?'

'Why can't you ask a straight question?'

He shakes his head as if trying to clear it of a confusing dream. 'I'm going in. You do what you like.' He holds a hand out for his quilt. She drops it off the garage roof and onto the front drive. It's the closest he's come yet to screaming. 'I can't believe you just did that. If my Father sees that he's going to kill me.'

'He's in bed, isn't he? So how's he going to see anything? All you've got to do is help me do this one thing.'

'I don't want to go back up there.' Blunt and true.

'You do, and I know you do, I know it.' Funny how her eyes blaze fierce in the night, black lights in the darkness. 'Your mum's up there, and until we put this right those idiots with my granddad won't let you back up there. In fact, if they find Neuman first, they'll come after you next.'

He's not going to let this girl see him cry. He pushes past her to climb down off the roof. 'None of this would be happening if you'd stayed away from me.'

Her voice is cold. 'That's not quite true, is it?'

36

They haven't spoken since leaving his house. They're both in pyjamas and slippers, steering as clear as they can of the bright glow of lampposts. Very few houses have any lights on; all have blinds and curtains closed. So far, there's only been one slightly drunk man to avoid, which wasn't a problem for two nimble kids. Caleb's heart races anyway. He has no idea what Misha's home life might be like, but sneaking around the streets in the dead of night will mean big trouble for him.

Dead don't think dead.

'You're sure it went this way?' she finally asks.

'Yes,' he whispers, 'and keep your voice down.'

'Why? I'm not the one worried about being found.'

'I'm going home.' He turns one hundred and eighty degrees. She grabs his hand and pulls him back. The fingers pressing against his palm give him a small warm shock.

'Take it easy, I'll whisper if it'll stop you having a hissy fit.'

It's a full minute before either of them speaks again. Caleb rubs his palm with his thumb. 'What had he done?'

'Who?'

'That guy you were burying alive.'

Her laugh is loud, sharp. He's sure that everyone in the street heard it. 'That was my granddad! He can be a bit much, but I wouldn't put him six feet under. Old swine would only find a way to get back anyway.'

'So what was going on then?' What he wants to ask is – *What lie are you going to tell me next?*

Her humour comes and goes quickly. 'You don't need to understand any of that. Best if you don't, really.'

'So how am I meant to—'

'You're not meant to anything. You said yourself that you don't want to get involved. So don't. You couldn't handle it.' They reach a crossroads. A right-hand turn here would lead them to the shopping centre and the big supermarket. They catch sight of a flicker up ahead, and the death of an echo reaches them. 'Straight on,' says Misha, full of all the confidence that Caleb lacks.

'Pernicious House is up this way,' he says, swallowing the throb of his own heart.

'Uh huh,' she says, turning the eight-ball over and over in her hands. It is blacker than the sky and reflects the stars.

'You take that thing with you everywhere?'

'Don't be ridiculous. I couldn't take it in the bath, could I? That would be stupid.' She tucks it under her left arm, the side furthest from Caleb.

He shakes his head. 'The way you carry on, it's no wonder...'

'What?' She stops in the middle of the street. 'No wonder what? Go on, spit it out.'

The heat returns to his chest. 'Nothing. I wasn't saying anything.'

'Really? That's funny, because I'm sure I heard your lips flapping about...' The sound of metal in pain from somewhere up ahead cuts Misha off. 'We'd better hurry,' she says, giving him another of her many looks. This one, with pursed lips and wide eyes, tells him that he's far from off the hook.

Their pace quickens, slippers slapping on pavement. Houses come to an end. On their left is a high wall, some twelve feet, to their right, trees. The metallic wailing has ended, just out of sight around the road's curve. The pair shift gear to a job, and Caleb can only wonder at his own stupidity. They're practically running towards the mad monster from the graveyard. Towards it. What kind of idiot would do something like that?

Me, he thinks. *I'm that idiot.*

But he's sure Misha is making some sense, even if she's a bit dotty. Put things right, even if none of this is his fault. Show the suits he's on their side, even if he doesn't know whose side they're on. Then they'll all leave him alone. Then life can be normal again.

Idiot.

They're at the locked wrought-iron gates of Pernicious House. Several of the iron bars have been snapped and bent to allow access. 'In we go, then,' says Misha.

Caleb doesn't want to go in chasing monsters. He doesn't want to go in at all.

He hasn't been here since Mum died.

The fountains are off. The lights are out. Darkness dominates. It has weight. He will have to push hard through it. Misha's already stepped in. 'Come on,' she says. 'You've come this far. Look, I'll even ask Eight. Should Caleb keep going?' She shakes the ball, waits for the answer. 'Wow. Okay. Eight can be a bit rude sometimes. We're old enough to make our own decisions, right?'

Caleb laughs despite himself. Misha doesn't laugh, just looks at him apologetically. It convinces him that their wavelengths are light-years apart.

He steps through the broken gate.

37

'For the last time,' says Crosswell, fingernails pressing into the meat of his palms, 'you must have done it wrong, you must have!' In the glow of the light-map his jowls take on a ghastly pallor, and his eyes look washed out and dead. It does nothing for an already unattractive man.

'You were here too,' says Grayson.

A sausage finger points. 'You were on the harmonics.'

'And I was flawless. As always. I wasn't the one arguing with a child.'

'Don't you talk to me like that!' Crosswell has to draw in a long stream of air through his nose to calm the anger. 'I wasn't arguing with the brat, she was arguing with me.'

'There's nothing wrong with the map. The weave is solid. It'll hold for as long as we want it to.' He points into the map, to the miniature version of the graveyard. There are two white lights close to each other and, between them, something that could be an incredibly tiny version of a map. Around them, all around them in the miniature graveyard, are very dim blue lights.

'If there's nothing wrong with it, then explain this to me: why isn't it doing it's job? Why isn't it showing Neuman?'

38

Pernicious House didn't look like this when Mum brought him here, back when he was six. His blazing sun memories paste themselves over this after-dark alter ego. He's free of Mum's guiding hand, running for the first of the three spouting fountains. She shouts at him to slow down or he'll fall in headfirst, and that sounds all right to him, and when he gets to the crystalline water, dappled with spray, he almost flips right on in. Bronze and silver wishes are scattered across the bottom and he wants to reach in and grab them all, but he'll get his sleeve wet, and then he really will be told off. He wishes he had a garden with fountains in. And look at the house! It's massive! It's bigger than Mum said it would be, and more so! Tall columns and doors for giants to get through and dozens of windows and—

'Are you coming or not?' Misha's halfway up the first flight of stairs. The front gardens sprawl across three levels, and there are more stairs before they reach the courtyards. He treads after her over gravel paths, stepping over foot-high hedgerows to cut corners.

Pernicious House is a huge slab in the night. It looks years dead. It feels abandoned, hopeless. It's a monstrous mockery, made to hold soulless creatures terrified of the light. 'If that Neuman thing's gone in there,' he says, 'you can just forget about it.'

'We go where Neuman goes. We need her back.'

'I won't go in.'

Misha walks on like she didn't hear him. They're up top now, crossing the courtyard, looking for open or broken windows. All sealed so far. 'Can't see any lights in there,' she says. Caleb knows that she means Neuman's eye-lights. 'I think it's gone around the back.'

'Why would it want to get in here?'

She shrugs. 'Who says it does? There's acres of gardens here.

Neuman's probably going to wander until she finds...'

'*Kay.*' A clear, strong voice at a distance.

Misha jogs to the far corner of the house, Caleb trying to stay close, trying to show he's as unafraid as this girl. 'Coward' is something he doesn't want to be called more than once in a day. He expects her to stop at the end of the wall and peek carefully around the corner. Instead she goes right on round. Caleb doesn't let himself think, he just follows.

After all, if there's anything round there, she'll get it first.

Where the front gardens are constrained by brick walls and iron fence, round here the landscape unfurls. The cobbled path is broad, the lawn is long and finely mown, and up ahead lie the stable to the right, fields of sunflowers to their left, and a forest opening up directly ahead.

Twin lights flash between the trees as a figure shambles about. 'That's her!' cries Misha. 'Come on!'

'Keep your voice down,' says Caleb in a panic.

'Why? We want it to follow us!' She goes running. Caleb doesn't have the heart to shout after her that he doesn't want any following, that he wants them to fail at this, that shouting and running around at this time of night is bound to cause trouble.

He has to run after her. There is no time to think of a different plan, to find another way.

Misha doesn't pitch headlong into the trees; she takes the gravel path running alongside them. 'Hurry up!' she shouts at Caleb. 'We need to get to the other end before Neuman!' He tries to speed up. It's frightening to run in this darkness. He could trip on a rock, run face-first into a low-hanging branch, get jumped on by God-knows-what.

Neuman crashes through the trees like a bear. 'Kay.' A woman's voice, twisted and deepened. 'Kay.' A demand of desperate hunger. 'Kay!' The twin lights slice through the trees, the silver-blue beams turning the trunks into brittle icy bones jutting out of seared dirt.

'Whatever you do, don't look into those lights!' warns Misha. He's too busy huffing air into his lungs to tell her that he already knows. Misha seems unaffected by the exertion. Where does she get such fierce energy?

This place of languid sun-washed walks with Mum as she named the flowers and the birds then let him play while she sat and wrote, this cannot be that place, because here he is running for his life.

His legs are burning. His lungs are exploded tyres. He won't make it much farther. And the Neuman monster will get him.

Misha cuts through flowerbeds, Caleb several paces behind. Neuman crashes through branches, stumbles out onto the path close behind him. 'Don't look!' shouts Misha. Caleb won't. He's desperately trying to keep his feet.

'Kay!'

His skin shudders: that syllable felt like it was right down his neck. Just like that, he forgets his agony and knows he could run forever. Juddering spotlights transform the ground. There are dark squirming shapes beneath them that Caleb wishes he couldn't see. They react to the lights, turn towards him.

With them comes panic.

Surrounded by night in the garden labyrinth. Neuman bellowing at his heels. Misha pulling away. Unknown hungry things reaching for him. *I'm going to die screaming.*

Misha slows slightly. 'This way!' She veers left, getting slower. Is she tiring? Because this is the worst possible time! Caleb blasts past her – and the ground drops away. She reaches for him, but his knees have already buckled, and he rolls downhill through scratching undergrowth, tumbling end over confused end. He grabs for something to slow himself. All he gets is a sting.

The fall ends with a splash. He lands on bruising stones, head under water, cold-shock lancing along his veins. He thrashes, kicking up plumes of water, firing off one of his slippers. A gasp floods his throat. It burns. He screams for air, gets more water.

A hand grabs his hair, yanks him up to the surface, coughing and heaving.

The hand doesn't let go. Caleb grasps blindly at the wrist to shake it loose. He can't clear his eyes. There's light everywhere. He's coughing up endless water. His legs are boneless.

'Let him go!' Misha screams from somewhere higher, and then Caleb finds the fight. Neuman has him.

'KAY!'

He can't get free. He doesn't mean to, but he looks up. No passing glimpse this time. Caleb looks deep into Neuman's eyes.

38

Too much is what he sees. His brain falls into unconsciousness, three short words on repeat: LET HIM FALL.

39

Stumbling. Legs refuse commands. Head won't lift. His only desire is to curl into a small ball. Someone drags him on, though. A very insistent someone who won't let go. He feels like something's thundered through him, a corrosive substance that swept into his system and left nothing undamaged. His breathing is weak; he can't get enough air.

Questions surface.

He tries to ask one, but his lips are unfamiliar and his tongue is slack. It drains from his mouth in a monotone slur.

'What are you on about now?' Misha. That voice belongs to Misha. The graveyard girl.

He shrugs her off. Needs a seat. Raises his head long enough to see a rickety-looking fence. He slumps against it. 'Neuman. Where?'

'We should really keep going,' she says. She looks nervous, which is a first.

'Where is it?'

'Back there somewhere. In the gardens.'

Propping himself up, he looks around and behind him. 'That's…'

'Daisy Hill. We're on the opposite side to the chapels. These are the rambling trails that cut along behind the gardens.'

'And they lead into the graveyard.'

'The back end, yeah. Where no one goes, except Granddad. It's where he keeps all his bits of wood and other rubbish. It's a pretty good place to hide out.'

'Who from?' He doesn't think he should be interested, but he is.

She shrugs. 'Anyone. Everyone.'

'Like Vic Sweet?'

She's about to tell him to shut up, to mind his own business, go to hell, something like that. It's in the hooded way she looks at him. The way she turns away, the way her shoulders draw up. She looks down into that eight-ball. It reminds him of when he was eight himself, holding Brown Ted, looking into those big plastic eyes for answers. They were so big, so open, that there had to be something in them, some explanation. There never was, though. Caleb was left with the never-ending why.

Some questions never have an answer, he thinks, *no matter how hard you shake the ball.*

She doesn't turn back to him, but she talks. 'You've got to get away from it sometimes. All the crap. All the hate. Because you really feel it. It's like a pressure, a crushing pressure. You feel it here.' Misha runs a hand along her shoulders, the nape of her neck. 'Makes it hard to shrug off when it's always here.' A hollow laugh at her own joke. 'My granddad can be so dumb sometimes, you know. I made the mistake of telling him about Vic once. He said that Vic didn't really hate me; he couldn't because hate's too strong an emotion. Hate's a vicious thing, he said. It's harmful; it wants to hurt. Kids don't know enough to hate that much, he said. Well that's what Vic wants, him and his friends and others like them. They want to hurt me bad, and they want it more and more, and I don't think they can help it. They know I deserve it, for what I am. And it's right, isn't it? Life would be better if I wasn't around. I'm not wanted. I can't even do what Granddad wants me to do.' She stares at the distant trees of Pernicious House. The only lights to be seen are the so-far-away stars. 'It gets a bit heavy, like I might snap. So I go to one of my forgotten places, and I stay there for so long that I can start to believe that it's the only place that's real, and I'm totally and completely alone. That's kind-of scary, and kind-of okay. It makes me ache when I think of everyone and everything else disappearing, it's painful, and I like it. That's where I go, that's what I do.' Finally she looks at him. No cocked head or arched eyebrows. She's almost defiant. 'You've got to be careful with questions, Caleb. Sometimes you end up getting an answer.'

Instead of telling her to shut up, that he didn't want to hear any of that, that he can't cope with that stuff, he says something else. 'My mum told me a dumb thing once as well. She said that when we die we all go up to the heavens, every one of us, and that each star is another soul. She said it was a fact and she could prove it. The soul is energy, and energy can't be destroyed, it just changes forms, and without a body to hold it then the soul has to go somewhere, so up it goes to join all the others and become a star. It made a lot of sense when I was little. I liked the idea. We'd all be up there, even the pets.' Caleb swings his feet as he sits on the fence. He starts to shiver as the chill of after-midnight sets into his skin. 'She died a few months after she told me that. I'd look up at the sky, whenever the stars were out. They all looked the same. Some brighter than others, but they were all just dots. It didn't seem right that when we're dead we become a random scatter of dots in the night. It was pointless her being up there if I didn't know which one she was. I couldn't work out why I couldn't recognise her. It's my mum's soul. I should know it. I should recognise it the way people point out constellations. I wanted to say, there's Mum, there she is just above Orion's Belt.' He looks up. There's an unending sea of black crystal above him, imperfections twinkling. 'I read up about stars. A star is a huge ball of gas held together by gravity. They're really hot at the centre, and when they heat up they shine. It's a load of hydrogen turning into helium. Nothing about souls. Just gas. I asked my d...father about it. 'Mum said we all become stars.' He said to me, 'Your mother also said she'd be around forever.' She told us all lies. She's not up there with all of them, and there's not much of her in the grave now either, is there?' He wants to throw things. 'It was a stupid lie, a stupid thing to say. And after I found out that stuff about stars, I kept reading. I couldn't stop myself. The universe is bigger than we've got any hope of imagining, and it's expanding so everything's getting further away from everything else. Between all of that is this dark matter stuff, and that's what most of the universe is made up of. So there's all this dark matter up there and it's all spreading out, and look at us. We're all living on this one planet. There are no other planets that we know of that have got life on them. Planet Earth is like the odd one out. The only one with life. All the others have got nothing. This planet is a mistake. We're not meant to be. That's why I sleep on the garage roof. I can't help it. I look up into the sky and all this stuff's in my head and I try to look at it all differently and I can't. I sleep on the garage roof. It's what I do.'

This is where she's meant to laugh and call him a whacko, then walk away. She doesn't. 'Where do the souls go, then?'

He yawns. 'Bed, if they've got any sense.'

She sits on the fence beside him. 'Come on, seriously, tell me.' She's so intense, so close. 'Because what you're saying is that there's nothing. But you don't believe that. You visit your mum, like, all the time, so you must think there's something. And after what's happened tonight...'

'I don't know what's happened tonight, I don't get any of it. I don't know what that Neuman thing is, and, and I don't care about it, I just want to be left alone to do what I do. I just want to be bored and ignored and visit my mum if I want to.' He looks towards the moonlit graveyard, tries to figure out where Mum is; he's lost his bearings. He talks to cover the absence of all other sound, and he talks low because the night demands it. 'I go because that's where she is, and I have to go somewhere. Whatever's left of her is there. She's not in the house anymore. That place is dead. There's memories and stuff, but... There's a stone with a name on it, so I talk to that.'

He's noticed that she never looks away when he talks. Her attention is total. 'That's not all there is. It's not just a stone.'

Caleb's feeling like he's tipping over. 'We're not going back after that thing, are we? I don't think I can do it. It's so late and I'm so tired, and I know we were going to and I know why, but I really can't.'

Misha swings her legs over to the graveyard side. 'We'd best go round the bottom of the hill. Crosswell could still be out messing around with light-maps, and you don't want to bump into that old loser, trust me.'

At this ungodly hour he'd trust pretty much anything as long as it gets him home.

40

After she pushes Caleb through one of the gaps in the far end of the fence, Misha drags herself back through her window and slumps into bed. She doesn't take off her muddy slippers. The grown-ups are still awake and agitated, going back and forth over the Neuman issue in the front room. She should, perhaps, tell them where Neuman is. She should, probably, go in there and let Granddad know what happened. But she doesn't want to. She asked Eight why she didn't want to.

IT DOESN'T MATTER

Her last few minutes of consciousness are a swirl of thoughts, and they're all about why Neuman went to Pernicious House. She thinks she can work it out, but it slips away before she can grasp it.

41

The quilt was heaped and waiting for him on the drive when he got home. He dragged it back up onto the garage and into his room. His sneaky night out hadn't been discovered. Caleb's fairly certain he knows why he got away with it. To be found out, somebody has to be looking, somebody has to care.

Mum would've known something was up. She had this sense of her son, of when he might be up to mischief.

She knew him.

He's overtired. Head too heavy, legs too twitchy, can't find that sweet spot to sink into the mattress. He hovers, then, in half-sleep, the blurry borderlands where his dreams are trying to pull him further in, trying to lull him even though he's still aware of their shifting wrongness, their tricks and deceits. It's that house and its gardens, and some of this is true memory, slices of hazy-coloured recordings, of unending days with Mum that ended too quickly, and he can taste the breeze, air that's always sweeter on this side of the gates. And he's running, he can feel his skinny legs fleeing. But he slows, he stops, the house too large, extra stories, more windows, and it's infinite black like compacted storm clouds. It's okay, though, because Mum takes his hand and leads him on. There are no gardens. It's the graveyard; Daisy Hill flattened and spread out towards the horizon. Mum sits on one of the graves, takes her notebook and pen from her bag, and beckons Caleb over. His breathing accelerates and he refuses to go. Her eyes are hollow. She's empty. And the land tilts down, like the props holding it up just got kicked out, and as the earth drops the graves explode, and Caleb jumps wailing out of the dream, clutching handfuls of his sheets. He buries his face in the mattress, pillow on the floor somewhere, and cries.

42

It's late. The morning got up without him and left him behind. The only time he's ever been in bed after eleven was when he had the flu. Caleb aches as he gets up, like his limbs have been glued down to his mattress for hours. His neck is braced-in-a-rollercoaster stiff. Dreams have attacked him all night, and he feels worse than before he dragged himself home.

Clouds are already gathering. They're deep, heavy and stacked; a dark inverted version of Daisy Hill. Looking at it gives him the shivers. He thinks of hollow eyes and bursting graves. He thinks of Neuman, and people in suits.

He has to go up there, though. He has no answers, only confusion.

He dresses quickly, tries not to panic about whether or not Neuman is still in Pernicious gardens and what she might be getting up to. Whatever happens, he's not going up there, he's not hunting that thing again. Let Misha and the suits go hunting.

With any luck that might be exactly what they're doing. He might just get himself a bit of space to do some investigating.

43

HENRY HUNTER
1832–1902
UNTIL THE DAY BREAK
AND THE SHADOWS FLEE

He's not comfortable being this near the grave again, the one Misha and her friends dug up last night. He scribbles down the inscription, then backs away until two rows of the dead stand between him and that cursed pile of earth. Caleb can't recall ever being this jumpy. Every shudder of a breeze-brushed branch is a Neuman charging out to strangle him. Every fluttering bird is a suit swooping over to grab him and bury him alive. His nerves jump like night-time crickets.

Stop being such a coward, he tells himself. *Misha would just laugh.*

And why does he care what that stupid graveyard girl thinks? She's dangerous; she got him into all this.

'That's not even true,' he says in a whisper, afraid to wake anyone. 'I came here in the first place, and I came back.' He didn't like that admission. He didn't want to think about what it meant. Instead he drew a diagram. Notepad turned sideways, he puts Hunter's grave in the centre, a tiny rectangle with a number one in it, puts a '1' beside the inscription he'd just jotted down. Then he traces his way back to Easton's grave, traces his way back two days, and has it really only been two days? Honestly? Time surely lies. He fills in a portion of the plots between Easton and Hunter, '2' and '1', leaving a thin space between each row for the barely-there pathways, and already he can see that he'll need a bigger piece of paper. Even at this small scale he can't hope to fit everything on.

Another inscription catches his eye.

A S MCLEAN
1822–1897
COME MY FRIENDS
'TIS NOT TOO LATE
TO MAKE A BETTER WORLD

That's number '3', jotted and numbered. Like the other two, nothing else. No mention of beloved wives, husbands or anyone. Just the message, which to Caleb almost sounds like an invite. COME, it says, 'TIS NOT TOO LATE. Caleb would love a better world. His world's been no good for too long.

The next stone along is completely illegible, but the next one over? That interests Caleb too.

JANE AND THOMAS MOORE
'68 AND '80
ON THAT BRIGHT ETERNAL SHORE
WE SHALL MEET TO PART NO MORE

The words resonate where he beats and breathes. They mean more than they say, he thinks. It's a sentence of hope. It hopes that there's an eternal shore to be found. It hopes that, even though Jane and Thomas's time together in this life has ended, they will meet again. It hopes that if there is another place and if they find each other, there will be nothing more that can come between them. It hopes for an end to misery. And what happened to Thomas? Did an accident take him, or were twelve years without his Jane beyond his ability to endure, so at the end he gave up?

Caleb can't choose which is worse. To be Jane and have happiness and your partner so suddenly gone and replaced with darkness, or to be Thomas and live after she's gone. To endure. To battle on through time as your memories slip back, away. Would he find her harder to remember? Would she fade?

What about the places they went together, the things they did, the moments they had, moments so vivid they could never be gone...

Two weeks ago Mum's face wouldn't come to Caleb. He'd run from the house after one of Father's longer tirades, a rant about mouldy cups hidden under beds, and there was only so many times Caleb could hear that he was useless and lazy before the tears came. He had promised himself that he'd never let that man see him cry again, not after what happened at Mum's funeral, so he ran, and he kept on going until he had no more go left, finding himself at the far end of the sports field. He sat hard on the grass, and wept, and hoped that by the time he went home Father would have decided that he couldn't take any more of his waste-of-space son and be long gone. It hadn't been anything like this when Mum was alive. There had been laughter in the house. It had been a fun place. A home.

Caleb tore up tufts of grass, throwing them as he shouted a stream of swear words, all the things he'd been storing up to hurl at Father. The thought of Mum stopped him. She wouldn't want to hear him going on like that. She'd have given him *that* look, the disappointed one that cut him deep. And he couldn't picture it. Mum's face wasn't there. Not just the disappointed version either. The pleased one, the concerned one, bored, excited, tense, tired, proud, and fretful, none of the expressions that yesterday had been so familiar to him were anywhere to be found in his memories. He thought hard of the places they'd been. He closed his eyes so that the present-day world couldn't overlay his recollections. He made himself concentrate on all the colours and all the names of the flowers in the gardens of Pernicious House, the names and where they could be found, and the words of the songs that Mum would sing when they were alone, and was he really remembering her voice properly. Was that the way she sounded? He could remember colours, smells, names, and songs, and so many little details, so why was the most important one gone? Why wouldn't she come back? Why couldn't he summon the image of her face?

Father was right about him. He was useless, a waste of space. He couldn't even keep the simplest promise in the world, one that he made to his own mum.

At the graveside, as she lay alone in her box, Caleb had promised that he would never forget her.

He would think about her every day, about their walks, their days out, their curl-ups on the sofa as she read books and he flicked through comics in Saturday morning sunbeams. She was so clear to him, always shining.

And he'd let her go. He'd promised that he'd keep her forever, and then he let her go.

He wanted to punch himself in the head. He couldn't think of any other way to numb this pain.

He ran to his grandfather, begged him to pull out all the photo albums, and he stared hard at every single picture of Mum, absorbed them. The curve of her cheek, the slope of her nose, the set of her chin, the wrinkles at the corners of her eyes, he pasted her back into those walks, days out and curl-ups on the sofa. Gramps brought him a cup of tea and asked what was wrong and he said nothing, it was all okay now, except it wasn't, not quite. It couldn't really be okay, could it?

What kind of son forgot his own mother's face. Perhaps he was turning into a cold creature, like Father. A genetic failing, an irreversible process. It's not Time chewing up his memories, it's his own DNA rejecting them.

Pain in his scalp. He's pulling at his hair again. Clumps of it gripped in his hands. He lets go, opens his eyes to see splashes of pain-stars disrupting his vision, unclenches his tight jaw. His chest and neck are fierce-hot. His lungs feel swollen, inflamed. He looks around self-consciously. There's no one in sight, no one's seen him acting oddly, unless they're spying from somewhere secret. There are a lot of places for a girl to spy from, but at least he feels alone. That'll have to be enough.

He needs a break.

He goes to sit with Mum.

44

Caleb used to watch how other people did it, wondering if there was a right way and a wrong. He soon learned that there are as many ways as there are people. There's a lady who comes every week to change the flowers on her mother's grave. She spends a while fussing with them, trying out different arrangements before standing back, nodding in satisfaction, then walking away. There's an old gent that Caleb spots on occasion, he brings a foldable stool, and sits with his wife for a time, and with his head bowed he talks quietly, and if anyone walks past he nods and says hello. He's said hello to Caleb a few times. There's the young guy who turned up and tipped half a bottle of whiskey onto a grave and drank the rest himself, ranting at God before staggering away. There are the families who come and don't know what to do, except for the really young who run and play. Those who fuss over the state of the grave. Those who stand and do nothing. Those who are ashamed of their tears. Those who look around to see who's watching.

He's seen all of these people doing it their own way, and still he wonders if there's a right way, a way that will be heard.

45

Cross-legged on top of the grave, Caleb presses his hands against the inscription on the stone and says 'Hi, Mum.' He tries to say it from his heart, to push the words through himself and onwards to wherever Mum might be. He sits upright, hands clasped as if in prayer, and he looks at her name as if it's her face. 'I think I'm in a whole bunch of trouble. I can't tell Father about it because, well, you know what he's like. He'll just shout at me on and on, and say coming up here all the time's made me demented, like when I was seeing all those shapes that time. I don't even know how to tell him about it anyway. Him or anyone. I'm not sure I could even tell you if you weren't...you know.' The sky is piled high with bloated clouds. In front of him, past the gravestone, the great oak tree shudders. 'I don't know how to get out of it, Mum. This isn't like when I was getting into all those fights just after you died. There was an obvious way out of that. I had to stop, that was it. But this...it's happening anyway, whether I stop or not.' He pauses. One of the deep-downs is coming. They always do when he sits here cross-legged and talking. The deep-downs are the secrets he'd never tell the living. 'I need you, Mum. I need you here, more than ever. It's not fair. You'd hate me for saying this, but I don't care. I'd swap if I could. I'd swap Father for you. All he does is put me down. I know his life would be easier if I wasn't around, and my life would better if he wasn't and you were. There. I've said it. And I'm not taking it back, I'm not.' The oak's leaves shake at him, like they tremble at his petulance, like it's a force that should be denied.

This time he manages to let go of the anger. He doesn't let it take over. Whether Mum can hear him or not, Caleb doesn't like these times to be spoiled. 'I wish you'd answer. I wish you'd find a way.' The squeeze of her arms around him; his ribs ache for it. 'I suppose once you're up amongst the stars there's no easy way back down.' He immediately feels bad for saying that. It's a cheap shot.

There's that bitter voice, though, the one that lives alongside the deep-downs, and that voice says it's a shot she deserved, and that it's okay to say these things here, it's really okay, because where else can they be said?

A raindrop spatters on the bridge of his nose, another on the back of his hand. The boy scowls at the swollen, bulging sky. It's never looked so heavy. It will break soon, and there will be a deluge. He always feels like there's so much more to say, but can never quite work out what that more is.

He hates that.

'I can't work out what the point is, Mum,' he says, and then the spitting flecks of water make way for the rain proper, and there's no more to be done here.

46

She's getting all kinds of hell. She could make it stop quite easily. One sentence would do it, a short sentence at that. But she won't. She'll never tell. Let them suffer. Let it drive them mad. Let them stare at their light-maps and all their other tricksy atomic manipulations and wonder why none of them work.

Granddad hasn't the faintest idea that she might know where Neuman is. How could she? Silly little Misha knows nothing about anything. He's too busy blasting her for roaming the town in the middle of the night. Crosswell dropped her in it, of course. Bitter old bastard. The fattening slob had waited until she was certain that he'd forgotten all about it, then seconds before heading out the door, he gave Granddad a 'By the way...'

Granddad looks older than ever. It's like his clock's been ticking a lot faster lately.

'What if you'd had an accident out there, alone in the dark? What then? Would you roll your eyes or shrug as you lay bleeding in the street, Misha? Would you think yourself so very clever as the bone jutted from your leg and there was nobody around to help you? And these are not the worst things that could happen to you. There are men who look for opportunities...'

And there's a revenant lurking at Pernicious House, she thinks. A monster hidden in plain sight.

She watches through the window behind Granddad, watches Caleb retreat from his mother's grave as rain splashes the glass. She should have been up there listening to him instead of in here being a disappointment. She liked to hear the things he talked about. She liked to ask Eight the questions that Caleb never got an answer to. She can only imagine the conversation she's missed out on because of Crosswell and his big mouth.

'Are you even listening, Misha? You never listen! How many times do I have to tell you? All of your problems are because you refuse to listen! Why such a clever girl can't concentrate for more than five minutes is beyond me. You could be so much if you would only do as I ask…'

'I don't want to!' It bursts from her, this anger. A shaken bottle exploding. 'I can't do it and I don't want to! I just want to be left alone!'

'Before long there won't be a choice!' He snatches Eight from her hands, and hurls the ball across the room. The shelf it hits bursts into pieces, dropping its books in a tumble. 'The foolishness has got to end! We can… *You* can do something great, something important. You can help us change things, you know that.' He finds her single hot tear hard to look at. The sigh wheezes in his chest, and he goes to retrieve Eight. 'Crosswell is right about you,' he says, and the words are strained. 'But that doesn't mean he has to stay right.' He checks Eight over before placing it on the table. 'Only one thing is happening today. We're getting Neuman back. We can't leave the revenant out there. It will ruin everything. If it's seen…' The world weighs him down, and right now she hates him. That's the way of it. 'Don't think you're wandering off today. We're putting an end to that. Today you light-weave and spirit-link and any other damn thing I can think of that might help us put things right, and we'll do it before Crosswell does.'

Misha doesn't have the energy to argue with him anymore.

47

Through rain-lashed glass the figure is distorted and featureless. Gramps watches it, hands in his pockets. 'That fellow's been standing there for about half an hour. Just standing there like that, in this weather. And people say I'm wrong in the head.'

Caleb got bored with watching the not-moving man after a minute. He's lolling on the sofa and staring through the news on the telly. 'Any crisps, Gramps?' He's not really hungry. He only asks because it's a question he usually asks.

'Your favourites, salt and vinegar, in the cupboard. You know you can just get them, no need to ask.'

'Yeah, Gramps. I know.' And Caleb knows that he'll ask next time anyway, and Gramps will tell him not to like he always does. Caleb checks the snack cupboard, finds no salt and vinegar, only cheese and onion. Cheese and onion is his favourite. 'Gramps, do you ever see weird stuff up at the graveyard?'

'What do you mean by weird? This fellow's certainly odd. I mean, you wouldn't in this weather, would you?'

Caleb roots around in the fridge, finds some drink called sarsaparilla, decides to give it a try. It's the least adventurous thing he's done in forty-eight hours. 'Weird, Gramps. Like...I dunno, things that don't look right.'

'Why do you ask?'

Caleb pours himself a glass of the strong-smelling drink, and tries to ignore the slight tremble in his hands. 'It's where all the dead people are, isn't it? So if anything's going to happen anywhere, that would be the place, I guess.' He tastes the sarsaparilla. He reels back from the rich aniseed flavour and vows never to touch it again. Not all adventures are worth having.

'So, it's ghost stories you're after, is it? There's a suitcase on the kitchen table. Bring it in for me, would you?' Caleb wonders if there's actually a link between ghost stories and the suitcase, or if Gramps is having another of his blips, but he does as he's asked. The suitcase is heavy, and he ends up dragging it into the front room instead of carrying it.

'You going on holiday?' he asks. 'You never mentioned it.'

'No holidays for me. Lift it up onto the sofa for me, Caleb. My back's not what it used to be.'

Caleb reckons his back won't be much use either if he has to keep lugging this thing about. It lands with such a thud that he fears the sofa will snap in half. It's probably rammed full of train carriages. The old man's hobby has really got out of hand in the last few years. The boy plumps down beside the case, but Gramps doesn't yet come away from the window.

'We have senses, don't we, Caleb? We use them to interpret the world around us. We use them to make judgements, to choose what to do next. If you see a car coming towards you, you will step out of its way. Without sight, you might hear it coming instead. Without hearing, perhaps you will feel a change in the air itself. It's that prickle along the nape of your neck; the one that always means run. Without any of these, what hope do you have? The car will hit you. You will be mown down. And there are a lot of cars out there.' Caleb doesn't know what he's on about, but this doesn't have the usual feel of a Gramps ramble, of those times when the old man has forgotten where the thread of a conversation lies and roots around in randomness. There's a steel *hereness* to his eyes. Gramps has the thread; he has it good and tight. 'Without sight or hearing or those prickles, it's good to know that we can rely on others to drag us out of harm's way. Can't always rely on that, though, can we? What if that person sees, hears and feels the danger, but leaves us to face it? Sometimes we can be left in the headlights, Caleb, and only know it when we've been flattened.'

Across the boy's skin, goose bumps rise.

Gramps perches on the end of his recliner. He can still glance out of the window from this angle. 'There was a girl when I was seventeen. Back in fifty-five, this was. Evelyn.'

'Grandma wasn't called Evelyn.'

'I know. As your father can't be bothered to tell you anything of the world, I guess I must tell you what I can before all my marbles are scattered. There will be more than one love in your life. Your grandmother was my heart and soul from the moment I met her until the last second of our goodbye, and she left an ache in me that I feel to this day. But I existed for twenty-eight years before I met her, and twenty-eight years is a long time. Well, until you get to my age, and then it looks like the blink of an eye.' And Gramps looks like a man cheated. 'Your opening ten years are the ones of wonder; and your third decade is your first as an adult, with a man's choices and burdens. But those years between? Those hold your first real tests, your challenges, and they show you who you are.

'Much like you are being tested now.

'I'd had what you kids call crushes before, fleeting fancies that brought me confusion and nervousness and little else. When I saw Evelyn, though, this willowy girl all long hair and smiles, all those childish uncertainties were swept aside. There was no confusion. I needed to know her. I stared as she stood in line for the pictures, oblivious to me, giggling with friends. There was joshing from my own mates, you know what mates are like when it comes to boys and girls, all the elbows and the whey heys. Before that day I'd always argued with them or pushed or got someone in a headlock when they started. That day, though, I let them jostle me and crack their jokes and I just smiled at it all.

'I can't remember what the film was. I don't think I remembered it seconds after it finished. I spent the whole film working out what to say to this girl whom I'd never met, whose name I didn't know, who was entirely a stranger to me. I could walk up to her and introduce myself, but that seemed a bit boring and official. I could persuade one of my friends to stroll past her with me and laugh on cue at one of my great jokes, but I couldn't think of a joke and the friends I had were the kind to purposefully make a mess of a plan like that. I needed some brute to make a grab at her so I could step in and be her gallant knight, even though I'd never actually been in a fight. It seemed that it should be the easiest thing in the world to work this out, and yet I couldn't find a solution to the puzzle.

'All too soon we were piling out of the theatre, and I lost track of her. Around and around I looked and no sign of the willowy girl all long hair and smiles. It was a crushing disappointment. I convinced myself that I'd come up with the perfect opening line, one she couldn't possibly resist and, in the style of the greatest romantic melodramas I'd been denied my chance to woo her. My first real teenage despair.

'It didn't last long.

'I tripped in the lobby. A small stumble. My shoelace was undone. I bent to tie it, and in my abject misery completely forgot about rule number one. Before stooping to tie shoelaces, always check the location of your so-called mates. That's how I ended up with a toe rocketing up my backside. It came from Eddie, seizing an increasingly rare opportunity to deliver what we called a "ring sting". I've never felt anything like it, before or since. Ed must have taken one hell of a run-up, because I actually shot out of the movie theatre entrance like I'd been fired, bent double, from a cannon. There was even a loud cracking sound, made me think my buttock bone had snapped in half. I crashed headfirst into someone, knocked them flat on their face, and landed with my head on their bum cheek.

'It was, of course, the willowy girl with the long hair. I couldn't yet see her face, but the smiles seemed a lot less likely. You ever heard people say how they wanted the ground to swallow them up? That wasn't enough for me. I wanted to stop existing. I wanted to blink out, like I'd never been on Planet Earth at all. That way I wouldn't be able to hear all the laughing. There was a *lot* of laughing, and hooting. I jumped up to my feet, went to help her up, but her friends pushed me back like I was some kind of robber. I was nothing but shame from head to toe. Every inch of my skin glowed red. I was never, ever, ever going to live it down.

'She brushed herself off, and turned to look at me. Even without the smiles she was a knockout. She lifted her eyebrows the tiniest fraction. It was a question. Did I have any kind of explanation for my behaviour? For some reason I couldn't find the truth, that my friends were idiots. It was like I'd forgotten everything. My wish to stop existing had only got so far as wiping my memory. It was a long few seconds of saying nothing. Really long. Oh boy, did it stretch out! I had to say something before my head popped clean off my shoulders, so I cleared my throat, which was the loudest and ugliest noise I ever made, and I said, "That's not normally where I put my head". She said that she was glad to hear it, and one corner of her smile was back. I was one lucky boy. The object of my desire had a sense of humour. I asked if she was hurt while clutching at my own backside, which felt like I'd been sitting on a bomb when it went off. She looked at my strange pose and asked if I needed to go anywhere particularly quickly. That set off all the laughter again, mine included.

'As simply as that, we were talking, this whip-smart girl and me. We only shared a few minutes, as she'd made stern promises to get herself straight home, but such wonderful minutes! I lived off them for a full week. I had to. She said she'd be at the flicks same time next Saturday, and I spent seven days convincing myself she'd be there, no she wouldn't, yes she would, no she wouldn't.

'She was there. We sat next to each other. I don't remember that film either. We whispered the whole time. Close, so I could smell her hair. Everything was wonderful, Caleb. The days were a little bit brighter for a while. But it all went wrong, you see.'

48

Crosswell's driving round the same slick streets and seeing nothing but blurs through the rain. It's a waste of time, and all he's doing is waiting for the call that says it's too late and Neuman's been discovered or killed someone or whatever. He's been cruising for hours, sick of his life. The damned thing can't have disappeared, there's something they're doing wrong, a fault in the weave. Anger swarms through his thoughts. The old coot thinks he can fix it with that dumb girl, and Crosswell yells in wordless frustration as he passes Pernicious House for the third time

49

where the lights are still out and there's a hole in the gate and there's a Neuman slumped against a tree trunk and although she can't see it directly, she stares in the direction of

50

the graveyard, where a girl is ignoring another of many diagrams as a stubby finger taps at the parts of greatest importance, and it's all meant to make sense. They've gone over positioning and stacking and the mysterious subject of convergence, and Granddad's recapped incantations and the Reach and the confusing topic of Intra-Corporeal Transference. She knows she is supposed to take it all in, this girl. She should take it all in and do something with it. Granddad's said as much about a gazillion times. But she wants to run away. She's just a girl. A girl in a graveyard across the road from

51

an old man telling an old story he'll never tell again. He sits sometimes as he talks, but it's never long before he's back at the window, looking towards a graveyard in which a girl is brimming with frustration. The standing man bothers him, and the bother makes Caleb anxious.

'Happiness is not a constant, Caleb. It sits on a tide, comes and goes. I suppose it stops happiness getting too familiar and taken for granted. It has to be appreciated when we have it. Evelyn and I, we had such a time together, always chatting and laughing and making nonsense jokes, and she'd always let me steal a single kiss before we parted. I carried that happiness onward through the night and the day before we could be together again. But Evelyn? She had to go home, and home was the graveyard.'

A stone thuds against Caleb's heart. He wants to stop the story and go home. This Evelyn woman is not Grandma. He doesn't need to know.

'Her mother died when she was very young, and it made her father a hard man. He worked hard, spoke hard, hit the bottle hard, and hit her hard. Donald Landy sent the better part of himself to the grave when his wife passed on, and there was nothing but bitterness to replace it. Evelyn didn't dare breathe one word about me anywhere near him. He would have come looking for me and most likely killed her, or near enough. And I quickly came to learn that he had the kind of friends who could make his problems disappear.' Gramps chuckles, the way old people do at things that aren't funny. He looks like someone who's never been on the shore when the tide comes in.

He's at the window when he tells the next part, restless. 'Secrets wriggle, Caleb. They're lively buggers. They want to be out and away. Wriggling like worms.

'The first hint that something was wrong was a bruise where her jawline curved to her throat. It was the size of a thumb. She explained it away easily enough, so I didn't think much of it. After all, she was the wonderful Evelyn. She wouldn't lie; she wouldn't keep anything from me. I suppose the signs went back even earlier than that. Any enquiries I made about her home life were always avoided, and she had nothing to say about her father.

'Then one of the boys, Eddie I think it was, took me to one side for a chat. She'd been getting knocked about by her old man and the rumour, which was spreading fast, was that Mr Landy had grown tired of her promiscuous ways and had taken to teaching her a hard lesson whenever he suspected her of disobeying him. Now, things were different back then. Meddling in a family's business was frowned upon. And people thought that a girl who went on like that had it coming to her. Nobody wants a daughter who brings them shame.

'Me? I couldn't believe it. My Evelyn was true to me, I was sure of it. And Donald might be her father, but that didn't mean he should lay a hand on her.

'You see how a young man can be filled with a sense of righteous justice?'

Gramps comes away from the window and spins the numbers on the locks of the suitcase. His fingers struggle with the small barrels. The case yawns open. There are books, folders, tubes, a broad metal implement. From the middle of the stack of books he pulls a leather-bound string-tied journal. He doesn't hand it over straight away, but holds it and flexes the cover. Caleb is glad. He doesn't think he wants it. A journal locked in a suitcase he's never seen before cannot be meant for him.

'The rest of it's between these covers. It's probably best if you hear it in my voice from back then.' He sits between Caleb and the case, blocking the boy's view of things he's sure are private and for others. 'Your father's of no help in what's coming. You know that. I'm losing my mind by degrees. You know that as well. It's sad that the best advice you get is from your mother up on that hill. But while I'm with it, you must listen to me. It's time to stay away from that graveyard. Well away. It's turning. It's turning to bad.' He points to the window, to a spot in the graveyard. They both know without looking that there's someone still standing there. 'That's not a man. Not any more.

'Read, and I'll make tea.'

52

12th April

If things turn out badly, I know you'll find this eventually, Mum. I'm sorry, but I got into something I never saw coming. You can't hide this away or destroy it, even if you don't believe it. You'll have to find someone who'll know what to do with it. I think you might need to be careful whom you ask in this town.

You must promise, and you must be careful.

Evelyn asked me to stay away, because of the way her father is, but after what I'd heard, I couldn't. I hadn't seen her for days. I had to know.

I climbed the fence, sneaked over to the house, peered through windows until I found her, sitting on her perfectly made bed, surrounded by old books, very old books.

She looked up. Pardon the language, Mum, but that son of a bitch had blackened her eye.

Evelyn was not pleased to see me.

53

She's gone again.

He got two hours out of her this time. Granddad sighs so deep he can feel his soul sagging. He's the oldest of the Belvederes and the entropy is carving big holes through him. He has nowhere near the energy he once had, nowhere near. The others won't admit it, but they aren't much better off. If only for her youth, they need Misha. Her vitality, her unblemished power.

'I need a two-minute break, Granddad,' she said, and stepped outside, and she cast a look at him before the door closed, and both of them knew she would not be taking a two-minute break. Darkness will fall before she returns.

It's long past time for him to give up on her, Crosswell is right about that. But Granddad knows he can't. He knows that, if Misha had the focus and self-control, she could have prevented the Neuman incident single-handed. He knows this because he has seen, but Misha has forgotten.

So many hopes for the future. How have the elvederes become so few?

Well, he's not like Crosswell, and he won't give up, even when he should. He puts away the book he was showing Misha, pulls out another slender volume. It is called *The Inherent Dangers of Soul Dominion.*

54

Evelyn flipped closed the books before I could get a clear look at the pages, and waved me away. She looked frantic, but after seeing the state of her eye, there was no chance of me leaving without a lot of answers. I was so indignant and outraged, so sure of my ability to settle some scores and put matters right.

Oh, Mum, what have I got myself into?

I stood firm. Angry, she drew her curtains. I rapped lightly on the glass with my fingernails, not loud, but steady, just so she knew I wasn't going to go away. I thought she'd leave me tapping, but she eventually gave in, whipped open the curtains, cracked the window to speak. The books were piled up on the floor.

'Who did that to you?' I asked. She said I needed to mind my own business and go back home before I was seen. Her anger was gone, replaced by terror. I'd never seen her face without a smile before. I offered my hand, told her to take it. She nearly did, so nearly. And if she had? Oh, we would have ran so far and so long that this would all stay behind us forever, and you know, I would never have asked her a thing. I would have left it all in the past. I've never seen fear like it. The tremor of her lips.

She did not take my hand then. She shook her hand instead, and so took the path that leads me to write this. 'You can go,' she said, 'and if you go it's fine. I'm not your responsibility. This isn't your fight.'

Well, of course it was. I had already chosen.

If she wasn't coming out, then I was going in.

55

A fine drizzle chills her face and peppers her hair as Misha makes her way to the hollowed-out tree. She needs to be out of reach for a while. She's given Granddad's lessons more effort than she'd intended to, she actually really tried, and she listened, and she understood, she always understands, but she's just not sure, and it's so much to think about that her head gets all crowded, and Eight! Eight's no help at all. She wants to smash Eight sometimes. She wants to get Granddad's sledgehammer from the shed and bring it down on Eight with all her might. Stupid Eight and its stupid answers. One blow and she could do away with them all.

She might also get to see what's inside that damned thing once and for all. A little peek at Eight's innards.

The ball will know she's been thinking like this, and won't like it. Misha climbs into the hollow guts of the tree and tells herself she doesn't care whether the stupid thing likes it or not. Tucking her legs under herself, leaning so as the left side of her face presses to the tree, she convinces herself that Eight can throw a huff if it wants and she just won't care.

Except the last time it got upset... The words it spat against the window, one after another, more and more spiteful, violent. A stream of promises. A torrent of vile warnings, each image bloodier than the last. It stopped abruptly, leaving Misha wondering if she should dash outside and dig a hole and bury the horrible monster. Eight heard what she was thinking.

YOU

DARE

flashed across that screen, then nothing more, even though she watched it for hours, sitting there on her plump quilt. She watched, and dared not think much of anything.

And if Eight wants to act like that again, so what? Let it. Words are words, nothing more. They can't do harm. Misha's heard them all. Eight's curses. Vic Sweet's spouting mouth.

Crosswell when he drops his above-it-all mask. Town gossip. Letters posted. Graffiti on the walls, the gravestones. All words. All hate.

Every day. Every single day.

It all washes off.

It's Granddad's eyes she can never shake off. He's so sure he's right, that there is no other way. The Turnings, the interference, she doesn't want any part of it.

All she wants is alone.

'Here you are, you disgusting little ghoul.'

Her guts turn inside out, hollowing like this tree. The only escape from here is past that voice. Vic Sweet's voice.

56

'Tell me it all,' I demanded. 'I'm not leaving until you tell me everything, so you might as well start now.' She shushed me, shut the door, and dragged me away from any windows.

'If he comes back early and finds you here he'll kill you, and no one will find what's left.' We argued back and forth about who would kill whom and what Donald could and couldn't get away with, when she came to a decision. She seized hold of my hand and led me through the house, to the scullery, to a trapdoor in the floor. She handed me a lantern and said, 'You won't be able to go back after this. You'll want to, but it'll be too late.'

The words dried up in my throat. If I had spoken my voice would have cracked, and I suspect my courage would have snapped too.

Down we went. Thirteen stairs. I counted to keep calm. It was a struggle to hold my lantern steady whilst my brain conjured up a dozen grim discoveries that could be waiting for me. What had Donald been up to? What could drive a man to punch his own daughter in the face?

As it turns out, Donald's been a very busy man. The original basement walls are all gone. There are tunnels. A lot of tunnels. I don't mean ones you have to crawl down. You can walk along these.

Evelyn led me into one of them, her fingers warm in my chilly hand. Our lanterns cast out a lot of light, but still the tunnel trailed away into darkness. The air was uncomfortably dank, hard to breathe. I almost immediately broke out into a sweat. I won't lie, Mother. I wanted out of there. I had no doubt in my mind that it was a bad place. I could feel that this underground maze stretched out far in front of me, I could feel it under my skin. I had to press on, though, didn't I? For Evelyn.

We soon came to the first of the branches. She led me into a kind of chamber, within which stood rows of mud columns, carved out with care. There was a hole cut into each at chest height. I knew right away that above each of these columns there'd be a gravestone.

Evelyn held up her lantern to one of those holes.

57

Caleb lowers the journal to his lap. Gramps is watching, no, studying him as if waiting to see what reaction might come. Caleb can't be sure exactly how he looks, but he feels pale, like his skin's been dusted with cold chalk. 'The place in this journal... it's that place over there, right? That graveyard.' Gramps nods. 'And Evelyn's house? It's the same house that's there now, right?'

'No,' says Gramps, and Caleb almost goes light-headed with relief. 'The old house got knocked down. A new one was built in its place. Not the same house. But the same spot.'

'I know the girl who lives there.'

'I know you do. Cup of tea?'

Caleb nods, and feels like crying. He feels like it doesn't matter what he does, the spiral will pull him down further.

Down, down, down.

58

Huge, he swarms into the tree. No chance of getting around him. She tries anyway. Vic's gorilla arm swings out, sweeps her up, pulls her in. He stinks. It's a guttural stench, unwashed menace. 'You're going nowhere,' he growls in her ear.

59

It took me a few moments to work out what the lantern was illuminating. It was round, it glistened. The top of a human skull. I'd never been so close to a dead body. I recoiled. It only took two short steps backwards for me to hit the column behind me. I felt a rush of claustrophobia, sure that the walls were narrower than they'd been a minute earlier. 'What is this?' I asked.

'Every grave is like this,' she said. 'He's made his way around every single grave.'

'But what is this?' I asked again. I didn't want to sound so desperate, so panicked, because Evelyn had given me a way out. My own insistence had brought me to that gleaming skull, not hers. I hadn't taken her warning seriously. I had thought myself to be the big man. It was time, then, to play the role, but it wasn't easy, not with the walls constricting and the thoughts of tons and tons of dirt crashing in on us.

My stomach turns to think of it.

A door slammed above us. It was Mr Landy, of course, full of beer and bellowing for Evelyn.

We ran.

60

Pinned to him, his hand awful against her, Misha screams, tearing the sound up from her very roots. He cuts the sound off with his other great paw, and here's her chance. She swings down with her fist, and the air whuffs out of him as he doubles over. She's off, scrambling out of the tree, heartbeat at maximum.

If Vic catches her now, she's dead. Really dead.

61

The urge won't go away. It's an anxious prickling at the base of his throat. That Misha girl, she's awful and dangerous and she might not know that the bed she sleeps in stands above some weird labyrinth created by a madman.

'Gramps, I've got to go…'

The old man's already nodding. 'You're me through and through, God help you, lad. Take the journal. When you're done, we'll go through the rest of the suitcase. There's no other way but one step at a time with something like this.' Caleb snaps the journal shut, gets to his feet. 'And stay out of that bloody graveyard. There's nothing good left in that place.'

Caleb leaves behind an untouched cup of tea and no promises.

62

Her feet have perfect memory. She has known this terrain for a whole childhood. No need to think, to pick out a route. Misha can simply go. She flees past row after row of gravestones, uphill, towards the top, muscles already burning. Over the summit lies the trick, an end to the chase.

Vic is powerful, thumping after her. A steam train. A red fury. *Faster. I must be faster.*

63

He'd heard Gramps perfectly clearly. How could he not? Caleb knows exactly what he was told and he understands it completely. There's an awful lot wrong with that graveyard and its occupants, but Caleb's known that for a while now, and it hasn't yet kept him away.

Besides, he's made no promises.

Why pretend? He could easily avoid the graveyard for the rest of the day. Easily. He's got dozens of places to go. Loll about in the playground. Mooch around the school field. Laze around in his bedroom. Drift around town. He could do the same thing tomorrow and the day after. He could do it the day after the day after, and day after day, and while he was in the playground he'd climb to the top of the fort, sit cross-legged and stare up at Daisy Hill. On the school field the kids would have a kick about as he thought of things coming out of graves. Up in his bedroom the window would always be there for him to gaze through – that window and its irresistible view. Drifting through town, he'd be pulled round in ever-decreasing circles, drawn by the gravity of dead people and monsters and mysteries and Misha.

There is a measure of time between Caleb now and Caleb passing back through those gates. Does it make a lot of difference if that measure is a week or a day or an hour or a minute if the end result is the same? Caleb has an unfinished story of horror underground, he has experience of a midnight chase, he has measurements, he has a peculiar man who Gramps says is not a man to investigate, he has all of this and he cannot let any of it go.

That's why he goes straight from Gramps's house to the graveyard, because he's going to do it anyway, no matter what. There is no hope of stopping now.

He looks back to see if Gramps is watching, but he's not there.

Through the gates once more, he turns right. Gravel crunches as he heads towards the man who might not be a man. The crunching noise of his footsteps seems very, very loud. He steps off the path, padding softly over soaking wet grass. The not-man is over there, not far off, facing away from Caleb. It looks like he's shivering.

Caleb stops at a grave, acts like he's there to visit. Messes with the flowers, plucks at weeds. Reads the inscription.

BELINDA SANDERSON
1900–1964
THE SUN HAS SET FOR NOW, MY DEAR
BUT WILL RISE AGAIN WHEN YOU ARE NEAR

The not-man, hair lank, clothes sodden, turns his head a fraction, as if hearing Caleb read the engraved words. There remains a fair bit of distance between them. A large measure. Enough for Caleb to be confident of escape in the event of a chase. He wants the not-man to turn around. He wants to see what it looks like. It is evidence. It is another part of the larger mystery. If he misses a part then he might not be able to see the whole picture.

But the not-man is listening for him, and who's to say it's not listening *to* him? To the slamming of his heart? To the shudder of his veins? The straining of his lungs? The thoughts in his head? Caleb doesn't know what the not-man is, what it's capable of.

Look at it shaking. Is that a symptom of cold, or of hunger?

Caleb's wondering about the distance between them. The not-man would have to run like a cheetah to catch him. The not-man might actually run like a cheetah.

It's turning. With slow, shuffling footsteps. Like it's getting used to feet.

A shout of pain, of anger. Caleb looks up over Belinda's grave, up the incline of Daisy Hill. The shout was male, but that figure in the swooshing dress is Misha. He takes the excuse gladly, ducks low behind hedgerows, weaves through trees.

Observing the not-man is one thing; being followed by it is not an experience he wants.

It follows anyway.

But Caleb quickly forgets the not-man as he jogs to the top of the hill. The shout is forming words now, not just noises. Threats, all aimed at Misha. He's picked himself up, and he's hobbling after her. Vic, red-faced and angrier than Caleb's ever seen. He means every word he spits. 'I'm gonna kill you, you little bitch! I'm gonna snap your legs off for this!' She's backing away, but not fast, like she wants to see his fury, like she wants the danger. A mouse taunting the cat. A crazy girl grinning at an enraged bully. A boy stalking a ghost.

He's losing track of who's actually crazy.

She is, she is, she is, look at him, he's steaming, he means it, he'll rip her to pieces.

Vic is so focused on her that he hasn't even noticed Caleb. He's frothing at the mouth, telling her the ways that he wants to make her bleed. Pit-bull eyes, throbbing temples. Limping, throwing himself into each step. He's going to lunge, and grab.

And Caleb hates that.

He runs at Vic, who's still too focused to see him, and it's clumsy but Caleb kicks, and it connects with the side of Vic's left knee, and it's a rough blow, feels gristly, and the bully boy howls like something important has snapped, and Caleb feels immediately sick.

Whatever he has done this time cannot be undone.

Vic totters, then crashes to the rain-drenched ground, clutching his knee, making an unbelievable noise through gritted teeth. Misha looks from Vic to Caleb. She is disbelief all over. In shock, she laughs out loud.

Vic barks. There are tears dripping from his eyes, real tears, and he's looking right at Caleb. 'You are dead! I won't stop until you're dead!'

Caleb turns to Misha and shakes his head – he's not sure why, it simply happens – then walks away. He doesn't wait or beckon her on, or sweep her away or any of those hero things (*why am I thinking about heroes, this is nothing to do with heroes*). He goes, because there's a hot band around his chest and he's in a world that's stopped making sense. He doesn't know where to go in such a world, but he goes, because listen to Vic. 'I'll smash your door in and kill you while you sleep, aaaaah God, I'll get you both,' and on it goes, so loud it must blanket the whole town, it'll bring everyone out to look, and he really doesn't want to be here for this.

kill smash get you get you get you

Oh God.

Misha skips after him, around him, clutching the sides of her head in amazement. 'There's no way you did that! There is no way that was you!' Caleb can't bring himself to look at her. He'll end up screaming with laughter. It's already bubbling up as her energy infects him. And Vic keeps on howling, and it's like she's dancing to it. 'That has got to be the craziest thing I have ever seen!' The craziest? Seriously? After last night's business? After Neuman?

Why is she so damn funny?

'You ninja'd his knee into the next life! Like, woop-pah!'

It explodes from him, a great gale of laughter, rushing up and out and tearing at his throat and closing his eyes to slits, and he hasn't felt like this since forever, and how can he be like this when he's probably done someone terrible damage?

As clearly as Caleb hears Vic swear, Vic hears Caleb laugh. Vic keeps hearing him, even when Caleb's long gone. He hears that laughter ringing around his head when he eventually hobbles home. He hears it all night long as he lies motionless in the dark. He hears her too. He hears her loudest of all.

64

Gramps backs away from the bedroom curtain, nodding. It's turned out almost the way he thought it would.

65

A fine drizzle is unusual this late in the day, at least according to this summer's rules. It gives the world a hazy sheen. Metal slickly glistens. The air tastes of crisp grass. Droplets pepper their hair and clothing, streams of fine beads. Caleb sticks his tongue out and thinks he can feel the slightest chilly tickle. Misha tries to pinch his tongue between thumb and forefinger, startling him. She's always doing weird stuff like that. His surprise makes her laugh again, yet up until an hour ago he'd never heard her so much as giggle. He feels himself flushing red as he fails to ignore how much he likes the sound. Hopefully the drizzle will cool his face quickly. Very quickly.

Subject change. Now.

'I shouldn't have kicked him like that.'

'Oh, come on, tough guy, don't go all mushy on me now.'

'I'll be dead by the end of today,' he says, swinging his bully-kicking legs. There's a pretty good three-hundred-and-sixty-degree view from up here on the fort. They'll see anyone coming and have plenty of time to climb down and run. Gangs intent on revenge, grandparents on the rampage, fathers out of patience. Any and all will be left behind. 'He'll hear about it and as soon as I walk in the house he'll kill me.'

'You're so funny. He's not going to kill you, is he? Not proper actual kill. Madmen and criminals do killing, not dads.'

His legs swing faster. 'Madmen can be fathers too.'

A jaw drops so fast it's almost audible. 'What? Is your dad like a mad killer? Is that what happened to your mum?'

It's such an outrageous accusation that Caleb laughs. Again. Two laughs in one day, and both about grim stuff. Maybe there's something wrong with him. Maybe Caleb's the madman. 'He didn't… That's not what I meant to say… It's just that people aren't always the way they're meant to be, are they? Like if you've got a father, he's meant to…I dunno, he's meant to care,

135

isn't he? I mean, that's the whole point, right? He's meant to be interested and want to spend time with you and you'd have all these jokes together and…right?'

She's been watching him the whole time and her gaze doesn't drop. 'I wouldn't know about any of that. No daddy, no mammy.'

'So you're saying I should shut up and stop moaning because I don't know how good I've got it? Well, no, because that's crap. Because I live with someone who hates me. He'd be happier if it was me that was dead instead of Mum. He looks at me like that every single day, like it's a piss-take that I continue to exist, like it's offensive that I take up air. If I touch anything in the house I'd better leave it as clean as I found it, like I'd never touched it in the first place. Like he doesn't want any evidence of me being anywhere in the house. It probably helps him pretend I don't exist, at least when he doesn't have to actually look at me. That's every day, every single day, and it's going to keep being every single day. Yeah, before you say it, I get it; you've got every single day of no parents at all. Well, take mine. Keep him. Him and his misery. Him and his endless rules. Him and his hate. Keep him and stick him.'

She remains quiet for a minute. The drizzle cools him. Then, 'Got that out of your system?' He wipes his face rather than answer. 'Something bad-ass got woke up inside of you. Nice rant!' He doesn't want to grin: he can't help it. Seconds later he's not grinning at all as Misha thumps him one in the shoulder. 'That's what you get for making assumptions about me.'

'Ah God, that hurt! What you do that for?'

'I told you. Don't go thinking you know me or what I'm going to say. You will get the biggest thumping of your life, and you'll deserve it. Lose the gormless look, it doesn't suit you.' She rolls her eyes when she sees that he is still confused. 'You assumed I'd give you grief about who's having the worst time when it comes to parents, right? Well, guess what? I'm over it. I learned how to deal with it long ago. They've been gone pretty much forever.'

Here's that time, the moment when he gets to ask what he wants to ask, what he's waited to ask for months. 'People say they were murdered. Some people do anyway.'

'Those are the people who don't bother to check around, do some investigating. Wouldn't something like that be in the papers?'

He clutches the journal under his sweater tight to his chest. 'Yeah, it would.'

'I knew you were the other kind of people, the ones who think. I knew you'd look.'

'There's others,' he says, courage flourishing. 'They say your parents did the murdering, then they ran away, leaving you behind.' It feels okay to say these things out here in the rain.

'They ran off without me? Does that make sense?'

'Maybe they thought you'd slow them down.'

'Yeah. Yeah, that makes sense.'

'Of course it does. I said it.'

She feigns shock. 'Oh my God, have you found a sense of humour somewhere? Caleb, I think you'd better give it back before it's missed.'

He wants to say something witty to follow that up, because then he'd be that little more cool. But nothing comes. He'll think of it later, in bed, and he'll kick himself for not being quicker. 'What happened to them?'

'Accident. Mum died straight away. Dad hung on for a bit. I ended up with Granddad. Living with Granddad is pretty much all I've known. He's a whole different kind of problem.'

Caleb remembers the opening of Gramps's journal. Evelyn, her father, the bruises. 'What did he do to you?'

And just like that he's aged her. He's looking at a teen who can no longer hold the world up, and all she can do now is stand back and watch it fall. He's scared again, and realises something. Gramps is wrong. They're nothing like each other. Caleb doesn't want answers, because when you get answers you have to do something about them. 'He thinks he knows what's best, okay? He thinks he knows what needs to be done.' Misha raises her face to the sky and lets the fine rain douse her face. 'Why me?' she whispers. 'Why not someone else, somewhere else, a thousand years from now?' Her knuckles tap him on the back of the hand, and goose bumps shiver. 'Lie back,' she says. 'Lie back and look up.'

'Why? The stars won't be out for hours.'

'Caleb, the stars are always out. Do as you're told.' She lies back on the top of the fort, and it's only a few moments before Caleb does the same beside her. The wooden slats of the roof are cold against his back. He's worried now about the journal pages, hopes water won't get all the way through his layers. It's grey up above. No glorious depths of space, of jewel-sprinkled blackness that lures him outside at night to sleep in air. Just thick, miserable clouds. He doesn't know if he's meant to say anything, so he keeps his mouth shut. 'It's huge, isn't it? The sky. Super huge. Enormous. But it's even bigger than that. Really, look at it. Ginormous. Say it.'

'What?'

'Look up at all of that and say ginormous. Just do it. And really look.'

It feels like a ridiculous thing to do, embarrassing. A frown folds over his face, and she turns to look at him, expecting a response, and he doesn't want her to see him frown, and the only other thing he can do is as she asks. He looks at the mass of silt-grey clouds, and he says, 'Ginormous.'

There's a hint of a smile in her voice. 'You're not really looking.'

He is. Of course he is. His eyes are open and pointing in the right direction. What else could he be looking at?

'Say it again and keep looking.'

Caleb opens his mouth and only breath comes out. He hangs over a vast and muddy froth, a churned-up mass of moors,

softened by rain and earthquakes. He is miles and miles above
it; he will fall for an age before thudding into those folds. A
dizzy sickness plunges through his stomach. It goes forever, it
seems, this clumping lumpy soup, and he can hardly bear to
be dangling above it a single second longer, and yet the thrill
is irresistible. Right here, he's before the endless. Strange ships
could cut through this sludge.

'Now you're seeing it,' says a soft voice by his ear, and how
has he not seen it like this until now? All those nights staring at
stars, thinking about how many and how far, but there's more
to it than that. 'It's the second you stop thinking about it, that's
when it hits you.'

'Yeah,' is all he can say, because the movement of the land-
sludge miles and miles below is making him slightly queasy.
That, and the way Misha reads him, directs him.

'There's no one else looking at the same part of the sky that
we are; no one else is seeing it from here. Not one person in this
cursed town, no one else on the whole planet. That's billions of
people not looking.'

'Some must be looking up.' His words sound flat in his head.

'A few. Maybe. But not at that, not from here.'

'Yeah, and we'll be the only ones on all the planets in the
universe...'

'We're the *only* ones in the universe. There's nothing on any
other planet looking our way or at their own skies or watching
TV or whatever.'

'Nobody knows that for sure...'

'I kind of do. But shut up. Those clouds, yeah? Behind them
are your endless stars and empty planets and wasted space.
Beneath them, this miserable planet and...and all these wasted
lives. We think we're so special simply because we exist, but
look at it all. Look. It's empty. The only rock in all of existence
with anything on it is this one. We're not meant to be here. We're
freaks. There's no meaning to anything, so why get worked up

about it? The way I see it, people get themselves all heated up thinking they can make a difference and that their life will be worthwhile, and then one day they realise.'

'Realise what?'

'They'll die and the world will keep on like they'd never been around. They made a difference? The world kept moving on. They sat on their backside and did nothing? The world kept moving on.' She turns to one side, leans on an elbow. 'Parents die. Does the world stop and cry its eyes out? No. It spins the way it always does.'

He doesn't want to look at the sky any longer. He mirrors her pose. 'Why are you being like this?'

'Because you asked. You wanted to know about the problem with Granddad. What you saw, up at the graveyard. It's called a Turning. It confuses evil souls that are taking over dead bodies. It slows them down. Stops them coming back so quick, if it can be done without any interruptions.'

'Oh.'

'Yeah. Now we've got a revenant running around that's not really meant to be running around yet.'

'That's what Neuman is? A…'

'…revenant, yeah. Souls aren't like us when they come back. They're…they're like broken parts, the stuff that's left once whatever happens in death happens. It's never the good bits though. Always the rotten pieces, the hateful stuff, the parts that like violence.'

'That must make Vic a remnant.'

'It's revenant. And he's like one, but still human. I can't imagine how awful he'd be if he ever came back as one of them.'

'Wow,' says Caleb, feigning a shudder. 'Vic Sweet with only the bad bits. That's a genuinely horrible thought.'

'Yeah. Horrible. I mean, I don't want anything to do with any of this stuff. Turning bodies, chasing possessed people, messing with the fate of the world. It's not for me. I'm not that girl. There's no part of me that wants to *be* that girl. But Granddad thinks I am. I'm his family, I exist here and now, and he wants me to be like his apprentice, and it's all so very important, and so what?'

Caleb's heart only rushes like this when he's running hard. 'Do you know what's under your house?'

'What do you mean? Caleb?'

66

The not-man shuffles too slow to keep up with them. It had lost them for a while and had done the only thing it could: stood still and waited. The rain, the chill, the shivers, it noticed none of this, waiting only for that boy and that girl.

And, unblinking, it spotted them, and it slowly-slowly follows, badness at its core.

67

He sneaks her in because they need a dry place to read. They can't go to hers, given that Caleb's a wanted boy, and after the confrontation with Vic she doesn't trust any of her hidey-holes. Wouldn't Father have a fit if he knew that Caleb had a girl in his room? Of course, Caleb might have that fit first.

Heating on, scooched up against the radiator, towels rubbing hair. The leather cover of the journal is damp in his hands, but the pages have mostly survived, flecked with only a little water along the edges. As long as he's careful turning the pages it'll be okay.

She nods at him to read from the journal. Caleb does so quietly, knowing that Father is busy on the laptop, knowing they could be discovered any minute.

It's a thrill.

Nightmares are made of less than this.

Running, our footfalls echoing with hard slaps. Tunnels that roll on and on. Stumbling over loose dirt, bouncing against the rough walls, tearing the skin from our shoulders. Lamplight swinging around, only showing twenty feet of tunnel before us, and when you're running that simply isn't enough. Any second we would hit a dead end, and the howling monster giving chase would be upon us. When I say howling, I mean that Landy was raging like he could pull down the tunnels with his voice alone. He thundered about betrayal and punishment, and as Evelyn led us farther and farther, his fury bounced off corners at odd angles. In one instant he sounded far off. The next, right at my neck. The next, up ahead and pounding towards us.

Betrayal and punishment, down there amongst the dead.

We had to be going in circles, because it couldn't be possible for one man to dig so much, so far. Chamber after chamber of those grave columns we passed, and then I realised we weren't doing circles at all, couldn't be, because the ground was gradually sloping. The gradient was slight, but I could feel it. The tunnels were burrowing further down. The world of open air and skies was far behind. More and more heavy, heavy soil above us.

My lungs couldn't find enough to breathe, and suddenly I wasn't so sure that the tunnels were Landy's. Something could have dug its way up just as easily.

'What are you doing in here?'

Caleb leaps to his feet, skin pulled taut. So stupid! He shouldn't have brought her here; he talked too loud, stupid, stupid, stupid.

Father's not in the room. He hasn't burst in and found them.

'Who are you? Get the hell out of my house!' He's downstairs. In the kitchen. His anger is peppered with fear. 'Get out! Now!' A thud, like someone bouncing off a door or wall.

Caleb wants to tell Misha to run. Wants to see who (what) Father's facing.

Shouldn't have come here. So, so stupid. Pernicious House, should have gone there, and never mind the revenant, it's not there anymore, it's come here, looking for me. And now it's in the garage.

That realisation makes up his mind.

'We've got to go,' he tells Misha, stuffing the journal into his school rucksack. 'Out the window. Onto the garage roof. Careful.'

The window screeches and clatters as she throws it open. Caleb winces, and follows her out quickly, trembling. There's a lot of shouting and thumping downstairs. Misha is sure-footed as she scampers across the slanted roof and leaps onto the garage. He slips, lands heavy on his elbow's edge. His whole forearm flashes numb, a blast of white pain then nothingness to his fingertips.

'I thought I was the one meant to be careful,' says Misha, coming back to help him up. 'Good job being quiet, by the way.'

She takes his good hand. The warmth of it almost distracts him from the rubbery misery that was once his right forearm. She leads him onto the garage roof, where they both stop and listen. Shuffling, scraping, a metallic clang. A struggle under their feet.

Caleb's own father, fighting a dead thing that Caleb himself brought here. He'll catch holy hell for this.

Misha prods him, shrugs her shoulders. *What now?* He clambers down to ground level at the back of the house, waits for her to land beside him. She's so light on her feet.

There are windows high up on the back wall of the garage. He grabs the ledge, pushes against brickwork with his feet. It's hard work boosting himself with a misbehaving arm. He holds himself up long enough for a short glimpse inside. Father, with his back to Caleb, stepping away from a staggering assailant. Caleb's only up a few seconds, but he sees what he needs to, and drops.

'It's not Neuman.'

'You sure?'

'If it is, she's worked out how to turn her lights off and become a weird-looking grey man who shivers all the time.' Misha looks her question. 'It's a man that's not a man, it was lurking around in the graveyard before I heard you and your situation.'

'So what are we going to do?'

'We're going to go.' And he walks.

She skips to catch up. 'What about your dad?'

'He'll be fine,' says Caleb with no idea if that's true. 'He looked like he had it all under control. And if he sees us there, what do we say? When the not-man thing goes right for me, how do we explain it?'

'Hey, I think I'm pretty clever, we can come up with something...'

'No.' He's never used the word so firmly. 'He'll be fine.' Caleb doesn't see the way she looks at him, like she's tilted a picture and noticed something new in the light.

'So where are we going?'
'I don't know,' he says. But he does know.
The rain stops.

68

Crosswell's hitting it hard. He came here intending to drink his fill, and that's exactly what he's going to do, right up to kicking out time. He beckons over the barmaid, puts on his faded smile, orders another pint. She obliges without offering much of a smile in return. To her, he's just another dirty old man who looks her up and down. To him, she's just another girl to look up and down. 'One for yourself,' he says, handing over a note. Her smile increases by an increment.

An ongoing battle, he thinks. *She'll come around one day.*

She walks off with that wiggle, and it reminds him that he's sick of females anyway. He's had a bellyful of them. Half the pint is chugged in one go. The taste has him now. There won't be any shaking it off.

The old man's going to be one person down for tonight's gathering.

'Senile old bastard,' Crosswell growls to himself. There's no one else in the pub. Him and sports news mumbling low on the enormous television over the fireplace. He hates sports. Who's got time for games when there's so much to deal with? Another example of how pathetic the world has become. Pathetic overpaid games.

Neuman's playing games. Best game of hide-and-seek ever. Vanished off the damn planet. Impossibly vanished. The brat too. She's one for games. Playing at being dumb, 'accidentally' messing up the Turning, and isn't that how they've ended up with Neuman the incredible vanishing revenant? No, that's not quite the whole how. That stupid old man's been playing his games for too long, stupid games with that nasty little brat of his.

A horrible little girl who should have been killed along with her parents.

'What a horrible little thought to have,' he mumbles before

chuckling. It's a truth he's mulled over every night for months. Every single night. All day, all evening, all night. With every single drink he becomes ever more sure.

One way or another, the girl has to go.

He knocks back the rest of the pint, and clicks his fingers for the barmaid to return. Five o'clock is whiskey o'clock.

69

Things have gone very quiet in the garage. Silent. It's five minutes since a dog stopped barking at the garage door, riled up by the strange noises inside. It's ten minutes since Caleb led Misha away, a boy who thinks he's finally taking control with a girl who's glad to let go of the reins. Those two are heading further into trouble, but there are problems enough here to be dealing with.

Not-man and Not-Father sway slightly on their feet. The fight is over. Both bear marks. Torn shirts, scratches, bruises.

Three knocks at the front door, followed by the bing-bong of the bell. A momentary pause, then repeat: three knocks, bing-bong. A muffled 'Hello?'

Not-man shambles, making his way from the garage, stumbling into the kitchen. Not-Father staggers after him, misses the first step as if he didn't know it was there. Both of them conduct a very small circuit of the kitchen, trying to work out where they're meant to be. The neighbour's muffled voice pipes up again. 'Hello? Jeff? Everything alright in there? Margaret says she heard something going on, wanted me to check in on you. Would've been over sooner, but... You in there, Jeff?'

Three knocks, bing-bong.

Not-man gets his bearings, speeds up, targeting the front door. Gets there in time to hear the neighbour huff and turn away. Not-man looks the door up and down, unsure why it's still in his way. Not-Father bumps him to one side and grapples with the handle.

A shoulder heaves Not-Father out of the way and Not-man bundles his way outside. Stands on the front step. Swivels, searching. To the left. The neighbour, heading back into his home, huffing and grumbling and not noticing that someone's come out of Jeff's house and is watching. Back indoors goes the neighbour.

Not-man drops down off the doorstep, shambles across the drive and then the lawn. Not-Father is about to follow.

'Hey there!' A voice behind him. It's the neighbour from the other side, a middle-aged man whose eyes are always screwed up despite wearing glasses. Not-Father faces him. 'You got a minute?' He's standing with hands on hips, like he doesn't really have a minute spare himself and this needs to be dealt with quickly. Not-Father starts shuffling over. 'It's about that kid of yours. Not that it's any of my business, it's just that he's been seen out all night, sleeping on the garage roof.' It's a short lawn, and Not-Father pauses at the edge, unsure of what he was intending to do. 'I'm not one for butting in, I'm sure you know I keep myself to myself, but it's an odd thing, isn't it?' Not-Father does a wobbly about-turn to see what Not-man is up to. He's rapping on the first neighbour's front door. Three knocks, then looking for a bell to do the bing-bong. Glasses continues bleating on. 'It's probably not for me to say, but the way things are this day and age it's not all that wise for children to be sleeping out of doors where any kind of funny character might find them.' Not-Father hears the words, but none of them mean anything to him. He watches as Not-man's knocking is answered by the huffing, balding neighbour, and then Not-man presses forwards into the house, grabbing two handfuls of the man's face. 'Hey, sorry, are you…are you listening? I'm in the middle of telling you something here.' When he turns back to Glasses it takes a moment to steady himself. 'Why are you looking at me like that? I'm just trying to do you a favour.' Not-Father walks at Glasses, forcing him to back-peddle. 'Hey! Back off, pal!' Not-Father keeps going, forcing Glasses to retreat towards his house. 'You lay one single finger on me and I'm calling the police, I mean it!' He swings the door, meaning to slam it in his assailant's face. Not-Father raises an arm. Wood bashes against bone. If there's a blast of white pain, if there's a flash of numbness, Not-Father doesn't show that he feels it. He pushes on in, and Glasses turns to run farther into the house. Not-Father lashes out, a wild, unfocused arm-swing, and a flat hand slaps Glasses hard on the ear, destroying his hearing on that side. Glasses drops to the floor wailing as Not-Father kicks the door shut.

The screaming doesn't last long.

70

They've talked all the way here without managing to say very much. The words are taking up space, filling up time, keeping them from thinking. Stupid stuff. What they prefer in sandwiches. Which crisps are best. The worst weather they've played out in. The longest they've ever stayed awake. The earliest they've got up. The ultimate animal they'd have as a pet. What they would call that pet. Anything but the things that worry them. He doesn't want to talk about the father he's left in the garage, or the thing he left Father with, or the things he's seen in the graveyard, or Vic Sweet, or any of that, not yet, not for a little while. She doesn't want to talk about Granddad or graveyards or Eight balls or what Caleb just did or Vic Sweet, not yet, not for a little while.

'I'd call him Dave,' she says.

He considers this. 'I'm not sure Dave's the kind of name that suits a giraffe.'

'I think that probably depends on the giraffe.'

'What, like they've got personalities?'

'Well, yeah. There's grumpy giraffes and happy giraffes and crazy giraffes, and ones that like dancing.'

'You're sure about that?'

'Yeah, they love it. They just keep it hidden in case the other giraffes find out.'

'What'll they do if they find out?'

'You don't want to know. They can get really ugly.'

There's an image in Caleb's head that he may never forget. 'I thought some of them were meant to be nice.'

She's solemn as she imparts the terrible truth. 'They can change. All nicey-nicey one minute, the next they're vicious monsters.'

They've reached the gates, and the laughter dies away. There's still a big enough gap to climb through; no one's bothered to fix it yet.

In daylight Pernicious House is less threatening, though it remains austere and cold. Caleb's walked into a broken memory, a dead recollection, all of its guts torn out. He and Misha are the only souls in this place. Everything other than scenery has been removed. Life, sound, action, all long gone. Lonely. This feels like a lonely place. Pernicious House is dead and alone.

There are no twin headlights swinging about, nothing to chase. Last night these grounds were lively.

It's a long walk over the front gardens and up the flight of stairs. The gravel underfoot snaps and pops, louder than space dust in his mouth.

There's not even any traffic to hear.

Caleb tells himself that he's not freaked out. He's really not.

'If she shows herself, we run. Not too fast. And not into any ditches.'

'Har har. Funny. Not.'

'Now that you're a tough guy, are we breaking in here or what?'

'We're not breaking in anywhere. Come on.' Round the side of the mansion they go again, but not towards the gardens. He leads her to a second building behind the main house, smaller but equally ornate. Pernicious Hall, built solely for hosting the largest of banquets, the finest of parties, the best of performances. Caleb remembers being in there, perched on Mum's knee, overwhelmed and drowning as an orchestra played. It was meant to be an outdoor performance, but rain as heavy as any this summer threw itself upon them, and as the day's visitors were ushered into the Great Hall, the old man warned them the music might be a tad louder indoors, and there was no tad about it. The sound swallowed up the air, it throbbed behind his eyes.

At the top of the stone staircase leading to the entrance, under the broad, elegant arch, he sits, back to the pillar. Misha sits opposite, legs curling up under her dress.

Beyond the courtyard is the lawn, which runs for a hundred yards before ending in an abrupt drop-off, like a large slice has been lifted away. Then there are swathes of trees, a resplendent green patchwork grown strong from the canyon. Past them, crowds of flowers laze along the slope on the other side. Then there are fields, golden and yellow, rolling like waves of molten treasure.

There are no graveyards in this view.

'Read it to me,' she says, and he does.

I imagined the fires of Hell nearby, stoked by the Devil. The thin air burned in my throat. I expected to turn a corner, see flicking flames around which demons danced.

My heart almost gave out when I realised we really weren't alone down there.

As we flitted past yet another chamber, I saw a figure within. In the next there was something struggling on the floor. The next, a slithering mass pulling itself from a hole in one of those columns.

I saw these things. They're real. They're down there. Now, in those tunnels. God alone knows how many have risen from their graves.

'Evelyn!' shouted Landy. 'If they get you there's nothing I can do! You'll wish I killed you first!'

One of those dirty, greasy creatures tested its voice, a crackling rasp that sounded like dry skin snapping. I was ready to throw myself on the ground, see which one laid hands on me first, Landy or the corpses.

A split-second before Evelyn's gasp of joy, I tasted fresh air. It was the finest breath that has ever entered my lungs. She grabbed my hand again, but this time I needed no spurring.

We rounded the corner. A dead end! Then I saw the ladder, and Evelyn wasted no time climbing it. Neither did I. Nothing will move you faster than the fear of dirty, greasy dead hands reaching for your ankles, the fingers rotted down to taloned bones, tearing at your flesh.

I kicked out at hands that weren't there. I'd left my calm, rational self far behind in those tunnels.

Evelyn dragged me up the last few rungs. We were out! I had no idea where we were, and I still don't. Somewhere at the back of the graveyard I think. We were amongst trees. Evelyn didn't give me much chance to think about it. She took the lantern off me and dropped it with hers before we were off and running again, despite how much my legs ached. I understood that out in the open those lanterns would have made us easy to spot and track, but as we ran helter-skelter along barely-there tracks, scratched at by branches, snagged by thorns and creepers, I wished desperately for some form of light. My heart pulsed hard in my head. One trip and I could smash my face in. One trip and I'd be caught. That monster of a man, his bellows chased us out of those tunnels, a troll spat out of the very earth.

'Get back here, Evelyn! Get back here now!' He screamed so loud I was sure that something must tear in his throat. 'Both of you! Get here now!'

That voice gave me energy I didn't think I had. I would run until my lungs exploded before even thinking of surrendering to that howling animal.

Evelyn led us on a baffling route, darting left and right and over fences and through trees and anywhere that provided at least some cover. She stopped so suddenly that I bundled her over for a second time, and didn't we make a tremendous crash as we fell through a hedgerow? We ended up on our sides, facing each other, her breath hot on my face. 'You have to go,' she said, 'and don't argue.' I tried to argue. Instead she picked herself up and bade me do the same. 'He hasn't seen you, he doesn't know who you are. At the end of this path you'll come out behind the school. No, no buts, don't worry about me, I can deal with him, I've been dealing with him for years. Go, now! He's coming!' She pushed me towards the path. I grabbed her hand to take her with me, but she resisted. And Landy's shouts were getting closer. 'I know him better than anyone!' she insisted. 'I know what I'm doing, I promise!' Then she was gone, shouting at Landy to 'Go away!' so he would follow, so she could lead him away from me.

I have never forgotten the last touch of our fingertips.

I ran, keeping low, looking over my shoulder over and over again. When I reached the school I stopped looking and kept moving. I was reduced to a jog, but I refused to slow any more than that. I had something to do, and I didn't think I'd have much time to do it in.

As I expected, the Landy house wasn't locked. The monster man had been in too much of a hurry to dish out some punishments. I found a satchel, went to Evelyn's room, filled it with most of the books she'd hidden under her bed, carried the remaining two under my arm, and the whole time I thought of that open trapdoor leading down to the cellar, to those tunnels and the dusty, greasy creatures that shuffled around in the dark.

I couldn't get out of that house quick enough.

But I didn't leave the graveyard, not straight away. I'm only so much of a coward. I lay low, keeping out of sight while watching that house. I wanted to see her come back. I wanted to see Landy, if he would return dragging Evelyn along by the neck or if he'd be alone. I watched to see the dead rise from the tunnels and spill out into our world.

I saw none of these things.

That house was silent for hours. I was left alone, cold and tired, with only assumptions for company. I told myself she was leading him the merriest of dances, and he was still chasing her somewhere in the night, maybe in big circles. I imagined that the creatures weren't coming out because they were awaiting their Master's return. I told myself to believe in Evelyn, that she could deal with him, because she would never lie to me, would she? My Evelyn.

I would hunt her out the next day, and she'd have a frightening tale to tell, and together we'd work out what to do next.

At some ungodly hour, then, I headed home, and in the absence of sleep I read a book.

Caleb lowers the journal. He wants to look at Misha, wants to see her reaction. Her gaze is diverted towards the drop-off and beyond. He wonders what she sees. Is it the girl, running,

running but eventually caught? Or is it the boy, sneaking home with books and fear? Or are her thoughts elsewhere, back home, beneath the floorboards?

Her chin is set firm, like she's ready to fight. 'Your Gramps is an old man now, right?'

'Yeah. Properly old.'

'All of this happened years and years ago.'

'Yeah.' Decades ago. What an odd thought. Caleb's only a little more than a decade old himself. Decades just don't makes sense to him.

'So either the tunnels collapsed or got sealed up. I've never heard of them or seen anything that might have come out of them.'

'We haven't finished the journal yet.'

'So what? You said yourself Landy's house got knocked down and replaced. There's no cellar, Caleb. No trapdoors. Or if there is, somehow I've never seen it, and unless it's been hidden under the rug in my bedroom all this time, then I really don't know where it could be.'

'What about that guy?'

'Which one? The one you left in the garage with your dad?' It isn't said with venom, but its still got fangs. 'That didn't dig itself out of the ground. Not dirty enough. That was something else. You're getting distracted by old stories when they don't really matter. There's a lot to deal with right now.'

'Gramps gave me this for a reason; he wants me to read it...'

'And we've read it, and it was great, but I don't know what you want us to do with it. We can't go down there even if we wanted to. We've got stuff going on right now that we don't know what to do about. There's Neuman who could be anywhere, and Crosswell's going to be a real pain in the arse, and Vic Sweet's going to get his gang to kill us, and Granddad's not far from raising the dead. There, I've said it. You wanted to ask, I know you did. It's been killing you. Well, there it is, that's what you saw. He's trying to control it so they all come up at once. The old coot's totally crazy, and Crosswell and the others are just as bad or maybe worse because at least Granddad's excuse is that he's mad, and you know what, Caleb? Do you know what? Once we're done here, you get to go home. Your Father's there, I know, and that's terrible for you, but you get away from it all. You close the door behind you, and leave the world outside, and it'll be like all the monsters are miles and miles away. When I go home, I'm right in the middle. I sleep with monsters all around me. And then Granddad wants to go out playing with them.' She stands, and he has a feeling she might take a run-up and kick him in the head. 'This is all a big scary adventure for you, Caleb, but for me this is life, every single day.' She walks off, heading towards the broken gate. Caleb scrambles to his feet. 'Don't bother,' she snaps. 'I need to get home before Granddad comes hunting.'

And so Caleb is, once again, alone. Just a boy and a journal.

71

Not-Father stands in the corner of a kitchen that's not his, watching the heaped human on the floor, the small blood splashes marring the linoleum. First the right foot twitches, then the left. Fingers grasp at nothing. Creaks and cracks as neck and shoulders jerk. Shudders run up and down the legs, the arms flap like rubber wings.

Then it all stops.

And Glasses stands. He's a little wobbly, but he's upright, and staring at the microwave. His reflection is dim in the jet-black door of the appliance. With a shuddering hand he rights his skew-whiff spectacles.

A bump in the garden outside.

Glasses shuffles to the back door, struggles with the handle. Not-Father steps forward to assist. As soon as the door opens, Glasses shoves Not-Father away and bundles out, staggering on the step down to the patio. There's a ball in the middle of the lawn, and a small face peering over the fence.

'Excuse me? Can I have my ball back this time please?'

Glasses heads for the small face, arms out-stretched and desperate.

72

An eight-ball, heavy on a bed. It's the only thing in the room shaking. When it stops a short message appears in its window: HUNGRY I ACHE

73

He long ago gave up calling out a 'hello' whenever he gets home. Once upon a time it resulted in Mum calling something cute right back at him before coming through from the living room, or upstairs, or wherever to hear about his day. Now, noise tends to alert Father to Caleb's presence, and the boy prefers to get in and get to his bedroom with the minimum of fuss. He doesn't want to know what happened in the garage, doesn't care if there was a scuffle when Father threw the intruder out on the street. So he enters via the back door, kicks off his trainers on the mat in the kitchen, and heads upstairs without seeing that the front door is open.

Caleb doesn't intend to stay home for long.

He needs to get back out there. He has to be in the graveyard. So what if she told him not to follow? So what if her granddad and his goons might be lurking around and looking for him? A million 'so whats'. There are measurements and drawings and investigations that will not wait. There are things that must be found out, and Caleb has to record it all.

He must.

Must, must, must.

In a minute.

As soon as he's got up off the bed. Only a minute or two. He's thinking about what to do next. Closing his eyes to think. A couple of minutes while he makes a decision about something. Whatever it is. Important. That's what it is, important. But it can wait. Five minutes.

That's all.

74

She approaches home cautiously, spends the minimum time possible in any sight lines from the windows. There are no cars parked out front, which is good and bad. Good, because it means there's no Crosswell or any of those other idiots hanging around. Bad, because it means Crosswell and the other idiots aren't around to distract Granddad. For an old man he can be surprisingly alert. She can't face any more of his disappointment. It's been too long a day already.

Round the back of the house she goes, slips through the window into her room.

Eight sits on the middle of the bed.

Misha takes a good long look at the silent ball, feels it is eyeing her right back. She drops a towel over Eight, something she's never done before, then changes into pyjamas.

She thinks that maybe she'll leave the towel over Eight for the rest of the day.

There's a soft hiss of shifting material as the towel trembles. Misha knows she shouldn't have let that thought out. She doesn't want to deal with Eight when it's angry. Maybe she should scoop it up, pop it in a cupboard out of the way, get a few hours peace. Or a few days. She could live without its predictions for a few days. Didn't exactly help her with Vic Sweet, did it?

The shaking under the towel becomes more violent.

She feels pale. She's let her thoughts run too far this time.

'Alright,' she says, 'I was only messing around.' Deep breath, and she draws the towel away. 'Take it easy, okay? Don't freak out. Nothing wrong with having a sense of humour.'

Eight regards her in cold, blank stillness. No words, no shaking. She turns her back on it, folding the towel and placing it on top of the drawers. She wonders if perhaps now would be a good time to go and face Granddad, get that unpleasant scene out of the way. If she offers to do a few weeks worth of chores then she might be able to take some of the heat out of the situation.

Even with her back to Eight, Misha knows a response has appeared. It's like an ice cube millimetres from her neck, her skin cringing away.

She thinks of Caleb, with only a miserable, hateful father to avoid. Poor boy with so little to lose. Alone in his bedroom. She wishes she could have stayed a while longer. It was nice there, away from the world, away from all this, even if it was only for a little while, even if it couldn't hope to last.

Now she must deal with this.

She turns to see what Eight has to say.

DON'T YOU DARE

A hard, dry swallow. 'Come on, I'd never stick you in a cupboard, it's a joke,' but it's a joke that feels lumpen in her throat.

Eight's words are an icy blue. ALL I'VE DONE.

'I know. You've done so much. I'm not saying you haven't…'

YOU MUST REMEMBER

'I can't forget, can I?'

No immediate answer, except the darkness is answer enough to her snappy words. If it launches itself at her, Misha won't be surprised. Then, I AM YOURS.

'Yes.' The lump in her throat grows.

YOU ARE MINE

Those are the worst three words of all. 'Yeah, but look, I could do with a little bit of quiet before Granddad finds out I'm back…'

FOCUS ON ME. This last word grows to fill the screen, simmers as if hot.

Misha reminds herself not to think of anything. Now is not a good time for thinking. There's all too much trouble in thoughts.

I'M IN CHARGE. This is a crimson shout.

OLD MAN NOT

'Try telling him that. He's got a world to change and he'll do it no matter what.' And if Granddad ever finds out about Eight there is no telling how badly he will react. The only guarantee is that the reaction would be very, very bad.

CHANGE IS GOOD

'So I've heard.'

CHANGE IS RIGHT

CHANGE IS NEEDED

OLD MAN FOOLISH

BUT ALSO WISE

She'd almost prefer Eight's violent outrage to this gobbledegook. 'I get this rubbish from him all the time,' she snaps, and reminds herself to keep her voice down or give herself away. 'I've heard all of this. I just want a break…'

CHANGE IS IMPORTANT

BUT NEEDS CONTROL

I'M IN CONTROL

CONTROL CONTROL CONTROL

'Okay, I get it, I get it. I bow down to you, the all-seeing, all-knowing Eight. But you didn't tell me about Vic. You didn't say that he'd get me up at the tree.'

The last CONTROL fades from the small round window, and she watches it hard, and the answer is several long seconds in coming. LEFT ME HERE, says Eight.

She frowns, reading the message again, and again. 'Did you know he was coming for me? You had to know. You always know.'

DOES IT MATTER?

'You got in a huff with me over something I hadn't done yet? I can't believe this. You left me to him.'

ALL NEED LESSONS

A horde of violent thoughts push and shove to the front of her brain. Throwings. Smashings. Burials. All possible endings for Eight the Betrayer.

'That's not fair. You're not fair, I brought you here. It's because of me that you're here and not still stuck over there!' Heat in her throat, tongue boiling. 'You made all these promises, and you're just like everyone else, you all say the same things, and you said you were different and you're not, you're as different as everyone else and that's no different at all. The only thing that's in that ball is the same old bull.'

DON'T YOU DARE

Eight shakes so hard that the words disintegrate and she thinks the ball might explode. She cowers away as small words expand: ALL I'VE DONE, ALL FOR YOU, ALL I'VE DONE, THROWN AT ME, HATE HATE HATE.

Misha drops to her knees before Eight, leans over the bed, finds the courage to bring her face up close. Her reflection bends and distorts. 'But it's true. You did leave me to him, and you did make promises, a pact you called it, a pact, and you were meant to stick to it.'

YES A PACT

Then, WE BOTH DID.

She sinks down upon the quilt, resting her head in the crook of an elbow. 'For a little while I thought you were on my side. I really did.'

ONLY ONE SIDE

'Yeah. Yours, right?' *Cool now, Misha, cool.* 'I was never off your side.'

STUPID EIGHT ANSWERS

She's been expecting this, but it's still cold shivery awful. Her own words. Her own thoughts.

GET GRANDDAD'S SLEDGEHAMMER

SEE WHAT'S INSIDE

STUPID STUPID EIGHT

'I was angry, alright?' Her honesty is all she has left against Eight's venom. 'What else do you want me to say? I said those things, yeah, I know. And you knew I was going to say them, right? And you know why. So it doesn't change anything.'

WORDS ARE WORDS

She looks away from Eight, to the wrinkles of her knuckles. Having her own spite thrown back up by this ball is wearisome, rapidly so. Soft quilt. Sleep is coming. She pulls the rest of herself up onto the bed, curls around Eight. 'I couldn't get rid of you. We both know it. Because I wonder how you know what you know. It's like writers who can see how the story will turn out, because it's their story.'

YOU ARE MINE

'You keep saying that.'

BOY IS YOURS

Did her stomach really flutter then?

KEEP HIM CLOSE

'I know what I'm doing. It's like you said. He's into it now, he won't let go.' She waits for more answers, but there are none, and she drifts.

75

It's a bang so loud it vibrates the walls and Caleb jumps up, gasping. That was the front door. He knows from the times he's slammed it and been verbally blasted as a result. It has to be Father who has almost taken the door off the hinges. No one else ever comes in (except for Misha, she was here, a girl in here).

Father never slams doors. He can shout and bang fists on tables and throw things at bins, but never door-slamming.

Caleb eases himself off the bed, nerves frazzled and spitting fireworks after the abrupt wake-up. He pads across the carpet, slips out of his bedroom, and listens with ears well attuned to the house he's lived in forever.

Some kind of...snuffling. Caleb's skin prickles. Dogs snuffle when hunting through grass. Hunting.

Caleb feels fragile and edible.

It stops, and is the house always this silent, this breathless?

Someone (thing) is in.

It must be Father. To shut the door, he had to let himself in first. It needs a key. Only Caleb and Father have keys. The door was definitely shut. He saw it was shut. Didn't he?

No. No he didn't. But why would it be left open? It's never left open. And people never jump out of their graves, and no one would ever dig a labyrinth of tunnels under a graveyard, and revenants don't exist.

Solid footsteps tramp down the hall, real solid footsteps, like Father's but not. More deliberate. Measured. Someone relearning the basics of walking might stomp like this.

How long are revenants away before they come back to this life?

Stop it! Caleb is stern with himself. It's Father. It can't be anyone else. It wouldn't be the Not-Man, back after wandering around in and out of the house, looking for Caleb, never thinking for a moment that the boy has already sneaked upstairs and been in bed for who knows how long (and how about that for an idea, a Not-Man looming over a sleeping Caleb and taking hold of his face with cold throbbing hands and squeeeeeeeeeeze). It's Father. Has to be. He got rid of the Not-Man and it was a great struggle and in that struggle Father got hurt. That's it. That's why he's walking strangely. It might be a blow to the head. Concussion. Caleb's heard of that. It makes sense.

If that's the case, why can't Caleb bring himself to call out? Just a few quick words. Or go and look. If Caleb thinks Father might be hurt, then he must go and look.

The footsteps are going in circles around the front room. Tight circles, increasing in speed.

Caleb retreats to his bedroom. He could drag his wardrobe across to barricade the door, but it would make a lot of noise. It would give him away. He could stack up boxes and books, but they wouldn't be enough to stop that man (*a man, are you sure it's a man? It's a not a man, it's not, it's not Father*) if he wanted to barge in, if he wanted to bash right in, grab Caleb's face in two strong hands and squeeeeeeeeeeze. (*Why do I keep thinking that? Stop stop stop.*)

Still not knowing who or what is downstairs (but he knows, oh God he really does know that this is all his fault. He's the one who turned and walked away. And what kind of boy does that? What kind of child could see their own father in danger and then leave them to it and think it will be okay? Caleb leaves the window open for a quick escape, then sits on the floor, back to the door, bracing his legs, and the footsteps move through to the kitchen, going round and round, as if checking every possible corner for boys.

For him.

It's the Not-Man. It's killed Father, and that's Caleb's fault, and Caleb will be next.

No. It's worse than that, so says his gut.

And here come those footsteps, steady up the stairs. Caleb's stomach clenches hard enough to hurt. Footsteps are at the first floor now, and coming.

Thud

Thud

Thud

right up to Caleb's bedroom door and it'll only take one hard push for this boy who weighs next to nothing to be thrown across the room.

Thud

Thud

Thud

those footsteps go right on by, past the bedroom, past the trembling boy hitching back tears, past the bathroom, the toilet, and Father's bedroom door is slammed shut so hard that surely wood has cracked.

Caleb allows himself one solitary sob. Even that sounds loud enough to summon the dead. Or summon the thing in Father's bedroom.

(*It's only Father. It's not, it's not him. I can't know that, I haven't even seen him. I don't need to see. I can hear. I can feel.*)

Caleb can't sleep here. Can't stay here.

There are only objects left by which to name this place home.

With infinite care he opens drawers and wardrobe to stuff his rucksack with a change of clothes and his smallest photo album and a few other items that will fit. He'll leave the bedroom window open in case he needs to come back for anything. Back here, where the monster lives.

He climbs out one more time, and it's like Gramps is waiting for him when Caleb turns up at his door, and they have beef stew with crusty bread and no questions. Caleb's not hungry but he manages to put away two bowls of stew and three chunks of the warm bread. They tidy up quietly, the old man offering only his wrinkled smile, then the boy heads up to the spare room which has never been spare it's always been his, and he flops down into sleep.

His dreams are dark, and everyone in them is not who they're meant to be.

76

Misha sleeps right through.

She doesn't wake when Granddad takes a peek in case she's sneaked back in. She doesn't wake when he retreats, reasoning that he might get some sense from her when she's awake and fresh. She barely stirs when the Belvederes arrive and the hot topic of Crosswell and whether or not he's right dominates the house. She is unmoved when they eventually leave dissatisfied and more fragmented than ever. She sleeps right through the night and the random messages that blaze onto Eight's screen, vicious fragments from bad dreams. She sleeps curled around this poisoned creature, and for a while knows nothing of all the plans being made for her.

She sleeps on past the plum-coloured dawn.

77

Sausage, bacon and eggs, cooked by Gramps. There is no breakfast quite like it. There are fresh tomatoes and beans cooked in the pan until the sauce is thick and clumpy and triangles of crisp fried bread and Caleb cannot get enough, mopping up every last bit of grease. His stomach grunts and groans its appreciation.

'Room for any more?' asks Gramps as the frying pan spits and crackles.

Caleb amazes himself by saying, 'Yes please.' The way his hunger is revving right now there's a chance he could go for thirds.

'Can't remember ever seeing you eat like this,' Gramps chuckles, dishing up two more rashers of bacon and another egg. 'I should think it's going to get a bit musical in here later on.' Caleb frowns at him. 'All these eggs will give you a bad case of the trumps.'

'Not a problem,' says Caleb between bites. 'I'll take it outside. Plenty of air out there.'

'You won't be able to see the other kids for the green fog around you.' Gramps decides not to ask the boy if he wants any more. Caleb shows no signs of slowing, and Gramps is part worried part amused by the idea that he might keep saying yes.

'Not going near other kids. Got things to do.'

'What about the girl?' That's the first thing all morning to make Caleb hesitate. 'Will you stay away from her?' Caleb, mouth full of breakfast, nods his head and looks insincere. 'You'll do whatever you do. I might be old, but I remember being young, your age young. There's the you that you show to oldies like me, and then there's the you that you are when you're out of the door and you're presented with all the world of choices. Don't fret, Caleb. This is not a telling off. I don't have the energy for telling offs, for raising boys.' He turns on the taps to do the dishes. 'Children try to do the right thing, by and large. I was one, you know, a child. They mean to do as they're told, but it becomes difficult when the telling's in the past and there's fun or excitement to be had here and now. That's when children start bending rules to fit, or convincing themselves that they misheard what they were told, or that if they don't say anything about this then nobody needs to know.' The frying pan takes some scrubbing. 'I can't chase around after you. I can't second-guess what you're going to do next. Hell, I barely know what *I* might get up to next. I lose things. I go into rooms and wonder why I'm there. I talk to myself and wonder what I'm on about.' With his back to Caleb he doesn't see that they boy's appetite has ended mid-plateful. 'What I'm trying to say is, save us the pain of any lies. It'll save you the effort of coming up with them, it'll save me the effort of dealing with them.' Drying his hands, he turns to look at Caleb. 'The girl. Yes?'

'No.'

Gramps nods. 'I see. I suppose you're going to be here for a few days? And your father knows you're here? He's not going to come knocking on the door, frantic to know where you are then wondering why I've hidden you here?'

'He won't come knocking.' It's a truth. He's missed out the part that makes it the truth, but then he wasn't asked about those parts, so there's nothing to feel guilty about. He doesn't need to tell Gramps about the awful, stupid, cowardly thing he's done. It's not like Father would have come looking for him anyway. He would have been pleased to get rid of his useless boy, might even have smiled.

His father, swaying in his bedroom, choppy noises in his throat.

Caleb wishes he could tell. But Gramps is old and tired and loses his grip, and isn't it a kindness to leave the old man out of this bit? Isn't that the right choice to make? Didn't Gramps just say it was *his* choice to make?

'Tell me when you've finished the journal,' says Gramps.

'There's more for you to see. It might change your mind, if you've already made it up.'

78

Crosswell slips out of the office with barely a mumble to his secretary, squints against the day's light as he crosses the street to the coffee shop. Fresh air stirs up his sour stomach and he chokes back a belch. He stayed up too long last night, stayed for one more whiskey than he should have. Up too long thinking about how girls can disappear, how old fools can be distracted by such disappearances.

Morgan is waiting for him in the far corner with his usual double espresso. 'You look rough.' She grins.

'How can you tell? I'm always rough.' He drops into the seat opposite her. The plastic protests. 'Meeting go any better last night without me around?'

She stirs three brown sugars into her cappuccino. 'It was a few decibels quieter, and it lasted a little longer. Those are about the only differences.'

'Told you not to waste your time. There's no arguing with the grand poobah. Do you believe me yet? Did he say all the same things he says every time? All the same excuses? All the same bull?'

'Do you need to ask?' Her lipstick smears the edge of her cup. She seems to wear a touch more make up with every year that passes. Crosswell thought she was overdoing it fifteen years ago. 'We need to take the books off him. We break in, it's not like we have to be subtle. He couldn't exactly run to the police and say that some naughty people stole his magic books and now he can't do his hocus-pocus. It's time to man up, Crosswell.'

He smirks. 'Is that manning up, is it?'

'Striding in there and taking charge? Yes. That's exactly what it is.'

'Moronic is what it is. We could do that easily. Of course we could. After all the things we've covered up, that would be nothing. We can get the books. That's if we can find them.

We could take them no problem. But then, what do we do with them? He's had them squirrelled away forever. He's had most of a lifetime to work with whatever's in them.'

'Bully for him. We're no slouches either. We can do…'

'Parlour tricks. In comparison to what he does, we might as well be building castles with dry sand. Before you run your mouth, Morgan, I'll make this really simple. Whatever it is we need, there's one sure-fire way to get it.'

Morgan leans in, smile hardening to hunger. 'And we can't just take her, can we? In the grand scheme of things, I think you'll find that stealing children is frowned upon a little bit more than stealing books. Who's the moron now?'

He laughs because he wants to slap her. He wants to slap her so hard that her teeth cut into her cheek. Wouldn't that cause a stir? Councillor Crosswell beats up businesswoman in coffee shop. That would stir these miserable leeches right up. 'All I need to know right now is whether or not you're on board. We forget the softly-softly approach. Completely. Ignore the endless meetings, the phone calls, the recalculations, and we look at all this from a different angle. We figure out how to get rid of the girl.'

'What about the Turning? We can't abandon that. If they get out of sync and start getting up whenever they like, then we're all screwed. It's a lot of time and effort wasted. Bye-bye grand master plan. A plan, by the way, that we've worked on for…'

'Long enough, yes, yes. Long enough. Too long. If we can get the brat out of the way, and if we refuse to help him with the Turning, it'll really pile the pressure on.'

'On who? Him or us?'

He drinks the double espresso in one. 'Pressure's not a problem for me. Now, I've had a thought.'

79

He can stand. It's incredibly bloody sore, but the knee's taking his bulky weight. He tries some test paces around the room. There'll be no sprinting today. But Vic is up, and Vic is moving.

80

Mickey would rather be playing football, but he's been out-voted this morning. Sam's noticed there's a 'whacking' big hole in the gate to Pernicious House, and he wants to go in. Jay didn't need much persuading. The prospect of clambering through illicit holes is one the frazzle-haired boy will never pass up.

'We could do this any time,' says Mickey. 'We've climbed over the fence before, it's easy.'

Sam, already sporting a mud-smear, shrugs like nothing in the world really matters. 'We're here now.'

There is no counter-argument, so Mickey boots his ball over the gate and climbs through the bars first. It's always good to be seen as first one in. He runs to his ball, brings it under control, then back-heels it to the other boys. The kick-about takes them around the dead waterfalls, up the stairs, across the courtyard, none of them taking much notice of the heavy clouds above. It will rain today. It's guaranteed to. If it pours, they will stay out in it as long as they can, just like every other day.

Sam misses a pass. The football whooshes past him while he stares up at the house.

'Nice skills!' cackles Jay. 'You play like a grandma!' He always reminds Mickey of a crow, hectoring from the trees.

Sam nods at the house. 'Let's go in.'

Mickey groans. He saw this coming. 'If you think I'm going in there, you're even more stupid than you look.' Another Jay cackle. It feels good to score a point against the almost-leader of the group.

'That sounds like the squawks of a chicken.' He's fixated on the darkness behind those windows.

'I'm not breaking in there. I'm not Vic Sweet. That's the kind of think an arsehole like him would do.'

Sam's sigh is disappointment and defeat. 'Fine.' He trots off to collect the ball, which has rolled to a stop beneath one of those big bare windows, and Mickey sees a shape, a human shape on the other side of the glass. It's walking forward. It's bending over to charge headfirst, to smash through, to grab the boy leaning over for his ball.

It's Sam's reflection. It disappears as he picks up the ball, reappears as he stands.

Mickey feels foolish, hopes his friends didn't see any of the fright on his face. A glance at Jay, who's making himself open for the ball, is enough to tell him he's got away with it.

Stupid spooky house.

It's a spooky house that Sam's peering into, like something's caught his eye, like something's hooked him, like he's forgotten that he just said 'fine' and now he can't walk away.

He's going to go in after all, thinks Mickey, *and we'll have to go in after him because that's what we do.*

And it's Jay that snaps Sam out of it with a shout of 'On the head!' Sam grins as he turns away from his dark reflection, and he knocks out a long curling kick that Jay deftly heads with a frazzly flick. Mickey dashes across to bring it down with one knee. Then it's all running and passing and shooting at tree trunks or lampposts or a bin or any static target. Jay and Sam quickly get bored, and Jay starts shinning up the tallest-looking tree he can find. 'The view from up here is going to be sweet!' he squawks as he snaps and cracks up the branches. Sam's got his eyes on the stables.

'Could be anything in there,' he says.

'What, like crap and straw? Go and get it, Sam!' Mickey has a good loud laugh at his own joke. This far into the grounds it's unlikely that anyone from the road will hear them or bother to investigate. All this space. A massive playground, only for them.

'There could be dead things in there,' says Sam, and here's one of his obsessions. He's always craved the great gruesome find.

'Who wants to see a dead horse?'

'It's not going to be a dead horse, is it? They haven't kept horses in there for ages, not even when this place was open.' He whispers the next bit, in case whatever's in the stables might hear. 'I mean a dead body.'

'Sam. A dead horse is a dead body.'

'No, you dummy, a dead person is a dead body. Come on, it's the kind of place where criminals stash stuff, isn't it? If I bumped somebody off, that's where I'd stick them.'

'Why you always on about bumping people off? I can't be bothered with this. I just want a kick about.'

Sam shrugs it off. 'Tell you what. You stay here being all gay, and I'll step up and deal with the situation.'

'What situation? You're so...' Weird is the word he doesn't get round to using. Beams of light sweep and stutter, cutting through the trees. Mickey looks up to locate the source.

'Police helicopter!' panics Sam. 'We gotta go!' He runs.

'Wait! What about Jay?' Heart thumping, Mickey wants to run too. The police are here! He can't get caught! How do they know? 'Sam, wait!' He can't leave without Jay, but Sam's not going to stop, he's not going to step up and deal with the situation, he's going to get gone.

Then Jay cries out, 'What the hell?' and then he's crying out without words, an increasing howl of alarm, and Sam finally slides to a halt and turns back. He and Mickey pound feet towards the tree containing Jay. White-blue light flickers in rotary cycles, and Mickey hears the snap of branches as Jay scrambles down as fast as he dares, and Mickey realises that the helicopter is making no noise, and what kind of helicopter makes no noise?

Jay's scream is suddenly coming down a lot faster. Sam and Mickey are still fifteen yards from the bottom of the tree. The rapid-fire crash of snapping wood, like a huge weight falling straight down the middle from the top. A huge weight with bright lights strapped to it.

Jay's feet catch on the lower branches, slowing his descent. A backflip, and he thuds onto the ground. The impact stops him screaming for a moment. The lights shoot down after him, and a figure lands right on top of Jay, and Mickey and Sam slide to a stop. Mickey has a moment to wonder why whoever-it-is has torches attached to their head, then the whoever is grabbing Jay's face in both hands, trying to set those beams directly in his eyes.

'Get off him!' shouts Mickey, and Neuman's head snaps round to face him, beams flashing across his eyes

through his eyes

and he sees Oh God he *sees*

the world stripped bare, blasted by some terrible weapon, pasted in icy blues and steely whites, the trees stripped of leaves and bark, boney metal skeletons that lean towards him, grass seared away from hard jagged ground, and Jay is without clothes or skin or flesh

and Neuman is monstrous, a grinning, glowering invention of a mad god

and the beam is gone as Jay catches Neuman with a stray knee, kicking himself loose, boosting himself out from under his attacker, then he's off, and Sam goes after him, and Mickey gets off his knees (*what am I doing on my knees*) and he's running too, going wide around the thing with torches for eyes (*they're not strapped on they're its eyes*), and he throws up a little, still disoriented after seeing that other place, that terrible place.

Jay weaves, darting between trees at random, faster than Mickey's ever seen him go. Splashes of light soak the tree trunks and paint them as freezing steel rods. Torcheyes is sprinting after them, as heedless as the boys. It cannot let them go. Mickey hears Sam crying, and his own wish is selfish and mean: *we should have left Jay to it.* They're going the wrong way; they're leaving the gates behind. Jay disappears, reappears as he zigzags through these woods, stumbling as something pulls on his foot. If any of them trip, they are done for.

Sam's not crying.

Mickey looks round, and the Torcheyed monster has his friend, got him by the shoulders, lifting him off the ground, fat lasers boring in deep. 'No! Leave him alone!' screams Mickey, but Torcheyes won't be distracted this time. It's got Sam and it's keeping him. Sam's mouth slackens. His whole face droops.

It's taking everything that makes Sam who he is. Everything that makes him alive.

It can't end for Sam like this, lost and swallowed up by a monster. This can't happen to any of them, it's not fair, they're twelve.

He runs at Torcheyes. Jay's shouting at him, 'What are you doing, come back,' but he can't leave stupid Sam who brought them here, and he screams his last scream.

81

The day is grey like late evening. He feels like he's breathing the misery in, like he's becoming colourless. Rain feathers his hands and face as he keeps count. Caleb's measuring the graveyard again as he can't think of what else to do. His other projects involve going through the gates, and his feet wouldn't let him.

Hand over hand. Measure by measure. Sixty-three, sixty-six, sixty-nine.

Also, he can't go in there because there's other things he should do, he knows there is. He should check in on Father. Whatever happened to him might be over. It's possible he's got better. He might be out cold on the floor. Worse, Father could have wandered off. Caleb wants to take responsibility. And at the same time he really, really doesn't.

Eighty-four, eighty-seven, ninety.

If he went to check in, and if Father was still bad, he could watch Father carefully, observe him, work out a way to put him right. There's always a way to put things right.

One hundred and two, one hundred and five.

His chest hitches a little as more tears are smudged out by the rain. At least Misha isn't here to see him like this. He wants her here, though.

All these opposites, pulling at his insides, leaving him here, measuring fences and blinking away tears.

He concentrates on the tape measure. One hundred and twenty-three, one hundred and twenty-six.

It's a shame he's concentrating so hard.

82

Because Vic Sweet is watching. He's watching the little rat who tried to break his leg. A snarl twists his broad lips as the freak edges along, one tape measure length at a time. Hideous little freak, what the hell does he think he's doing? It's like a really crap geography assignment in the middle of the summer holidays. Freak. It makes Vic want to vomit. Some freaks shouldn't be allowed to live, especially leg-breaking sneaking rats who get between him and the little bitch.

Vic wants to storm over there, smash his head in, stomp on that melon until there's nothing left but mush. If the little rat sees him, though, the chance will be gone. The best Vic's capable of right now is a jog. So he has to wait for Blaine to turn up. Big dumb Blaine, who should be here by now. Vic's patience is straining at the leash. Where is he? Blaine's so dumb he'll probably stumble along and alert the rat too soon…

83

She's been in the room for around about two minutes. He hasn't moved. Granddad's got his elbows on the bench, head in his hands, staring at the toaster. The toast's already popped up, was already up when Misha walked in. He's looking at it, but he's not. It's white plastic, so there's no reflection to see. Straight through – that's where his gaze is set.

When he notices her, it is slow, like he's emerging from an anaemic sleep. It can't have been last night when she last saw him. Surely months have passed, hard months. It's painful to see his sallow skin, his deep wrinkles. He looks like he should be in a grave of his own. 'It's all coming apart,' he says, and his mouth sounds rusty.

'Think that toast's ready.' She's aiming for amusing sarcasm. He's not interested in comedy.

'You all know what's at stake. Every one of you.' He's older than she's ever seen him, way past his limits. 'You, Misha, with all of your talents, and everything I've ever told you, and yet again today you leave me hanging around. Do you think all this is funny? Do you think I'm joking around? You've seen them for yourself, again and again! All you had to do today, this one single day, was grow up, and you ran away like a spoilt little brat. If that's not enough, Crosswell's trying to split the group, and those other idiots are stupid enough to listen. And if *that's* not enough, we've lost Neuman when we can't afford to lose anyone. And if *that's* not enough, the revenant that took her has stirred up the others. Did you know that? They took notice, they saw one of their kind break through, and now they're all pushing harder. Yes, they're coming through faster, and that means all the timings are now wrong, and because you keep running away and the other fools are too busy pouting and stomping their feet, I'm basically on my own. I can't do it all. I couldn't do it all even without the added nightmare of all the recalculations.

And 'woof woof woof grump grump grump bark bark bark' is what Granddad's rant degenerates into. His lips whuff away, and Misha doesn't see why she should have to listen to it. She's grotty from heavy sleep, she's already had enough from Eight, she's had a bellyful of yesterday, and Granddad never ever seems to stop. This stuff's all he ever talks about, never anything else.

'You care more about those dead bastards than me.'

His hands slam down on the worktop. 'Because everything rests on them! And you know that! Nothing else matters!'

Misha walks away. He shouts after her, pleading, but she's heard him loud and clear and will hear no more. She passes her bedroom. Eight's still there on the bed. Restful, but always listening. She steps back to the doorway, considers Eight.

84

Neuman, revitalised. Lights burning hard. Skin cracking. She's fed deeply on her catch.

85

350.2m x 361.3m

Over and over he repeats these numbers to commit them to memory. They can't be right. They can't. That's a huge leap. It's an extra thirty-odd metres in either direction. He's seen a lot of madness lately, the incredible made real. But this is messing with the rules of physics. This kind of thing cannot happen without affecting the surroundings. You can't contain three hundred and fifty metres in the same space as three hundred and ten. It's not possible. People would notice. Either everything in the graveyard should look squashed up and crammed in, or everything out here should look stretched. Or there'd be gaps between the houses. Or there'd be something else between them to fill up the space.

Or something.

But the world around him looks as it always does. Same number of houses in the same neat lines. Pavements uncracked. Roads unstretched. Lampposts all in the same places.

The world outside the fence carries on as normal, whilst the incredible occurs on the other side. Why is it that he, Caleb, has passed the boundary between the two, when the world just keeps on spinning?

Ah, but it's bled out, hasn't it? The darkly incredible has spilled out of its burial place. It was there in his garage.

He walks. He can't really go home, doesn't want to go to Gramps's house yet, and his feet take control. With nowhere else to go, they veer into the graveyard, and he won't stay long. A little look around for clues and, you know, maybe he'll see her. He wouldn't mind talking about what happened yesterday, about what upset her. What if she doesn't want to talk to him? Misha made it clear that she didn't want him to follow. Was that a permanent order? Should he apologise? Caleb's not even sure what he's done wrong. Should he...

Vic Sweet lunges out from behind the East Chapel. Caleb takes a heartbeat too long to run away. Vic gets a handful of a sleeve. Stitches pop as Caleb yanks his arm away. He's free but off-balance, stumbling. Now Blaine's coming at him from the West Chapel, coming fast, dropping a shoulder, and he slams into Caleb, hard, knocking him over. Caleb hits the tarmac, teeth clacking, biting through his lower lip. Skin peels from his left elbow. He thinks of that for no more than a second: a pain-blast thumps into his backside. Vic just toe-punted him.

'Woah-ho!' hoots Blaine. 'You nearly took his arse off!'

A second kick lands in the exact same spot, and Caleb cries out, cries loud. Vic stands over him, prods him with a foot until he looks up. 'Bet you're glad to see me.' He hawks up a glob of phlegm, spits it into Caleb's hair. 'I'm going to make a real mess of you. You know that, right? I'm going to use you like a football. Nobody will be able to recognise you when I'm gone. Blaine?'

The two older boys grab Caleb, lift him up and drag him towards the West Chapel.

Caleb screams for help, screams for it over and over. There's no one coming, no one in sight. Vic is squeezing his arm so hard he can feel bone creak. The more Caleb screams the louder Blaine laughs, and Caleb can't stop screaming because Vic meant every single word he said, and they're behind the chapel now, obscured from the road, and he tries to fight but they are bigger boys, stronger boys, and the back door's been prised open and they drag him

in

and throw him to the floor.

He tries to get right back up, but a kick across the knees sends him crashing into the front pew. Vic and Blaine come at him. 'Pin him,' orders Vic. 'Pin his arms down and don't let go. I don't care how much he screams.' Blaine doesn't look like he cares either. He holds Caleb's arms in a death grip, and Vic stands over him emotionless, and that's the real source of Caleb's terror, that broad, blank face. He doesn't care how much he hurts Caleb. He doesn't care how big a mess he makes, what trouble it could lead to, because this mess needs to be made, here beneath the stained glass windows, here where Mum once lay in a coffin as people cried and Father stared off into nothing.

Vic lifts his foot high, drives it down. A desperate squirm shifts the target. The stomp catches Caleb's knee a glancing blow, hard enough for him to howl, and to know that if it had caught him full on the kneecap it would have shattered. 'Damn it, Blaine! I told you to hold him still!'

'I can only hold his arms or his legs, what do you want?' Blaine slaps Caleb across the face. Stars scorch through his vision, his tongue and cheek burn with fire. 'You heard him. Stay still or I'll slap you some more.'

Before Caleb's head can clear, Vic's massive foot tramps down on his stomach, and all the air is gone and won't come back. This is light years worse than the pain in his face. He wants to throw up; nothing will move.

'I bet you think that hurts, don't you?' growls Vic. 'I bet you think that's the worst pain there's ever been. I'm going to give you a moment to think about something. What you're feeling right now? That's the easy bit. In five minutes you'll be wishing to be here again, feeling like this. In ten minutes you won't even remember who you are.'

Blaine gets right in Caleb's screwed-up face, laughs hard. 'You're gonna be a walking bruise! We are going to break you!'

Caleb needs to clutch his stomach, can't so much as wiggle his pinned arms. A punch in the gut. This time Caleb is sick. It blurts out of him in a brown foam, a splattery mess that clogs his nostrils, trickles into his eyes. 'Oh no, oh God, that was horrible! Hit him again,' demands Blaine, 'see what else comes out of him!'

'Please,' is all Caleb can spit up.

'Please!' hoots Blaine. 'Pleeeeeease! You heard this kid? He wants more!'

'He's getting it whether he wants it or not.'

Caleb can only see blurs through the vomit and spit in his eyes. The Vic-blur is pulling back its leg-blur to deliver another toe-punt.

A figure swishing in behind Vic, swinging a white bundle. It slams into Vic's upper arm, and the bundle is heavy, very heavy, sweeping the bully sideways, and he crashes into and over the top of the first row of seats.

Suddenly Caleb's arms are free.

'You little bitch,' grunts Blaine, swinging a punch. It connects with the off-balance swishing figure. She cries out.

She.

Caleb swipes at his eyes to clear them, starts sitting up. Blaine thrusts him back down, clambering over the boy to get at Misha. She's stumbling backwards, struggling with the bundle and its inertia. Caleb kicks out, catches Blaine's right ankle, tucking it behind the left. He trips, stopped only by the pillar he catches hold of. Misha's stepping forward, swinging the bundle at Blaine. He's already fallen under her arm. She misses his head by inches, hits the pillar hard enough to knock out chips, almost drops the bundle, and she's there beside him, her hand grasping his, and in that blink of a second Caleb feels no pain, just detached amazement and her warm hand.

Then the roar, 'You're dead!' The threat fills the chapel, resonates, as Vic rises up from between the seats, and Misha and Caleb run.

The pain returns. It doubles, and doubles again, and he can't run upright. Misha's dragging him too fast. He falls through the back door, and he's a bad shape for falling, and pitches face-first towards ground. His hands come up to take the impact. Stones cut into the meat of his palms, stones that could have had his lips, his nose, his eyes.

'Dead!' The word blasts out of the chapel like a bear-bark from cave depths. It drives Caleb up and moving and chasing Misha.

She's going the wrong way.

They should head for the graveyard gates, the road, people. Misha's turned the opposite way. 'Move!' she shouts at him from the base of the incline of Daisy Hill. Every last ounce of his breath is accounted for, none spare for his voice. Already he's going after her, already his choice is made, already they're leaving the exit behind.

Caleb has no hope of escape.

Blaine is fast, scary fast. He slows to let Vic catch up. 'Go! Just get them!' screams Vic, still struggling with his leg. Blaine accelerates, and Caleb can't look back any more, must focus everything on getting up this hill. Ignore the burning in his belly. Ignore the way his knee wants to twist and give out. Urge his lungs to inflate. Urge his heart to pump hard and strong. Blood and pain rush through his veins in overlapping waves. Gravestones whip past, fuzzy blurs, as Misha pulls away, like the blades of grass under her feet are flicking her forwards. That grass is against him. It feels treacherous, ready to slide under his trainers and pull him down.

And Blaine must be right behind him. Reaching. Grabbing.

Faster. The world gets blurrier, hazy. Up, up, up as Daisy Hill steepens.

He can't make the top. It's miles away.

Legs burn, stomach burns, lungs burn.

Misha shouting at him to move.

Rough breathing behind and closing.

He can't carry on.

Blaine spears him, shoulder driving into the base of Caleb's spine. The spike bends him into a mid-air dive, arms and legs thrown backwards, then he's driven into the ground, sliding to a halt, nose inches from a gravestone.

H. A. SOWERSBY
1910–1965
BEYOND THIS ENDING
WE WAIT FOR YOU

Caleb may never take another breath. It sounds like Blaine is struggling to catch his. The grey is spilling out of the headstone, pouring into the ground, blending with the heavy sky, and he's passing out, and let Vic have him, let Vic do what he wants. This great big monolith is tilting to the right and taking the whole world with it, and he feels damp grass against his cheek, and a daisy brushes his eyelashes.

A scream, incoming. Something swooshing. A bag swings through his line of sight. A sickly clunk. The weight is gone from his back. He's rolled over. Misha's face is everything. Her hair tickles his forehead. 'This is the last time I save you.' She's dragging him up; the world whirls round and rights itself. Vic is a few gravestone rows away.

Caleb finds more energy to run. He's sick in his mouth. Misha lashes her fingers into his; he's not getting left behind again. 'Blaine...'

'Might be dead, I hit him hard. Shut up!' She's right. A single word costs him too much in air. Vic's snorts of exertion: a wounded boar who will have blood for blood.

Upwards goes their mad chase. Is Misha leading the bully to another trap? Another ditch for him to snap his ankle in? At the peak, past Neuman's open grave, no traps, no ditches, just the down of the hill, down, down, down. His legs get carried away. He feels them windmilling like he's a cartoon character. Full speed is exhilarating. Every second it takes for Vic to reach the top of the hill puts them further ahead.

Giddy laughter. Misha's. Lilting in loops.

Swearing from Vic. He's fallen! Caleb prays to Whoever that the bully's busted his knee, that his running days are done. He and Misha go

Go

Go

Go

She drags him so fast he almost crashes through the fence at the back of the graveyard. He risks a backward glance. Vic is a considerable distance away. They can lose him pretty easily. All Caleb has to do is keep his feet.

Over the fence, and it's the hardest climb he's ever done. It seems as if each part of his body has turned against him. Limbs that ache and resist movement. Back muscles that don't want to flex and bend. Head that wants to lie down somewhere.

Boy and girl drop down on the other side in unison. 'Pretend to fall,' says Misha.

'What?'

'Just do it?'

'What are you…' She pushes him, and he doesn't need to pretend. She's knocked him on his backside.

'That'll do. Come on, let's go, he's getting close again.' Up once more, and bounding along a rough trail through long grass as Vic reaches the fence, hurling himself over.

Nettles bend themselves to sting, branches reach out to scratch, the path bucks like an undulating snake, writhing through fat tufts of wild grass. This is helter-skelter running. This is life with everything against them.

They're pulling away from Vic again.

Misha throws herself to the ground, makes a big play of getting up.

'What the hell did you do that for?' Caleb's voice splits and breaks.

'If we get too far ahead he'll give up.' She takes flight again, and Caleb's in the middle of two crazies; chasing one, chased by another.

No way off the path. Hemmed in by trees and tangles.

All this because he was too stupid to keep his eyes open.

They burst out of this encroached trail onto a broad path that swoops left and down, a high wall running alongside them, and Misha feigns another fall. A guttural noise escapes Caleb's throat, a frustrated growl. It's either that or kick her where she kneels.

He takes her elbow to get her up.

'No! Not yet! He'll lose us!'

Twig snaps and bush rustle signify Vic's stumbling arrival on the path. He's red and sweating through pain. He stops, clutching his knee, a rabid troubling dog. Staring, and staring.

'He's done,' Caleb whispers, backing away, drawing a reluctant Misha with him. 'What's wrong with you? He's given up, let's go.'

To Caleb's cold horror she points at Vic, and shouts so her voice tears at the air. 'You're a loser, Sweet! Look at you! We beat you!' The bully limps forward, each step taking a heavy toll on his leg. How he glares, how he wants the blood that's so far away. 'I hate you!' Misha rages, it vibrates from her in waves. He feels it in his lungs, and it scares him

'I hate you!'	because he burned this hot
'I wish you	a fire that melts eyeballs
were dead!'	into tears, and he screamed
'You should	this at Father because Mum
be dead!'	was dead and never coming
'I hate	back, and here he was,
hate	right here, still living, still
hate	there with the nerve to live,

to keep limping on, like Vic would rather his leg snap than give up. Caleb's managed to drag spitting Misha to the bottom of the slope, under the bridge where it's cold and damp, real cold like dawn frost, real damp with water-slick stonework. 'You deserve to die!' Her threats reverberate and redouble and surround him. 'You think you've got the right to touch me, to do whatever you want, and you're disgusting, you're scum, and I want to stick a knife in your throat and watch you bleed!'

Caleb's nerve-endings thrum.

Vic has halved the distance. He bursts into a final charge. Close, so close Caleb is sure he sees tears streaking from bloodshot eyes, before he and Misha flee. His burnt-out muscles make his legs difficult to shift, and it's uphill again, and this couldn't be harder if he was wearing iron boots.

Caleb knows this part of the gardens. The path branches. Left goes to the Butterfly House. Straight on is the Tea Rooms. To the right, lights. Getting brighter. Approaching.

'Come and get us!' screams Misha, and Caleb hisses at her to shut up but she's too busy shouting at Vic, too intent on winding the bully up.

She's so intent on who's behind her that she takes the right-hand turn.

'Not that way!' He reaches out to her, to steer her, but she's got past him, heading towards the beams.

She's still shouting at Vic to 'Come on! Come on you scum!' and Caleb realises that it's not chance and random choice that's led them here. It's Misha.

The steel-blue splash of the beams is surging through the trees up ahead.

Caleb's no longer running; he's stumbling, staggering, between two monsters.

Vic is gaining ground fast. Ten paces behind, nine, eight.

Low branches snapping as headlamps race forward, blazing in the gloom.

Vic seven, six, five paces behind. Pushing harder.

Howling-yelling Misha takes Caleb's hand. He sees Neuman pounding through trees painted bone-metal with her lights.

Vic four, three, two.

Misha pulls on Caleb's arm. Sharp left, they veer off the path, slipping on loose stones and dirt. Vic turns after them. Doesn't see Neuman burst out of woodland, launch herself across the path. Caleb sees.

Oh God he sees

Vic Sweet, eyes fierce, mouth sneering, sure of victory, doused in the light scorching from Neuman's sockets, an airborne demon, all crackle-skinned and stretch-limbed, and in its lights the world is a seared wasteland through which jut the long, scything talons of thirsting devils, and under the ground glow the angry and broken half-souls of writhing revenants, and the light strips away Vic's skin and flesh

and Neuman crashes into the boy, driving him to the ground. He doesn't get the chance to cry out.

He will die with the taste of dirt in his mouth.

Misha drags Caleb to the path. There are no final bursts of energy for running from this awful scene. He must listen to the fading struggles. He must hear Neuman pulling Vic out from the undergrowth. He must listen. He shouldn't feel any pity for the boy who wanted to kick him until he was dead. He shouldn't feel anything but bruises and exhausted muscles and scorched lungs.

Her hand grips hard. It doesn't seem to fit properly in his.

Each breath is fire in his throat. 'Oh God, what have we done?'

'He did it,' she snarls, all hackles and bloodlust. 'He did it all, and don't you forget it. It's his fault.' Now she begins to tremble? Now she's scared?

They cut through flowerbeds and trample a patch of cabbage, only using the path when it goes their way. They hear no birds, see no animals. They pass a football, an empty plastic bag, a trainer, scattered rubbish. Caleb wants to be thrown away too. It would suit his aching legs if he were cast aside, left to crumple and heap.

No lightbeams follow them. The day's dull is theirs alone as they press on towards Pernicious House. Off the path one last time. One more shortcut through the trees.

It'll never end. He'll always be here, chased and terrified.

A boy in the deeps of gloom. Caleb's first thought, *Blaine!* is dismissed. Too skinny. Too small. 'There's someone…'

'I just want out of here, okay? We're in trouble, I know, I get it. Just move, will you?'

They leave the boy behind. Onward, around trunk after trunk, and the boy is over to the left now, still and watching, but he must have ran to get over there so quickly, he must have sprinted.

It (why it? The boy is a he, a he) is hunch-shouldered, miserable in stance. Miserable? Caleb can't see anything but silhouette. He's over-tired. That's no boy. There's no one there. A collection of branches with tight clumps of leaves.

There, to the right, and further ahead. The boy. Can't be the same boy. There's more than one.

Caleb stops running so suddenly that he almost jerks Misha off her feet. 'What the hell?' she snaps. He points at one boy shape, then the next, then the next.

'We're surrounded. That's what the hell.'

She turns in circles, looking from one black silhouette to another. 'Who are they?'

'Was hoping you might have an idea.' An awful idea: 'What if it's Vic's back up?'

'No.' She's shaking her head a lot. 'No. They're nothing to do with him.' She fishes an eight-ball out of the pillowcase, holds it up to look into its window. 'Who are they?' A shake. Glowing letters swarm together.

DEAD ALL THREE

Caleb feels cold water in his veins. Misha grips the eight-ball so hard her fingers turn bone-white. 'How can that be? How are they here?'

ONE QUESTION ONCE

She's talking to it. And it's talking back. 'Damn it, Eight! How are they here?'

THESE ARE REMAINS

Caleb tears his eyes from the answer (answer! It answers!) to see the boys (they're boys, not its [why does he keep thinking it it it]) closer. Like they hovered five steps closer. None are standing up straight. Shoulders sag, heads loll, arms hang limp.

'Oh God,' breathes Misha. 'It was Neuman, wasn't it?' Shake, shake.

SHE DRAINED THEM

The ball shakes itself.

VERY LITTLE LEFT

Two of the boys speak.

'Home.'	'Home.'
'So far from Home.'	'So far.'
'Want to go Home.'	'Take us.'

Misha drops the eight-ball back into the pillowcase. Through the thin cotton Caleb can see a single luminescent word repeated: RUN RUN RUN.

Echoing whispers, the darkled voices of shadows:

'We've been here	'It's all dark here
for so long.'	they're all dark.'

Misha spins the pillowcase to form a thin rope. That single word whips round, RUN RUN RUN

Caleb's pretty certain he has no run left.

'Where is Home?'	'I'm lost, I'm lost.'
'Take us there.'	'So empty.'
'You, Caleb, you.'	'Hate you, hate.'

He might have a little left in the tank after all. He and Misha make a break for it, and cold hands reach for them. The ball swings, cracks a forearm. No cry of pain from Mickey. That's who it is, Caleb's friend from school. A boy he knows. Just a boy.

'Caleb, we need you, Caaaaay-leb.' He looks back to see Sam behind Mickey and Jay, another boy he knows, but they're not boys anymore. They won't be playing football and they won't be going to school and they'll never go home.

86

The town doesn't see the two kids tumble out of a hole in a fence, doesn't yet know about the missing. The graveyard's secrets are spilling out, but for the most part the town is unaware of the miseries coming its way.

They are coming, though, and they won't be stopped.

87

He couldn't climb it. He barely made it all this way to the fort, and clambering onto the roof is too much to expect of his legs. And his arms. And everything else. So they're inside the fort, sitting opposite each other, the eight ball in its case to one side.

Caleb thinks he may never move again. He'll stay here in the playground, in the thin rain, and let Neuman come, or the thing from the garage, or Father, or any horror at all, let them all come, and let them all take him because he can't fight and deserves only the justice of the dead. (*Father's not dead, why think that, he's not, he's not*), but he is. Dead and gone. Like Mickey and Sam and Jay.

He leans forward, elbows on knees, head low, looking at his pencil-slim fingers. Misha leans too, touches her forehead to his, and he watches as she laces her fingers with his. After monsters and ghosts, the touch of her seems hyper-real, more real than anything has ever been. The racing of his breath slows and deepens. Eyes closed, he tries to listen to whatever might be in her head. If only she could hear his thoughts too. Speaking is too difficult. His heart gets in the way.

Will she stay here with him, even when the monsters come? Will she be here at the end?

The pulse in her fingertips, it bumps against his own.

'There's no point in us telling anyone,' she says, and when she speaks Caleb can feel small vibrations in his skull. 'You know that, right? It's too late. It's a waste of time.' She squeezes his fingers, as if to reassure him that this terrible choice is okay.

'We've got to say something. Their parents should know.'

'What? That they've been taken by a creature we call a revenant? That they're haunting the trees of Pernicious House? That they'll do bad things to Mummy and Daddy if they ever get home? Nobody's going to believe a thing you say.'

He lifts his head, frowning. 'We tell them their kids are

missing. That's what we have to do.'

'And how do you tell them that? Because if you know where they are, they're not missing, are they? And they'll want to know how you know. They'll want to know a lot of things. I don't think you're ready for that, Caleb. I don't think you're anywhere near ready.'

Hot sparks in his chest. 'Of course I'm not ready! I've not been ready for any of this! What has that got to do with anything? When has being ready mattered? They're boys I know, I played football with them, I had a fight with Sam every other week, and I know them, I went to school with them, Mickey was in my class, he's a kid, he's just a normal kid. And he's got parents, and his parents probably love him, so don't you think they deserve to know? We have to tell them something.' Misha's not holding his hands now. She's leaning back, leaning away.

'They're not coming back,' she says, 'so what are you hoping to do? Where's telling the parents going to get you? Done is done. It's over for them. I knew them too, you know. I'd seen them around. Boys like any others.'

He barks at her. 'They were kids, Misha. People.'

'And what does the world care? Has it ended? Has the world come to a stop? It didn't when your mum died, and it didn't stop today. Three dead boys aren't going to change that. It's all going to keep on going, the way it always does.'

'How can you say that? How can you think like that?' He's shouting now.

And so is she. 'Don't you get it? It doesn't matter what I say or think! It doesn't change the way things are. I can't change it, and neither can you! Do you think those three were ever going to make much difference? Seriously. Did they ever have a chance of doing anything that might help fix this broken world? No, all they'd ever be is another broken part of it.'

Caleb's on his feet. He wants to be away from her; he needs Misha to hear him loud and clear, needs it, needs it, needs it. 'Of course it makes a difference! They'll be missed. There are families that won't have Mickey or Sam or Jay in them, and that affects the world, it affects someone's whole world, it's like tearing it up into tiny pieces and then giving someone a roll of tape and saying, "There, go and stick it all back together if you can".'

Misha's up as well, and her limbs are rigid with anger. 'You've got to open your eyes! You've got to be able to see past this crappy little town, past your own tiny little life. It'll all keep working without us, you know, without this town. The world's full of shit, Caleb. Look at Vic. Look at what he tried to do to me. You think I care that he's dead, that anyone cares? Is he such a big loss? Are we missing out on anything now that the scumbag is gone?'

'You knew what you were doing the whole time. You led him to Neuman. You killed him.'

'I'd stab him in the throat if I could!'

Every ounce of her means it. He can see it in the way she vibrates. This is something wearing Misha as a girl-suit. The graveyard girl herself is little but a memory now, a memory that maybe isn't real. 'People say things like that all the time, but they don't actually mean them, Misha, they don't! Look at what you did! You led him there to die! You basically killed him!'

And isn't she mad now! 'So I'm a killer, I'm a murderer, and that's fine by me. The things he wanted to do to me don't matter to you, do they? Caleb, the good little boy who's never done anything wrong, the good little boy who's been hard done-to by the world. He was going to kill you today. He was going to keep kicking you until you bled out of your eyes and ears, and then would have kicked you some more. Only I was stupid enough to save you, wasn't I? I come along and save your life and how dumb does that make me?' She's stalking now, walks three steps away from him before turning to stride right at him, like she's building up to charging him down. Stalk, stalk, stalk, stride, stride, stride. 'And I've got rid of him! I've got rid of Vic Sweet!

He's gone forever, and it's because of me! You couldn't stop him, nobody else could stop him, but I did. He can't bully anyone ever again, and it's because of me!' Her rage burns tears. 'He can't beat on you again because of me! He can't corner me again, can't grab me ever again, and the only person who stopped it is me. Tell me, Caleb, tell me how the world's going to suffer without him in it? Tell me how we're all so much worse off, why don't you? What does it matter that he's dead?'

'What does it matter if any of us dies then?'

'Exactly. Now you're getting it.'

He throws his hands up, pleading. 'What does that mean? You can't say things don't matter when they actually do.'

'Your mum died and kids still ran around in the playground screaming and laughing and playing tag. Your dad hates the fact that you exist and the neighbours keep wasting their time on what the pretend people do on TV. It's like that for everyone everywhere. We hate each other. All over the world, we hate each other. It doesn't matter how any of us goes because it makes no difference to anything.' She stalks back to the fort, picks up the eight-ball. 'So fuck the world, Caleb. Fuck it.'

She goes, and his guts sink. She is not his Evelyn.

88

Later, when he's curled up on Gramps's sofa and staring at the waste-of-time television, when he's seeing none of what's happening on the screen because there's too much spinning behind his eyes, Caleb wonders what he can do to stop the ache in his chest. He knows it's his thoughts that are hurting him, but they're like an infection he can't shake off. He pushes one away, two more come from behind it.

His head, resting on a coarse cushion, is nestled in the crook of his arm. He's sure he can smell her on his sleeve, that girl he first saw in the graveyard.

He wishes she'd stayed away, because he knows now that he can't.

89

It's back to being her tree again. A hollowed-out hidey-hole at a far end of the graveyard, away from all eyes and demands. Only Vic ever found her here, so determined to have her to himself. He's never coming back. He'll never follow her with his gang or corner her again. He is gone for good.

For good.

That sounds fine to her. Vic being gone really is good.

Yet she can't step back inside her tree. He'll forever be here, pushing his way in, grabbing for her. That face, those hands, his stink. It's a stink that's all over this place.

How can he be gone but still here?

Hanging in the pillowcase she's still holding, Eight answers. Eight answers all questions.

90

While she wanders around the outer edges of the graveyard, thinking about the boy, and thinking about ways to stop thinking about him, her grandfather is alone by a graveside, on his knees. He looks like a man mourning a loss so great it has punctured his heart and deflated him. A blue glow fades at his fingertips. Barely any sleep in four days, no recollection of when his last meal was, and he can't remember the sigils he must hold in his mind, and he can't concentrate on the notes he must hit, because he's empty.

Stephanie Parsons, 1964–1999 rests here, but she won't be restful much longer. She's next, in fact, and Granddad can't stop it alone.

There's movement down there. Faint knocking.

He would cry if he had the energy.

91

Nightmares wake him, and panic is electric in his chest as he finds his room is the wrong way round. The walls have shifted, his bed's been spun, his wardrobe's in the wrong corner. Father, the thing that's in Father's skin, it could come in here, could come in at any second and drag him from this wrong-room, and it will make him like Father, dead and not dead, trapped in a torturous in-between, and he'd never see Mum again, not on this side or the next and

Gramps. He's in Gramps's house. This is his room in Gramps's house. This is about as safe as things can get. No monsters in Father-skins, unless it has left the house and come hunting (and don't think of that), no Crosswells because Crosswell knows nothing of Gramps, no Vic Sweet because…well, because.

Although here in the first push of dawn, as deep blues take over from the dark, it occurs to Caleb that there is no reason to believe that Vic Sweet is gone for good. At least, not all of him. Neuman definitely isn't gone for good. Neuman is very definitely still around. She's killed four kids. Killed. Is that the right word? It tastes right, a metallic taste, a bone-white taste. Caleb saw Mickey amongst the trees, heard him, but that wasn't the boy from school.

THESE ARE REMAINS

Mickey's there in the trees. Father's in the house. So Vic Sweet, the remains of him, are still out there.

Is that better or worse than what they had?

ONE QUESTION ONCE

That ball. The one that told them to RUN RUN RUN. The one that knew. It answered Misha's questions. It could answer his. He has a lot, and no answers.

He hates that.

He sits up in his bed. It's way before early, and he's never been up at such a time in years, and he likes the feel of it, like it's too soon for anything to happen, bad or good. The day is stretching itself out, limbering up. There will be events later, happenings, occurrences. There will be awful things to face. For now it all waits. There are missing boys and an angry girl, and decisions, but for now it all waits.

Caleb wishes it could all wait forever.

92

'Are you sure about this? It's daylight. We don't normally do this in daylight.'

She fumbles a light-strand, looks at him like he just stood on her foot. 'You were listening to what I told you, right?'

'Uh-huh.' Crosswell scans the cul-de-sac. It's quarter past eight on a warm morning, and there's nobody out in the street. There should at least be someone heading out to work in their car, or some early-bird kid punting a ball about, or a dog getting walked, or, or, or. 'If anyone sees you making that, I'm walking away and leaving you to it. You know that, don't you?'

'No one ever accused you of chivalry, did they?'

'Accuse me of anything you like, just so long as you know I'm not stupid.'

Morgan hums a note that should be steady, stretches a fragile filament of light, and eases it into the map floating between her hands. It is a tatty neon representation of this cul-de-sac. It shudders like a construction with poor foundations. It wants to fall apart. 'Pack it in, you're putting me off.'

'Only looking,' he says, neglecting to tell her that someone seems to be 'only looking' from a bedroom window, third house on the left. Crosswell can't see them clearly through the blinds… but he can see them. He stares right back. Let them know he knows.

'Done,' says Morgan in faltering singsong. 'Look here.' She steps towards Crosswell with the map. It almost crumbles into sparks on her first step. She sings to it, an encouragement to hold its form. Her voice flutters like bird wings. Crosswell expects it to give up and splinter, but somehow it holds. 'See, in every single one of these houses. Just like I told you.' She sounds like a smart-alec ten-year-old when she says it, which makes the palm of his hand itch.

The two of them are golden pulses at the mouth of Puliver

Way. Something orange skitters across the road behind their position. Crosswell turns. A cat, streaking from one cover to the next. Back to the map. Each house is represented in minute detail, drawn by an almost-steady hand in brightest yellow. There's at least one blue pulse in each dwelling. No golds, only blues. It's a chilly, steely colour that flexes. Looking carefully enough shows the rhythmic pulse that runs through all the lines of the map. Crosswell looks around the three dimensional diagram, to the third house. A metallic-blue dot, on the first floor, at the window.

'Hmm,' he says, and narrows his eyes at Morgan. 'You sure you're doing this right? Because you remember what happened down in those tunnels…'

'I might not be the best at Constructs, but there's no way this is a mistake. Look at it. There we are. There all they are. This is what it is.'

He sighs. She has the right of it. 'There's ten houses here.'

'Yes.'

'Every single one occupied.'

'Yes.'

'Couples, and families.'

'Yes. And you know what? It doesn't look like any of them have moved. Since I called you I think they're all in the same position. It's as if they're waiting.'

'Chess pieces.'

'Huh?'

'Chess pieces stay still until the player is ready to move them.' He beckons Morgan to follow as he approaches the first house. The door is slightly ajar. 'This is because of him.'

'No, this is what happens when revenants are left to run around and do what they want.' She guides the map-construct between her hands, wary. He's not sure if she's worried about it crumbling down to its component atoms or if her trepidation is to do with those unmoving pulses.

'Morgan, all of this is what happens when we spend far too

long dancing to some crazy old man's tune. This is his idea of being in control.' He uses his foot to push open the door of number one. 'What have we got in here?'

'Back of the house.' She peers past him down the hall. 'Go in there, must be the lounge, then the far corner…' She tilts the map to check. 'Yeah, far corner, in front of patio doors.'

Crosswell's hands start to work, plucking violent atoms from the air. 'You coming in?'

'Any chance of giving this one a miss, boss-man?'

His eyes glitter, reflecting the mesh he's creating. 'Get in here. If it moves a single inch I want to know about it.'

She sighs. 'Isn't this a bit like poking a stick in a cave to see what bites?'

He's already in. 'Pretty much. Shush.' He leads the way, expecting her to speak up if anything starts coming for him. He moves slowly so as not to upset his weave. He'll never admit it to her, but he's nervous, and it's knocking his concentration. If he drops a single thread they'll be defenceless, and their only option will be to run. Crosswell does not like running. It's almost as bad as waiting.

The man, middle-aged and paunchy, is at the conservatory doors, rocking from one foot to the other. The sleeve of his shirt has been torn off, hanging like shorn snakeskin from a chubby wrist. Scratches have raked his upper arm.

'Excuse me,' says Crosswell, tearing a rope out from the bundle of woven light.

The man turns. There are thick scorch-marks around his eyes, charcoal remains of blazing fires. His lips bleed from chewing. There are bruises on either side of his head.

Crosswell snaps the rope like a whip. It snags hold of his throat. The Possessed bellows discordance, a chest-thumping note that pounds at the rope, shards of light splintering away. Crosswell retorts with a hard note of his own. Dust motes leap from every surface. The air shudders, the wooden floor thrums.

Holding the note, thickening it, Crosswell clicks his fingers at Morgan.

'Speak,' she tells it. 'Where is the source? Where is the one who made you?'

The Possessed increases its volume, and Crosswell's weave fractures. It will not hold.

'Speak! Now! Where is the Revenant?'

The noise cuts out. 'Not Revenant. He came. He's the one.'

'Who?'

'The Alpha. Here. Here!' It's angry that she doesn't understand already. 'Let go.' It has no eyeballs but it turns the sockets on Crosswell, and there are dark sparks in those cavities, pulsars light years away. 'Let go.' Morgan speaks, but in faint crackles of static. Crosswell's own voice comes out as distant white noise. The edges of his vision fizzle. He's passing out. His brain is vibrating. Behind its words the Possessed is making an ultra-high pitched sound. His lungs sink. The whole room seems to drop.

'LET

GO!'

The light rope shatters. Sparks spew out of holes in the Possessed's neck. It lunges for Crosswell even as its legs turn to jelly. Morgan gets to Crosswell first, pulling him away and out of the shuddering room, the house of screams. They bounce from wall to wall, scrabbling.

On the doorstep Crosswell wants to drop down, to sit, to sprawl. But she's insistent, won't leave him alone. He can hear clearly now

'Come on, come on, come on!'

Can see clearly now,

front doors are opening, blaze-eyed creatures are emerging,

and despite his weakened state can think clearly again, and he knows this is out and staying out.

93

How can I tell you how much it hurt? How can I get you to understand? Would I even want you to? No one deserves to feel like this.

Losing someone. Losing a love.

It's like a piece of meat taken from your chest.

It's like there's not enough oxygen in the air.

It's like your blood's so thin that your veins are collapsing.

And there's no respite from it. An end of a relationship is always hard, harder for one than the other when someone walks away. At least, though, there is a finish to it, nothing left hanging.

But my Evelyn…

I ache for those who met their love early and held them close through the years until some last sudden moment when they are gone. No more memories to be made. No more reaching out to touch that hand you know better than your own. No one to hold you when the world howls at the letterbox. Left alone and hollow. Tens of thousands of days together, and it ends, and those days are gone and can only get further away. Our wrinkled hands end empty.

I hurt for those who found their love, only to lose them after a few short years, after hopes shared and plans made. Do they think of all the times they said 'Let's just do that tomorrow'? Do they regret not staying awake a little longer each night? Do they look at the decades to come and wish that there were none at all? A heart made whole, now torn in two, one piece gone forever, the other just bleeding flesh.

I ache for those of us who were with another for moments, that look in their eyes of 'Here's someone I want to know, here's someone who I might allow to see my soul'. The air is rich and all lights are dazzling, and you know now that you won't be alone all of your life, and that someone wants to be with you. You'll get to know each other. You'll learn what you have in common, and the differences that keep you curious. They'll admire your laugh, you'll think of their smile as you go to sleep. But before you've had more than a touch or a kiss, they are gone. The future is dead. Your heart is still.

How can I tell you so that you'll understand? I never saw her alive again. I touched her hand, and before I could get to know her more she was gone. She didn't tell me she wasn't interested. I know she was. She didn't say she didn't like me. I know she did. She never said she couldn't love me. I know she could have.

Oh, how I wanted her.

But Evelyn's father killed her, and buried her, and she came back. God help me, she came back.

94

Caleb throws the journal down. There are no answers in there, no guidance. Or perhaps these really are the answers, and he doesn't like them one little bit. In fact he hates them.

He doesn't want to read any more.

He wants to finish it all now.

He hates it. He hates the journal. He hates Gramps for having it. He hates that reading it is the only thing he can think of to do.

What he hates most is how he's just lied to himself. He can think of other things to do. He just doesn't want to do them. He's too scared. Every single time he's gone out there everything has gone wrong.

And that's not all of it, is it? There's something worse. The things he's done, every action, every last one, has been pointless. Taking measurements. Talking to that girl. Watching people. Being chased. Arguing. Reading this journal. All of it has achieved nothing. He doesn't know what's happening. He doesn't know why. He doesn't know how to stop it. He doesn't know if it *can* be stopped. He doesn't know how to change anything.

He doesn't know one single thing.

And he hates that.

And he hates this stupid room that isn't his. Can't stand being within these walls. Wants to scream until they crack and split and the window blows out. He jumps off the bed and strides out.

He comes back for the journal.

There's busy noise coming from the kitchen. Gramps is on hands and knees, rooting through the bottom food cupboard. He's pulled out dozens of jars and tins and packets, stuff that's probably been in there for years and dropped far out of date. The way he mutters sounds to Caleb like the old man's annoyed by someone at the back of the cupboard. 'I need to ask you something, Gramps.' He tries to say it softly, but there's still the thump of a surprised head. The old man pushes himself out with a collection of creaks.

'Ah, Caleb, you haven't had it, have you?'

'Had what, Gramps?' he asks, already sinking.

'The tomato soup.'

Caleb looks around the stacks and collections on the lino. 'There's a tin there. And two there.'

'No, it's not that one or those.' Gramps sticks his head back in the cupboard. 'It must be here somewhere, I saw it the other day.'

'Aren't they all the same?'

'Not at all! Where is it, your grandmother would know...'

'Can't you just have one of the other ones this time?'

With difficulty Gramps retreats once again, has to use the worktop and Caleb to stand. It looks so painful that it make Caleb angrier. What use is this frail old thing? 'Maybe someone put it in this cupboard instead.' He pushes things from one side to the other, one side to the other.

'Gramps, forget about the stupid bloody tomato soup will you? You've got loads of tins here, loads! It all tastes the same! I need you to answer something.'

The cupboards are closed, and Gramps turns. 'What if I don't want to answer?'

'What?'

'You heard what I said. It's about the journal, isn't it?' His eyes have hardened to granite. 'There's a reason why I gave it to you. There's a reason why I wanted you to read it. If I wanted to tell... If I could have told you it myself, I would have. So before you start snapping at me again, you little pup, ask yourself why I might have shut the covers on these books and locked them in a case and stowed them in the corner of the attic.'

At last, Caleb asks the first of the questions he's wanted to all along. 'Why did you bring it out then? Why didn't you just leave it?'

'How could I? You weren't going to leave it, were you? Back

and forth to that bloody graveyard day in, day out, and didn't matter what anybody said to stop you.'

'I wanted to see my mum, that's my right...'

'What is there to see? A gravestone? How many things are there to say to someone who never answers back?' Thoughts of his father hunched over a laptop flash through Caleb's mind, and with them come spears of guilt. 'Weren't you told it was unhealthy? Weren't you told to leave the graveyard behind and try to live?'

Hot tears come. 'Why are you being so horrible?' He could take this venom from Father (dear dead Father, dead, dead, dead), but Gramps?

'We gave you every chance, Caleb, every urging to stay away before you saw something. And that's all it took, wasn't it? One curiosity, one off-kilter presence to catch the curiosity of the child.'

He screams now. 'And giving me this stupid journal was meant to stop me?'

Caleb has never seen Gramps this fierce. 'No, because there is no stopping! There is no going back, ever!' He sinks back against the oven, fury faded. 'You stupid, stupid children, why can't we ever teach you? Why aren't our words enough?'

'You said, "We gave you every chance". We. So Dad knew as well. He knew whatever it is you know.'

'Not all of it, but he put together enough.'

Here, then, was the second of the questions that have burned in Caleb every minute of the day. 'Dad is dead, isn't he? Something got in the house and killed him and now he isn't Dad anymore.' The words clunk hollow through the clay shell he's become.

Now the old man reaches out to him. Now Gramps is the figure he's always seemed, caring, gentle. Caleb steps away, kicking over tin stacks. He waves the journal. He's gripping it so hard that his fingernails bite into the cover. 'Why did you give me this?'

'Because there are things that can't be said aloud. Because words can be heard and diagrams have weight and the air is tangible...'

'Gramps, you're rambling, please focus...'

'I'm trying to explain to you! There are traps, Caleb! They can be anywhere, they can be woven from the air itself, and traps have triggers... Oh God!' He kicks out with a slippered foot, connects with a can of corned beef, thumps a dent in the cupboard under the sink. 'If I talk more, I forget more. That is my trap. I'll forget everything. Everyone. It's like needle picking at the stitches holding my mind together. The memories will go. The feelings will fade away. I'll come apart.'

It's cold in this room, like it's never known heat. Gramps has had problems for years – forgetfulness, confusion, obsessive behaviours, sudden mood swings – problems that Dad (dear dead Dad) said were getting worse, and Caleb's suddenly wondering where they started and how. 'So you couldn't...'

'Of course I couldn't. If I ever found someone I wanted to tell about all of that up there, of Evelyn and everything that's come after, how could I expect them to believe me? And I'd find it harder and harder to remember what I wanted to say, and I would become this tiny minded simpleton, and that would be the end of that.' He takes the journal from Caleb, runs a crumpled hand over it as if to smooth out the dents. 'At least some of my memories are in here. When my mind finally fails, this will be here. A piece of me, a piece of her. You know what's ironic? I can't even read this to fill in the blanks, because it just makes those blanks bigger. A grand trick indeed.'

'There must have been someone you could tell...'

'The police?' His bitter smile is no joke. 'Some government authority? The neighbours? It needs someone to see first to believe.'

'So tell me. I've seen, I believe. Now's the time, Gramps.'

He looks like a man the years have run away from. 'The more

I say, the less there will be of me.'

And now Caleb sees how scared his grandfather is, and understands what he's asking of this frightened soul, truly understands. He cries, and goes to the man, and hugs him like he may never get to again. He can't ask Gramps. There's only one option left. He needs that eight-ball.

95

The phone rings. Granddad answers, sweating. The walls around his heart are cramping.

'I've been warning you for long enough, and now it's finally happened.' Crosswell, at new levels of smugness. Granddad feels his stress step up a gear.

'I haven't got the time for your hectoring. I'm a busy man…'

'You're about to get a hell of a lot busier. You've been trying to contain things that won't be contained. Now they're out. Neuman's gone and done it. Whatever's in her has struck. It's a full street. Maybe two we're still looking into that.'

'No.'

'Like all your words, old man, "no" is useless, "no" can't change the facts. It's official, friend. You've lost control.'

The band around his chest tightens as he listens to Crosswell tells him where it happened, the number of houses, the number of families, the number of souls. 'It's not time, it's not…'

'Shut up. We need the books. You've messed around long enough. Hand them over, let us deal with this.'

'You can't have them.' Where's all the air gone? 'They're not for you.' He wants to tell Crosswell that he'll feed the books to fire before he'd ever let him near.

'Listen to how tired you are. What is it you think you can do? This isn't reversible, you know that. You're already struggling in the graveyard. And you can't keep that brat under control, and I haven't seen you out here helping with the search for Neuman.'

'If you had helped me…'

'What? Helped you do something I don't believe is right? You've been waiting for something that isn't going to happen, and now we're in a very dangerous position, and it's all your fault! I'm coming over. Get the books ready.'

These next words he means with every fibre. 'If you come, I will fight you.'

Hesitation at the other end of the line. It gives him a dark thrill to sense Crosswell's uncertainty. 'You're tired. I could bring you down and you know it.'

'I've always been ready for you.'

'I think it's time we find out.' The line goes dead. For the first time in days, Granddad sits in his recliner and thinks of nothing.

96

Her forehead blooms with sweat beads, her hand tremors make it difficult to weave, light-strands formed then fumbled. She is hunch-shouldered and sore. There's a needle-puncture throb in her finger-endings. 'This'll fall to pieces,' she tells Crosswell. 'This is beyond me. It's beyond him too.'

'I need it done, and I need it done fast, Morgan!'

'We can't do the full net! If you don't help it will collapse. Look at it!'

He looks at it, then her. There are days when he could happily punch Morgan in the face, and this is one of them.

97

He presses himself against the wall. He's nowhere near flat enough. She's bound to see him, and then she'll clobber him with the very object he's come for. Misha will smash his head in, and maybe she'll regret it and maybe she won't, but in this instant he feels very clearly that he shouldn't be here. Caleb hasn't thought this through at all. As he strode into the graveyard he'd envisioned himself demanding that she hand the ball over, that she owed it to him, that he's not going to take any argument. As he got closer, and he could see her house, it changed to a chat, a request, a favour needed. As he spotted her coming, he threw himself round the side of the house, heart tangled in his lungs, praying she wouldn't see him lurking.

And now!

He desperately wishes he hadn't hid! All Misha has to do is peer around the corner, and what will he say? What could he possibly say? After the way she raged last night, would she give him a chance to explain? But does he want to explain? He's angry with her. He's sad. Confused. He's...

safe. The front door opened, and shut again quickly. She's inside. He sags. It takes a surprising amount of effort to try to become a wall.

'What am I doing?'

He came up here to confront her, and all he's ended up doing is hiding. So much for his brave stomp up the hill, his conviction that he would take charge of the situation and get to the bottom of everything. Yet again, all hot air and empty promises. Cowering is about all he is capable of.

He hates himself for that.

He slides his back down the wall, sitting with a bump on hard ground. Perhaps he should leave and not wait to be discovered, but he can think of nowhere to go.

Angry muffles of shouting inside. The words come and go

as the argument moves around the house. He doesn't need the specifics: it's an age-old theme, the clash of generations. Where have you been, it's none of your business, it is my business when you live under this roof, why are you always on my case, and on it goes. He wonders if Misha looks the way she did at the playground. Seething eyes, pointed shoulders, throat pulsing.

He has to see her again. Now that he's here, he needs one look.

Caleb eases himself back up the wall. There's a window at his side. He slides closer, and he braces himself to peer in, and his mouth clogs up. Caleb pins himself to the bricks instead. Can't look. Can't move.

Can't stay here all day.

Why does he have to see her? Why does his breathing feel strange?

One look.

He leans out slowly, so he can see through the window a tiny slither at first, then gradually more, ready to jump back at the slightest hint he'll be spotted. Clearly he hears her granddad: 'Your childish behaviour will get you killed! You know what's out there!'

Misha, snappy: 'Surprise, I *am* a child! Can you believe it?'

'Here we are again with the attitude. And where did you get that from? Certainly not your mother.'

'Stop comparing me to her!'

Caleb's looking down the hallway now, as the inhabitants move out of sight – a brief glimpse of Misha with Granddad following. Caleb feels the pull of her, darts around the house, matters of bravery forgotten. Next he comes to a bedroom of dowdy browns and woollen blankets and a fade-old armchair and mish-mash stacks of cracked books threatening shelves. The door is shut. Caleb moves rapidly past to the next. This window is partially open.

The room is hers.

Purples and lilacs in here, softer than he would have expected. Unframed paintings on the wall of suns dipping behind graveyards, gatherings of well-ordered graphic novels, a collage pasted on the wardrobe of magazine cuttings and chopped-up postcards, figurines of kung-fu girls, and on her bed the eight-ball. The bed is beside the window. The partially open window. The gap is small. His arm is slim.

A message flashes up on the ball.

NOT FOR YOU

Caleb has never felt such a strong invitation.

Misha's bedroom door is also shut. The argument is very near.

Against his expectation, bravery burns cold in the cavity of his chest.

Caleb reaches in.

DON'T DO IT

A message in hot lava glow. It pulses, growing bigger, surging.

His arm won't go in past the elbow. Caleb pulls at the window. It's held in place on a latch. His fingers dance towards it, so close.

KEEP OFF ME

Each word bursts forward to fill the screen. Caleb flinches, sure his skin will burn if he touches the ball.

Her voice: so close! Outside the bedroom door. 'It's the same arguments every day! I don't want to know! I don't even want to be here, so why would I want to know?'

The door handle turns.

An old voice cracking, but still strong. 'You don't walk away from me again! You need to grow up and stop acting like a brat!'

The handle springs back, suddenly let go. 'I'm a brat? You're the one almost stamping your feet!'

Keep arguing, urges Caleb as he stretches for the ball, trying to push his arm in that little bit further. A ragged spelk of wood catches inside of his thin bicep, pushes into the meat. The pain is hot and precise. He wants to scream loud, hammers his knee against the bricks so he can feel something else, anything else. Agony hisses out of him on an endless keening breath.

Finger-ends brush over the surface of the eight-ball. It's warm then cold, warm then cold, a heartbeat pushing then retracting blood.

'Please,' says the cracking old man at the precise moment that Caleb begs the ball to come to him, 'please, Misha, I need your help, now more than ever, help me this one time...'

Her shout is also a plea. 'Leave me alone! I don't want anything to do with it!'

The handle turns, quick.

Caleb lunges.

Gets his hand around the ball; the splinter punches in.

BLEED BLEED BLEED

The door swings open.

Misha pauses in the doorway. 'And don't come knocking! I won't answer.'

Caleb pulls his arm out of the window. The splinter slides out slickly, popping out of his skin. The ball clangs against the window frame, as it won't quite fit through.

'I've had enough of you!' screams Misha. 'I wish I was dead like Mother!'

Stupid in panic, Caleb pulls again. It didn't fit last time; it won't fit through this time.

Except it does.

The thin frame bulges millimetres. It's enough. Out comes the eight-ball.

Misha's in the room and slamming the door.

Caleb drops to the ground, fast enough to catch his own heart in his throat.

Deadly silence. It's like the door-slam cut out all noise. The pain in his arm is so bright he wants to cry out, needs to let the pressure go, but he's already convinced he's bleeding too loud.

She'll hear.

She'll notice her precious ball is gone. She'll come to the window. And lean out. And see him cowering.

A silken blood-thread trickles up goose bumps to the crook of his elbow. The puncture wound gets hotter.

She's in there, above him, growling and caged, throwing things around. The rest of his skin prickles at the pulse of her fury. Something hard shudders the window – the force of her uncontrollable rage. The glass has to be cracked. One more blow and he'll be sprayed with cutting shards.

The eight-ball is flashing messages.

HORRID LITTLE THIEF

When Misha realises this ball is gone, she will go off like an atom bomb.

BURN IN HELL

The message swims as if melting in flames.

Bed springs bounce. Sobbing. She's thrown herself down, energy spent. The pillow does a poor job of quieting her tears. Misha's short hard sobs pull at him, hook into him deep. It's there, the want to do something stupid.

GO ON IDIOT

He wants to stand up, say something quiet and soothing.

TALK TO HER

He wants to be the one to stop her crying, make it all okay. He wants to be stupid enough to save her.

OPEN YOUR MOUTH

But what can good-boy Caleb say to murderer Misha?

SHE HATES YOU

It aches where words should be.

DAD DOES TOO

He crawls to the corner of the house, then runs. But it all keeps up with him.

98

Nights linger when pieces are missing from you. Sleep was of no use to me. It offered no respite, no relief. I would keep myself awake with despair and regret, and when exhaustion finally smothered me Evelyn would be at the edge of my dreams. Such awful, tiring dreams. Mazes, of course, narrowing tunnels, with hot breath on my neck. She'd be round the next corner, or the next, and I couldn't run fast enough to catch her. I'd snap awake, sweating as if I'd really ran for hours through snarling labyrinths, more tired than before I'd slept, dead awake in a pre-dawn world. The sense of her nearness would linger longer than the twisting horrors of those maze-dreams. I sometimes thought that if I could just turn around quick enough, I might catch sight of her, whole, real, and alive. It was a hope that fluttered in my heart.

It was a hope I'd come to regret.

Four nights later – or perhaps it was five, time becomes slippery with so little sleep – I was back up at that graveyard. I'd been there every day. I'd wander around for an hour, hoping for...I don't know what. Looking for some kind of evidence to show to others, perhaps, something irrefutable. Another entrance to those tunnels. Some kind of answer as to what had happened and why. All I found was line after line of gravestones – and the silhouette of Evelyn's father staring out at me from that damned house.

Dusk was fading into full night as I retreated towards home, but there was a figure blocking the way through the gate. It wasn't so dark that I couldn't recognise Evelyn. He'd buried her in the same dress she was wearing on that night I lost her. She smelled of soil, but even then I would've gone to her, would have reached out to touch her pale hand, if she hadn't spoken. 'He wants you.' The words crunched in her dry throat like grit under foot. 'I have to take you to him.' She didn't come at me straight away, waiting for me to surrender or flee. My Evelyn, a predator, a dead and hungry thing.

I have no idea how I managed to find my voice. My throat was taut with ropes of tension. 'I'm not coming, Evelyn. Your father's an evil man. The things he does are wrong.'

Did she smile here? I think so. 'My father made me. Does that make me wrong? You didn't think I was wrong that day you kissed me.' There were sheets of ice under my skin. I was talking to a ghost who sounded like her voice was still in the grave. Darkness was swelling around me. 'Evelyn, I have to leave, I have things to do, I have...'

'...a life to live?' The accusation was clear. Her fingers flexed. I heard brittle, thin bones crack. She stepped forward. Her dress whispered. I thought of cold bodies lying down in velvet lining. 'You've thought of me every night, all night long. Your dreams pulled at me. You brought me here, to this.' It was a lie! Her father had summoned her with whatever black arts worked in his soul, but a large part of me believed her all the same. This was my Evelyn. How could she ever lie to me? 'So come with me. It's better if you do. I promise you I will kiss you again.' Another step, stiff and stuttering, as if her legs struggled to remember how they should work.

I moved towards her, opening my arms for a cold embrace, and my pulse was up in the roof of my mouth. Her face...sunken at the sockets, drawn in at the cheeks, lips thin and retreating, a glimmer far back in her deflating eyeballs, a dull shudder of tarnished golden starlight. She leant towards me, and panic-tension warned me she was coming for my mouth.

I dropped my arms, dodged around hers, and ran. She was far quicker than I'd expected. Evelyn snatched at my throat; her splintered fingernails tore along the side of my neck, opening three deep scratches. I didn't stop running. I held a hand to the wound. She screamed after me, the predator denied. She screamed for me to come back or she would hunt me down and drag me to the grave.

I ran without thinking.

I ran home.

By the time I got back to my bathroom, the trio of scratches were burning like they were infected. I cleaned them as much as I could be bothered, then shut myself away in my bedroom so I could not be seen. My neck seemed to swell up, it itched from within, but I didn't care what it might mean. I couldn't care much for anything again. All I'd had left of Evelyn were a few wonderful memories, but they were all poisoned by that encounter with her dead soul. In all my recollections she would no longer be the beautiful girl with the easy smile. She would have those sunken sockets with those tarnished metal pinpricks staring out at me, talons grasping for my throat.

And I spent hour after hour that night going through every one of my memories of her, trying to remember the girl who was so full of life, not the one so full of hate for me. I couldn't. She'd been taken from me again.

When I went to close the curtains Evelyn was there on the other side of the glass. She placed the tips of her skin-tearing nails on the windowpane, dragged them up and down with a keening squeal. 'Daddy wants you,' she whispered, and the window did not silence her voice; I heard it in the very centre of my head. 'Daddy doesn't want to let you go.' She drew back a dead hand to smash her way in.

'Wait!' I cried. I didn't want that thing in my home. I didn't want it to wake my parents. I didn't want them to come in and see it killing me. 'I'll come. Just wait.'

'Come out the window.' That way she could get her hands on me immediately. Cold, dank skin.

'Just wait.' I backed away from the window and out of the room, and tried not to be terrified and failed. I left the house as quietly as I could, and Evelyn was striding rapidly around the corner on legs that knew exactly how to work. I walked fast. I kept a strong lead, heading for the graveyard.

'Let me hold your hand,' she cracked. 'Let me touch you.' I sped up as we reached the graveyard gates. 'Give me your hand. Or I take more of your blood.'

I didn't answer. Instead of going back through those gates I turned right, away from the graveyard, away from my home, away from my parents. I sped up. So did she, the hard slap of her feet catching up on me. Not a sound from her broken throat. No threats, no commands, no screams, no roars. I ran, and she ran too. Dead Evelyn, closing in on me and the blood in my veins.

I ran until I was nothing but hurt, until I was dizzy with exhaustion, until I had to stop and let her have me. She was no longer there. I was on the outskirts of town, and Evelyn was nowhere to be seen. I looked round, and round, in case it was a trick. Not that it mattered. I was utterly drained. I wouldn't be able to fight her off. I sat on a nearby bench, and I wept. The only girl I'd ever loved, and she'd been turned into a monster because of me. All I could think about was the way she hated me, the way she wanted nothing other than to kill me. It was impossible to bear.

I decided that next time I'd let her.

Eventually the remains of me dragged itself home. Evelyn had been there before me. She'd torn my parents apart. They were spread out across their bedroom, skin and blood.

It's blank for a while after that. How long for, I don't know. What I did in that time I'll never recall. When my mind fully woke up, I was on the run with a bag over my shoulder and wearing a change of clothes and with no idea where I might go, knowing only that I could never go home.

Turned out I was wrong about that too.

The wounds carved along the side of my neck blazed, but they were the very least of my cares. Let them rot. My parents were gone, murdered. My home was a slaughterhouse. My Evelyn was a demon back from the dead. The whole of my life was in torn bloody ribbons.

I kept walking. Through the night, through the day. I left town. Walked right through the next. Eventually I came to my great aunt's door. She lived in a village miles and miles from home. I didn't think I'd be able to stay long before I was hunted down for the murder of my own parents, but I was tired and hungry and near the end of my wits. I held myself together just long enough for Edith to welcome me with joy, ushering me to a comfortable chair and filling me with tea and cakes.

She threw a hundred questions at me, all about family matters. I *answered as if my parents had not been ripped to pieces.*

Inevitably she saw the wounds along my neck. I blamed it on some horrible beast attacking me on my journey. No lie there. Great Aunt Edith insisted I visit a doctor. I was even more insistent that there was no need. I won, but she still managed to sit me down and tend to the injury herself, cleaning and dressing it.

Edith was a good woman.

During the week I stayed with her, the throb in those deep scratches refused to leave. At times it grew stronger, so much so that no cream or cold compress could cool the heat. It brought on tremendous headaches, which gave me a good excuse to hide away in bed when my emotional traumas devoured me and became too much to bear. Every minute was misery. Poor old Edith tried her very best to make me comfortable, and she knew there was more wrong than I was telling.

The nights out there weren't merely dark, they were utterly black. Once the lamps were snuffed out nothing at all could be seen. Lying in bed with my eyes open, my sight would strain to find something, some tiny glimmer to latch on to, anything to confirm that the world still existed around me. I would stumble across the room, open the curtains and stare out into an endless void. Fields and hills and trees: I knew these things were out there, they were simply indivisible from one another. Evelyn was out there too. She could have been on the opposite side of the glass, right there in front of me, and I'd have known nothing about it. Inches from my face, Evelyn raising her fingernails, those jagged coffin-tearing splinters, reaching for me as my neck burned.

I told myself lies. I told myself Evelyn knew nothing of my family, of where they lived. I told myself she couldn't find me here. After all the damage done to me, after the destruction of my life, I would be left to my suffering. This last assertion made the most sense to me. I wasn't standing in a bedroom: I was suspended in death's void. I was inside the charcoal remnants of my own heart.

Morning eventually came. Exhausted after yet another restless night, I dragged myself to the kitchen. It was the first part of the day's pattern, pretending for Edith's benefit that I didn't want to lie in bed all day and torture myself with thoughts of those who'd died. She smiled at me, and for a moment I hated her for that smile. I'll never forget feeling that way. It was the smile of someone who's never seen a family member reduced to a bloody canvas. I wanted to tell her then, and wipe away that smile for good.

I heard the back door open. I turned, and there in morning daylight was Evelyn, and she hit me hard, lifting me off my feet. I banged my head on the pantry door and my vision span so I couldn't tell which way was up.

Evelyn dragged Edith away screaming.

I fought the oncoming rush of nausea. Edith's terrible gurgling screams tore through the house. I tried desperately to get up, to shake off the pains in my head, the scorching heat in my neck. I had to save Edith, save myself.

But I was too late for my great aunt.

Her awful, nightmare-haunting shrieks came to a sudden crunching end before I could leave the kitchen. There was silence. Then wet tearing. Then Evelyn: 'You made me do this! You think you love me, but you ran away! You left me.' Her footsteps approached down the hall. 'You might not love me, but I still want you. I'll take you back. When you're dead like me I'll show you what true love is. I'll show you.'

I fled. I ran from the house, left everything behind, left another member of my family slaughtered. Evelyn came after me. Took the door off the hinges as I sprinted across the road. The nearest house was two hundred yards to the left or right of me. I went in the only direction I could – straight on, into the trees, into the dark. Enough people were dead because of me. If I went knocking on doors for help innocent people would die. There was nothing anyone could do against the maelstrom tearing after me, a malevolent corpse ripping up fence-posts and hurling them at my head.

'You're mine!' she shrieked. 'You promised!' Her voice was thunder-bright in the midnight forest, setting off fear-flashes in my ribcage. There was no light to see by, but I knew that the deathly glimmer in her eyes allowed her to see me clearly. My wounds seared hotter than ever, churning the bile in my stomach as I bounced from tree to tree, and her voice seemed to be at the very base of my skull, and my skin tried to pull away from the teeth that I imagined were about to bite. 'You will always be mine!'

Arms out in front of me, I ran faster. Faster into thick darkness.

A low hanging branch caught my left hand, bending it right back. Two fingers snapped. The pain was like a pair of popping fireworks in my flesh. It slowed me down, and my limbs jellified under the duress of shock and pain and panic, and I could hear Evelyn crashing towards me ever faster, and then it was all I could hear, my own wailing and heavy breathing utterly smothered as she smashed the forest to pieces in her frenzy. The explosive splintering of tree trunks, the chunks of earth heaved from the ground, huge shadows rushing past me or glancing off my shoulders. She was pulling the planet apart to get at me.

Then the ground turned mushy underfoot, and I stumbled, and I fell into shallow water, gulped down a large choking mouthful of fetid liquid. I was out of the forest, and sprawled in marshland.

On hand and knees I vomited up a gutful of foul water, and pedalled my feet as hard as I could to get myself moving. Soaked, freezing. I stumbled onwards, knowing that Evelyn was still on my trail. That night stretched itself long. Splashing on through the marshes, water dragging heavy at my trousers, I was hounded by the noises that followed me. Sudden loud splashes nearby. Screams of rage that ripped my nerves to shreds. Bubbling laughter that gave way to flat silence. I begged her to stop, to turn around and go back to her grave. I shouted at her that none of it was my fault and she could go back to Hell. I pleaded for forgiveness. I told her all of my deepest hurts. I whispered to myself that it would all be over soon. Hysteria, terror, exhaustion, I had run to the very limits of my sanity. The dark was full of arms, all attached to the corpses of dead girls. All I could smell was the dank dirt at the bottom of graves. My blood felt thick and lumpy and cold.

At some point I collapsed. On the outer edge of consciousness I *waited for Evelyn to catch up with me, and pull me apart there on the marsh, alone and a million miles from anyone.*

My body was in a constant shivering state as a tangerine dawn bled over the horizon. I watched it through twitching eyes, sure I would never see another. I was unconscious long before the sun rose fully. I could have been out for hours or days.

When I awoke I was on a hard bed and knew immediately that I was terribly ill. Sweating, cold to my bones, shaking. I still had my marsh-damp clothes on under the covers. A thin old man, cross-armed, stared at me from the doorway. 'What were you doin' out there?' he asked, his voice flat. I couldn't answer. 'You have a think. Next time I come in here, you give me an answer before I get the police.'

I heard the door lock.

Part of me was screaming at the injustice of being saved from one bad situation only to wake up in another. That was a very small part, though. The rest of me was very far from caring. No piece of my body and soul was spared from agony and anguish. All of my desperate running was merely delaying the inevitable end. Evelyn would kill me: I would be in her service forever, the walking, talking dead. Every day until the end of time I would see my murdered parents and hear Edith's final screams. Every day there would ever be. Why keep fighting? One way or another it was all over. Let this strange man do whatever he wanted. Let the police come, if that was actually his intention. I was finished.

I couldn't close my eyes without seeing blood.

I could hear Evelyn in every creak of the house.

I couldn't take my thoughts from the helter-skelter chase through the forest.

I drifted through endless nightmares.

A loud bang, the kind you feel in your ribs. The strange old man shouting broad obscenities. Her voice, stronger than his by far: 'Where is he?' Then smashing, and screaming. His screaming. Whatever he had in mind for me was obliterated in an instant.

Despite my desperate desire for my misery to end, despite the certainty that I was only delaying the inevitable, I did not want that creature to get me.

Even at our last, we fight for more.

I slid out of the bed, hot and stinking. My legs buckled, I sank to my knees.

Outside the bedroom, those screams shifted pitch, higher, agonised. The grim stranger was dying. I'd already seen that doors were flimsy protection from Evelyn. Within moments I'd be next.

That thought gave my legs strength. My arms too. I picked up a stool from the corner, smashed the window with it, climbed out into the night, cutting my hands and forearms.

Wood shattered behind me.

I ran.

Such was my life for more than two years. I couldn't stay in one place for long. Evelyn was forever behind me.

I had two modes of survival. Whilst on the move I became quite an adept thief (although until then I grew incredibly weak and skinny). I developed a keen eye for spotting opportunities for a steal and a getaway. There were plenty of close calls, angry chases and the occasional shotgun to avoid. Every once in a while, however, I had to pause, had to take a breath. When the pulse in my neck lessened to a barely-there background noise, I would stop in some town or other, doing odd-jobs – any jobs – in return for money or a night's lodgings or food. It wouldn't be long before the throb would tell me she was catching up again. Or the police would get word about some thieving in the area, and I would have little choice but to move on. I didn't stay any longer than I thought necessary. I had enough deaths to my name.

I spent all those months believing that I'd stuck to this vow, that I'd fulfilled it. Now I know very different. I know of the trail of destruction I left in my wake. She thought nothing of tearing down doors and flesh. She showed no moment of hesitation in chasing me down. She pushed the price of my life higher and higher. Would I have come back sooner if I'd known? Would I have returned to face my demon sooner?

Many nights I have told myself that, for the sake of so many lives, I should have handed myself over to Evelyn. But even at our last, we fight for more, don't we? Whatever the cost.

I came home. I got as big a lead on her as I could, and I came home. I returned to the graveyard. This time I was armed.

99

The ache in her arms is dull and thick. They won't stop trembling. Her hands aren't nimble enough for the job. It's like she's wearing two pairs of gardening gloves for knitting. She doesn't know what's going on over the opposite side, whether Bartley's holding it together or not – the communication thread between them has snapped, and Crosswell is gone, leaving Morgan isolated and exhausted. The fact that this patchwork-wobbling fence is holding any kind of form at all is the only evidence she has that Bartley's still working on the other end.

Damn Crosswell and his ambition. Damn herself for listening to that stupid man.

She's so tired and so scared that she might throw up.

The Possessed have all come out into the road. A gathering. Waiting. One turns to face Morgan. There are thick scorch-marks around its eyes, charcoal remains of blazing fires. Its lips bleed from chewing, and there are bruises on either side of its head. If it comes for her, Morgan's pretty certain she's in major trouble.

Whatever Crosswell's up to, he'd better make it fast. Really really fast.

100

SHE HATES YOU

Caleb knows it's best to ignore the spiteful thing. It's been spewing up hate messages since the second he laid eyes on it. For a noiseless object, it is terrifying. Inside it must churn with hot poison.

DREAMS YOU DEAD

Some of its threats and evils are in small cold letters, like it wants him to strain to read it. Others blaze large. If they were any hotter the window would melt and allow its anger to pour out into the world.

SHE KILLS AGAIN

He hates these messages the most, the ones that sound like it knows the future. He really hates that the future always sounds very bad for him.

KILLS YOU TODAY

Then acts as if it can read his mind, like it knows precisely what he's thinking.

HA HA HA

He hates this thing. It's been fifteen minutes and he wants to hurl it at the nearest wall and smash it to bits. Perhaps he will once he's got what he needs.

WILL NEVER HAPPEN

'Okay, so you can read my mind. So you must know everything about me, then.' It doesn't answer with words. A smile peels open, fat, rancid lips that part slightly to show jagged rock-teeth perfect for flesh-tearing. They bleed, those lips. Like the mouth has chewed itself. Or recently fed. Caleb slams the eight-ball on the floor, with enough force to bounce that foul mouth out of the screen. 'I won't put up with your crap! If you know everything about me then you must know that!' He's shouting; he's got to cool it. He doesn't want it to know that it's got under his skin (but if it knows everything then it already knows that it has, but he won't let it see, no, he can't ever show it on his face), and he doesn't want anyone hearing where he is. Anyone, or anything.

Huddled in a corner of the main hall, Caleb knows it's madness to be here, and that's exactly why he came. Nobody would think to look for him here. Nobody would believe he could be so reckless.

He can hardly believe it himself.

The murky window nearby isn't easy to see out of, despite a hard rubbing with his sleeve, but at least it allows him to keep an eye out in case someone (thing) approaches. Plenty of space in this hall for escape too. Four sets of doors, lots of windows.

THEY ARE NEAR

'They can be as near as they like, it doesn't really matter if they don't come in here, does it?'

THEY CAN HEAR

'Then I'll keep my voice down.'

NOT YOU. ME.

A blunt and horrible threat.

Caleb doesn't know enough about this unpleasant ball, this haunted abomination that should not exist. Like everything else, he is too far into something he doesn't understand.

STUPID LITTLE BOY

He would love to crack it open like a skull, spill its brains. 'Say whatever you like, it doesn't bother me.'

I CALL THEM

'I don't believe you. You're just saying that.'

AM I REALLY?

Stalling. The idea comes to Caleb that bluntly. The eight-ball is stalling. It is distracting him and upsetting him and doing whatever it can to waste time and stop him asking his questions. Caleb needs to put up his shield, the one he uses when Dad (dear dead Dad) is at his worst, when Dad tells (told) him that he should be up in that graveyard instead of Mum, that he's a waste of every last minute, that Dad doesn't know why he should give time and money over to a boy he never wanted.

Dad might have done him one single favour. He'd given Caleb plenty of training in how to take torrents of crap and pretend he was still functioning fine.

'If I ask a question, you have to tell the truth, right?'

SHE HATES YOU

'Answer me properly. You can tell all the lies you want, but if I ask a direct question, do you have to tell the truth?'

A blank pause. Then, I ALWAYS TELL

This could be a part of its games.

'Are you dead?'

LONG TIME DEAD

That gives Caleb a peculiar thrill, excitement twisted with horror. He's having a conversation with a ghost. 'How long?'

BEFORE YOU ALIVE

An answer that's not quite an answer. He will have to be careful with this politician. 'What's your name?'

EIGHT IS NAME

NAME IS EIGHT

'No, what's your real name?'

A large question mark, flashing.

EIGHT IS NAME

NAME IS EIGHT

'What was your name before you died?'

NAME WAS MINE

A feeling in Caleb's gut. He peers out across the courtyards. There's no one. A fine drizzle smatters the glass. 'How long have you been in the ball?'

DO NOT UNDERSTAND

'Okay... How long have you been Eight?'

TWO YEARS LONG

'And Misha put you there?'

GIRL THE GIRL

This message flashes up repeatedly until Caleb says, 'Alright,

alright, I get it.' He's not sure why it didn't occur to him until now. Some dumb part of him (the bigger part, he suspects) simply believed that Misha must have stumbled across the ball and decided to keep it. But she didn't. She made it. She purposely made this strange and frightening creation.

If there is a God, thinks Caleb, *would He allow this to exist?*

HE DOESN'T CARE

Caleb chooses to ignore that. Perhaps there are some questions he really doesn't want the answer to.

YES YOU DO

YOU ALL DO

More distractions, it's all distractions with this insane ball.

'What's Misha doing?'

BUSY RIGHT NOW

Wrong question. Or rather, questions asked the wrong way. 'What's she up to at the graveyard?'

LOOKING FOR ME

Damn thing tells the truth, all right. It twists and turns to tell the truth it wants to.

SHE'S NOT HAPPY

Caleb has a vivid vision of Misha flipping her bedroom upside-down in the search for Eight. He's not far wrong.

And something's coming for him, but Eight won't tell.

101

Panic thumps its pulse behind her eyes. The room is throbbing, she can't see straight. She knows she left Eight in her bedroom, she knows it like she knows her own heart, but it doesn't matter how many times she goes round and round and round, there's no sign of it. She keeps thinking of a part of the wardrobe she hasn't checked, or a place under the bed Eight could have rolled to, and when she looks she remembers that she's already looked here five, six, seven times. And she remembers Eight can't be in any of those places, absolutely can't, because she put it on the bed, right there, there, there damn it there!

Granddad took it.

That can't be true. He hasn't been in her room since she came home. She knows he hasn't. She left her room to argue with him and shut the door behind her.

Eight rolled off on its own, then. That's the only explanation. But Eight's never rolled anywhere of its own accord before. It's done a lot of things, some very frightening, but never that. Eight's been taken.

No. She's over-reacting. She tells herself this as she tears the sheets back off the bed, as she yanks everything off the shelves, as she starts screaming in frustration, as she yells at Granddad to keep out of it, to stay away, as she rips down the curtains and flings them aside, as she breathes too deep and fast, as she forces herself to stop because she's making so much more mess. Never mind the room, *she's* a mess. Tears spatter down her face. Skin glows hot.

Granddad's knocking gently on her bedroom door. 'Misha, please, what's wrong? Open the door, let me talk to you, we'll just talk, no shouting…'

She's not interested in talking. She's interested in the slick splinter jutting out from the window frame. The window in that frame is open. Not a lot, but enough to make her belly squirm. A closer look. Drying claggy blood.

There's only one boy stupid enough to do such a thing.

She'll kill him.

102

The thing that once was Neuman peels itself up out of a heap in a garden. It collapsed some hours ago on top of a bush behind a shed, drained. Sparks cough from her throat, scorching flesh. She senses a band of energy nearby. She senses someone familiar. She is drawn.

103

Morgan glances at the discarded and dying light-map on the ground next to her feet. There are minutes left before it will blink out for good. There's a new pulse at the far side of the cul-de-sac. Stronger than the others. And moving.

104

TAKE ME BACK

'Not until you start answering my questions properly.' Caleb wonders if he could kick Eight around like a football. All the spinning might knock it so sick that it could start to behave.

I'VE BEEN ANSWERING

'Yeah, you have. When I ask the next question I don't mean what's the person doing right now. If you really can get in my head, then you know exactly what I mean.'

SHE'S AFTER YOU

SHE HATES YOU

Caleb tries not to, but he can't help thinking over and over shut up, shut up, shut up. 'What were these people doing in the graveyard?' Hard concentration to replace shut up, shut up, shut up with an image: dark suited people, an open grave, lights, a burst, a body lifted off the ground.

TURNING THE CORPSE Small letters, reluctant.

'What does that mean?'

SLOWING THE SOUL

SOMEONE IS NEAR

SOMETHING IS NEAR Quick, quick, quick the messages come.

'Slow down, I'm trying to follow. Slowing what soul?'

ONE IN GRAVE

'There's no souls in graves. Only bodies.'

NOT UP THERE

Questions with tiny answers, answers leading to big questions. What should he ask? And how? 'Are all the souls coming back?'

THEY WILL BE

SOON SOON SOON

'Are the souls good?'

SOME VERY BAD. Eight allows these words to slowly fade, then adds, LIKE THING OUTSIDE.

105

The light-map flutters and flashes like a battered laptop screen. Morgan misses a loop on the net she's attempting to strengthen and it sags towards her, and it's got no hope of holding anything in.

No hope at all.

She should run.

She remembers all of Crosswell's threats. Threats that were delivered as promises. Tags that mean she can run as far as she wants and will always be found.

She looks down again. No map. That big jagged blip could be anywhere. Could be closer.

A flicker. The light-map, taking a few last greedy breaths. All those blips, holding their positions, except one. Except that single one. It goes off the back of the map. Vanishes.

Bartley's over there.

106

Caleb looks out across the grounds through one window, then another, then another. He's watching for dead boys. None by the lifeless fountains, none creeping up the garden stairs. He goes to another side of the hall, squints hard at the trees. Difficult to see if there are any shapes that shouldn't be there, especially with an imagination in overdrive. Branches blend in differing configurations, becoming nimble arms beckoning or slender legs walking. Caleb stills himself with long, steady breaths, holds his gaze level, focuses on the corners of his vision.

No dead boys.

No dead Vic.

He knows they're out there. But do they know he's here in the hall? Are they coming? Has Eight summoned them?

Or is that stupid ball stalling yet again?

Caleb seizes it, squeezes, even though all that achieves is sore fingers. 'There's nobody out there! Just answer me. Why is he bringing them back?'

IS MEANT TO

BUT IS STALLING

'Oh God, you speak in tiny riddles.'

IS ALL TRUTHS

THEY ARE HERE. The word THEY splits into triplicate and vibrates.

Caleb ignores it. Let it throw up all the stupid nonsense it wants to, as long as in between it answers some questions. It's a lot harder to ignore his cold spine, however. The skin down the middle of his back seems to be pulling away from something he can't yet see.

So easily it gets into his head!

'Is Misha helping him?'

NO, SHE RESISTS

'But if she helped him… She must be really good if she made

you, right?'

SHE IS RARE

Caleb feels that in every fibre. That's exactly what she is. Rare. Forever endangered. 'So if she wanted to, she could…'

RAISE ALL DEAD. It holds the message so that he can read it again and again. RAISE ALL DEAD. Even after everything he's seen, it's just about impossible to make sense of.

'Why would anyone want to?'

THE HARD RESET. This is underlined twice.

Caleb's shoulders sag. He wishes he could crack this thing open and pull all of its words out and read everything in one go instead of this agonising…

A rattling window. Caleb throws himself into the corner, kicking up dust plumes. The ratta-tapping on the glass stops. Pounding, pounding against his ribs, the swollen tempo of his chest. Looks at Eight.

HA HA HA

The tapping starts again, a little harder, more insistent. An almost-there voice, too soft to hear clearly. Tap-tap-tap, tap-tap-tap. Stops again.

I TOLD YOU

Caleb is stone. Won't move. Can't move.

I DON'T LIE

Tap-tap-TAP. Tap-tap-TAP, threatening to smash its way through. Joined by another set, in time, rhythmic. Hard bony knuckles. Tap-tap-TAP. Tap-tap-TAP. Both windows to his left, tap-tap-TAP, tap-tap-TAP.

He could drop below ledge level and crawl. If he could get himself to move, if his dumb legs would budge. If…

Tap-tap-TAP on the first pane to his right. Tap-tap-TAP on the next along. And another. And another. The hall fills with the sharp glassy sound. Caleb pushes back hard into the corner.

HA HA HA

A loud piercing crack. Bang-bang-BANG. Bang-bang-BANG.

He dares to lean out, compelled to look. Fists bashing. A right fist on this pane, a left on that. One dead boy hammering away, two sheets of glass vibrating like the skin of a drum. And there's a rasping chant in voices of dust. 'Cay-leb! Cay-leb! Cay-leb!' These dead football boys chanting for his blood. 'Cay-leb! Cay-leb! Cay-leb!'

He's heard this before. A similar call. His panicking mind pushes that realisation away. It's not important. Escape is.

THERE'S NO ESCAPE

'Shut up.'

'Cay-leb! Cay-leb!'

YOU DIE ALONE

'Shut up.'

'Cay-leb! Cay-LEB!'

DEAD LIKE DADDY

'Shut up!'

'Cay-LEB! CAY-LEB!'

DEAR DEAD DAD

'SHUT UP!'

A shard storm shatters the hall. Every window bursts at once, a torrent of glass flooding in. 'CAY-LEB!' Three shrill voices cawing for him above the rain of splinters, paper-pale hands reaching.

Caleb runs, feet crunch-crunching, sprinting from the dead boys. The shards act like marbles underfoot and he slides and his legs are lifting sideways and he's up in the air over those sharp slivers.

Bloodless gasps of delight.

He lands on a blast of pain; hard floor and cut skin, all along his side, all down his leg. No time to worry about how he suddenly feels wet at the hip. MUST GET UP. The message flips over MUST GET UP and over MUST GET UP as Eight rolls away MUST GET UP. Caleb slices his palms open as he boosts himself up. His left leg wails at his weight. He stoops to get

Eight, stumbles, is sore-clumsy. The hall is electric-cold at his neck-nape. Anticipates strong-brittle fingers clamping on his shoulder.

'CAY-LEB!'

Slick and painful are his palms as he lifts Eight. MUST RUN NOW. Caleb's already away, and he's running senselessly, and he's plunging deeper into Pernicious House.

107

Gramps perches on the end of his armchair, clutching at the journal. He doesn't dare open it. He's struggling to remember what's on those pages. Everything's going fuzzy in his brain again, a heavy fugue behind his eyes. What is in here that he wanted Caleb to see? There is Evelyn, yes, but there's also something more.

He could read it. But how soon after would he forget? Gramps can't remember.

He fancies some tomato soup.

108

She climbs out of the bedroom window while Granddad's still prattling away on the other side of the door. He's veering between warnings about kicking his way in, and pleading for a chance to talk without shouting. Always pleading. Help me, Misha. Help me.

She doesn't care about the old man and his wrong ideas. She wants Eight back, her only hated friend.

The wind is riling itself up, the clouds are fattening. The graveyard feels unbalanced and wrong, like it's heaving, like the soil under her feet is a tumbling ocean. She expects Daisy Hill to roll like a wave, roll right down over the town, bury it in coffins and dirt.

She'd like that.

Skirts swishing, she stomps downhill towards the gate, and from there she'll head to Caleb's and from there she'll take what is hers.

109

The remains of Vic Sweet regard the girl with craving eyes, with deep-down need, a need that's crossed a boundary from life into undeath and has grown stronger, fiercer in the crossing.

He hates her.

It's one of the only things he knows, that hate. It burns coals in his guts, shovel after shovel. He knows it better than his own name. It flares and sputters so brightly that most other memories are gone.

This time he will have her.

She beat him, she beat him so badly, and that is one memory that sticks. He remembers looking into that Thing's eyes, and he remembers dying, and he remembers that it's because of her. The her he must have.

Vic peels himself up out of the empty grave, clambers over the plumed piles of dirt, and follows.

110

He can't remember the way. The window he broke at the back of the house, it should be easy to find! But his brain's all crazy-static and back here the house is dark dark dark and the thick air vibrates with the echoing hoots of boys at play, boys hunting. They're running through the halls and rooms around him. A door to his left is jammed. Shoulders it. Locked.

'WE WANTED TO BE FRIENDS.'

'WHY CAN'T WE BE FRIENDS.'

Caleb's panic-blind, bouncing off walls. His hip screams blood. Eight's words strobe-light, blinding Caleb then plunging him back into darkness, then flaring again.

GET US OUT

flashing so fast the words blur together.

Blam GET

blam US

blam OUT.

'I'm trying!'

'FRIENDS DON'T RUN AWAY FROM FRIENDS.' A familiar voice, whispery-loud and furious. The game is coming to an end. They're out-manoeuvring him.

Kitchen up ahead. Must be. That's how he got in! A boy-shape in there, coming at him.

TURN TURN TURN

'YOU'RE NO FRIEND OF MINE!'

TURN NOW NOW

And Caleb's off down another foreign corridor, this one narrow like squeezed-in ribs. The ghost comes fleeing from the kitchen and there's no way out that way now, and if he turns right a couple of times he thinks he'll come to the front staircase and can go up but up, isn't out, up's further in, there are only windows and drops as an escape. Up is dead, but there's nowhere else, nowhere, as he tumbles through rooms full of old

hard furniture and
    trips
    spilling over
    tucking and dropping a shoulder to take the
    impact.

His foot throbs worse than the time he ran into the sofa. He managed to keep hold of Eight this time.

DOWN DOWN DOWN

'Not the time for sarcasm,' he snaps, and he doesn't like the wobble in his own voice. It turns his nerves sickly.

NO, IDIOT, DOWN

Caleb can't hear footsteps piling after him, but do ghosts have footsteps unless they want them? (It's crawling across the ceiling towards me, crawling, crawling until it can drop down on my head.) Rushes of pain run up and down his left side.

OPEN THE TRAPDOOR

He can't make sense of what he's being told; he can't see much in the windowless gloom.

OPEN THE TRAPDOOR Eight repeats. One of the Os zooms in to fill the screen, turns solid white, becoming a torch. Caleb sees it, the metal ring he tripped over. A large square of pale floorboards, where once must have sat a rug. In that square, the trapdoor.

DOWN DOWN DOWN

The opposite of upstairs would be far worse than upstairs. But all of his options are gone. (The ceiling, the ceiling, there's a dead boy on the ceiling!)

Caleb hefts the trapdoor open, and it's blacker than anything down there, and he scampers down the ladder, Eight under one arm, slipping on the rungs, babbling to himself. 'There's a way out, there's a way out, there's a way out,' and up above they are screaming for him, absolutely screaming.

Eight lights the way.

It starts as a basement, a scattering of old boxes and a couple of broken chairs. Fat pillars support the ceiling. Caleb does his best impression of jogging on; his leg is a flare, and Eight's getting heavier. He quickly realises that the huge basement is tapering into a funnel, pouring him towards a passageway. Eight's torchlight has a limited reach. Ten feet in front of him things rapidly fall away into night, a thick abyss in which untold horrors lurk. But real horrors are chasing him.

'CAY-LEB, CAY-LEB.'

'YOU'RE A BAD FRIEND, CAY-LEB.'

'BAD FRIEND! BAD!'

They're down in the basement and they're fast and they'll never be slowed down by fatigue or pain.

'YOU'RE NO FRIEND OF MINE.'

'CAY-LEB! CAY-LEB!'

He bangs his elbow on the plastered tunnel wall, joggling Eight, and the light jitters wildly and it makes the path ahead look like it's jumping and heaving. He risks a single glance back. Ghost boys pushing into the tunnel entrance, one crawling up and around the arch, dim sparks where eyes should be.

Cayleb runs as best he can.

A three-way junction. No time to pause, think, ask questions. He goes straight on. He can't see Eight's message: NOT THAT WAY.

111

I came back home.

Not to my house. That, of course, was inhabited by a new family. I pitied them if they knew what had happened within those walls, and small towns don't tend to keep such secrets very well. I didn't want to be in that house, not with my memories of what happened inside it. I didn't want to be anywhere near. I found a B&B on the other side of town. A couple of nights at most was all I intended to stay for, and what little money I had after my helter-skelter chase back home wouldn't stretch much further anyway. My beard was growing in and my frame was scrawny. Mirrors told me I'd be difficult to recognise.

As it turns out I only paused long enough for a meal. Evelyn, I knew, would not pause at all. Not for food, not for rest, not for sleep, not for anyone or anything. I wished good luck to any poor soul that might step in her way. The pulse in my neck injury was low but ever-present: I imagined each beat matched one of her footfalls as she straight-lined her way directly to me. I imagined her driving right through family homes, ripping and tearing, and that's where I stopped imagining, and that's when I set out on the final part of my single-minded mission.

I went to the graveyard. I had a knife tucked into the waistband of my dusty trousers. I had the sense not to approach via the front gates. I had a burning hate in my chest. I had very little else. Two years of wandering alone, no local family connections, no ability to make friends or form any kind of relationship knowing what would happen to anyone I came near, always moving on, always sensing her presence whether near or far. So many nights I woke up in darkness, doused in the fear that Evelyn had caught up and caught me off guard, lurking just behind a doorway. On too many occasions that had turned out to be true. I knew little of genuinely peaceful sleep, and everything of terror's constant beat.

I wanted it all to end. I could not take one more day.

It was a cold thrill to trudge up the back of Daisy Hill, knowing what was under my feet. All those tunnels that Evelyn and I had run through, there amongst the dead. I wondered how much more digging her lunatic father had done since then. I wondered how it would feel to stab him in the heart when he refused to help. Even as a young, desperate man I was not so foolish as to believe the confrontation would smoothly go my way.

Did I, therefore, go up that hill and to that house with murder in mind? I have to say yes. I wanted him to stop Evelyn and I wanted him to put her to rest, but I also wanted vengeance, hot bloody vengeance for what I had suffered. If he would not cooperate, then I would bury the maniac in the graveyard, and I would be glad of it.

He was tending to weeds in the back garden as I approached. He stood slowly as would a man with a back complaint. 'Actually found a little courage to come back, did you?' he growled. 'Took you long enough.'

I pulled out the knife. 'We're going to have a little talk,' I said, 'whether you like it or not.'

There was a trowel in his hands. A brutal weapon. It made us rather even. And he dropped it. 'I won't be talking to you. Not today. Not tomorrow. Not any day after that. So kill me if you think you can, boy. Stick me right in the chest if you haven't used up the last of your guts coming here. Get it done with.'

I'd run through the scenario a thousand times on my way back to this town. I'd thought of as many possible endings as I could, all of them bad for one of us. This had not been one of those scenarios. I lowered the knife. There was no murderous instinct in me after all. 'All I want is for you to undo what is done. Call her off. Send Evelyn back to the grave.'

He was steel through and through on that slate-sky day. 'Why should I? It's because of you that my Evelyn's gone.'

My grip redoubled on the knife's hilt. 'You killed her. You brought her back. You sent her after me.'

'No! You killed her!' His bark was cigarette-and-whiskey rough. 'You stuck your nose in where there was no room for it! You chased after something that wasn't yours to chase! What else was I supposed

to do?' He started towards me; I threatened with the blade, holding the madman back, but his rage was building. 'My girl! She was my little girl! She was not for the likes of you!' He pounded his fist into his palm with every other word. 'Stupid little boy, trying to take her away from me!' He swung a hand to slap the knife out of my hand, only succeeded in cutting his fingers deeply. He didn't cry out, and I cringed from the splash of blood, my skin bristling.

'I wasn't taking her away!' I didn't like the wobble in my voice, the weakness. I took a step forward, stabbing towards him with the knife, a warning to back off. 'I didn't even know what you were doing here!'

'It was only a matter of time before she blabbed. You forced me into it! I should have killed her sooner! That little bitch took you into the tunnels!'

'It wasn't a choice! You were chasing us!'

I realised he was crying, thin tears tracing his cheeks. He didn't seem to know they were there. 'She was meant to stay with me. She wasn't meant to go after you. But she picked up on my hate and how much I wanted you dead, wanted everything about you erased from the earth. So she went after you, didn't she?' A bitter grin. 'And she's kept you running all this time. All that running, and for what? To end up back here, back where it started. You've run to nowhere. You haven't moved an inch in, what, two years?' Laughing. 'Almost makes it worth losing her to see what she's done to you. Almost worth everything I've been through.'

Bile rose in my stomach. 'What you've been through? What about me? You don't know...'

'I don't want to know about you! And you don't have a clue, boy! You don't know about all the years! And all the work! And it was me that had to kill her, not you! I had to strangle her because you wouldn't stay away! I had to squeeze her throat, squeeze until the life choked out of her! She was supposed to help me. I was supposed to train her for all of this! Instead I've been alone.'

The way his head lowered, the way his eyes dulled, I knew he was coming at me whether I had a knife or not.

I didn't shout. I didn't move. I didn't step out of the way. He ran right at me, and onto the knife. His whiskey-stale breath burst over my face, and his eyes drew sharp one last time, staring right into mine. His whole body tensed up, then shuddered, as if the life was being shaken loose from his frame by unseen hands. It took a painful age for him to slump to the ground and finally die. My hands were bloody and I felt sick. With a struggle I managed to hold onto my dinner. The last thing I wanted to do was give his corpse the pleasure of upsetting me.

It was only then that it occurred to me to look around for witnesses. There was nobody. I almost wrote down that there wasn't a single soul, but that would be far from true, wouldn't it?

I dragged his body into the house. Whatever leaves the body in death is replaced by weight. My back howled as I lugged that meat-sack over the doorstep, limbs flopping about and getting stuck on everything. It was a better fight than he'd put me through outside. I dumped him in the hall, near the kitchen, locked the back door. An intense hunger seized me like none I'd ever felt before. My body cried out for energy, now, now, now. After a little rooting about for everything I needed, I threw together a thick ham sandwich, got through it in four large bites. It wasn't enough. An apple was next, and I chewed it round and round while my stomach was already baying for the next piece of food.

Sitting at the kitchen table, I looked back at the body and wondered what I had become. The man, as vile as he was, had died on a blade I was holding. Coming after me was his dead, vengeful daughter. With the father gone I had no likely chance of stopping her. Yet there I was, waiting and refuelling, instead of running away from a crime scene and certain death. I hadn't felt so good in a long, long time. Not, in fact, since my first kiss from Evelyn.

We would meet one last time. She would find me in the house where I lost her.

112

She hasn't had an answer out of Bartley in five minutes, and the light-weave is pulling, like hers are the only hands holding it up, like it wants to collapse. It needs more links, it needs tightening, a second layer if she's to feel any kind of security.

A burp of light by her feet. The light-map, belching its last. The image has flash-burned onto the corner of her eye. A map with motionless blips in each house, and one other blip, one that's moving right down the middle of the road. Moving towards her.

A pain blasting into her hands and up her forearms, a javelin bursting through her wrists. The barrier disintegrates, fragments melting into the air. Morgan clutches her arms to her chest, gasping at the heat.

No map. No barrier. Defenceless. It's time to run.

Then she sees the girl.

113

Misha swipes her arm through the light-weave like she's brushing aside gossamer sheets. It crackles static electricity across the back of her hand as it spun-sugar shatters. A weak construct, hardly worth the effort of summoning the atoms to weave it with. Had to be the work of one of Crosswell's bunch, if not the scowling man himself.

It was put here for a reason.

Here. Caleb's street.

What else has that backstabbing boy been doing? What has he done to rile up Crosswell? Why would Crosswell want to fence him in when light-weaves don't even work on the living?

Possibilities flash through her brain, and Misha is surprised at how some of them make her ache. Crosswell has caught Caleb and killed him. Perhaps to silence the boy forever, perhaps to get Eight for himself, perhaps any other reason, doesn't really matter (unless Crosswell has Eight, then it matters, it really really matters). The boy is dead in this street, and Crosswell set up the light-weave to trap him here. Would ugly old Crosswell be scared of a ghost boy?

Would he be scared of a vengeful girl?

She hates Caleb.

She hates Crosswell far more.

She liked Caleb. Still does.

'No I don't. He stole Eight. He's a selfish bastard.' The boy with the dead mother. The boy just like her. 'He's nothing like me.' But he is, and if she doesn't care, then why is she so worried? Why is she frozen to this spot, afraid to approach his house, afraid to look inside and see his shell shambling towards her, eyes blazing.

She will kill Crosswell. She will rip his face open. She is burning; her chest is anger-swollen.

She doesn't even know if Caleb is dead.

'I just want to kick his head in myself.' That lying, thieving, backstabbing boy. As bad as the others. No, worse. Worse, because she thought he was okay. She let herself believe that he was an okay kid, and she liked him.

Misha will never forgive herself for that. Or him.

Without Eight she feels lost. So many questions, no one to give any answers. No help, no guidance. This is Misha, well and truly alone. She hasn't noticed she's alone until now. All the way here she'd been full of fury and certainty. It's all gone with the falling of the light-weave. swept away.

She has to know if that stupid lying boy is okay. She wants to punch something. His head will be a good start.

Misha starts walking towards his house.

Hands grab her, pull. She swipes fingernails, screams.

'Shut up!' hisses Morgan. Crosswell's mate. Which means Crosswell must be here. Which means she's right about Caleb. Her punch catches Morgan on the edge of her left eye socket, almost knocking the woman over. Misha tries to run past. Morgan spins her by the shoulder, bouncing her off a wooden fence. 'God, you little bitch!' She's holding the side of her head. She's all kinds of bad shapes, contorted fury; hunch shouldered, scowl-mouthed, blaze-eyed, crook-fingered. There's a will to slap, to hit. 'I'm trying to do you a favour!'

'You killed him, didn't you?' Misha hopes she looks equally angry.

'Killed who? I'm saving your dumb life, although right now I'm regretting it.'

'Stay away from me. You and that arsehole Crosswell...'

Single finger to lips. 'Keep your voice down when I tell you. It's in this street somewhere, I don't know exactly where.'

'What is?'

'Neuman.'

Cold burrows into Misha's bones as a hard dusty voice barks, 'Cay.' Woman and girl huddle up against the fence. 'Cay.'

That sounded close. Two houses away, three at most. 'Cay.' Somewhere round the top of the cul-de-sac, Misha thinks. 'Leb.' Can't hear footsteps. 'Leb.' Is it a little closer each time? 'Leb.' A little angrier?

'Cay. Leb.'

And what is anger if it's not a hunger?

'CAY. LEB.'

It's after that stupid lying boy.

114

The strobing of the light is making him sick behind his eyes, making it hard to run, to judge distance, to anything. 'Stop doing that!' Caleb gives Eight another whack. It's response is to pulsate faster. He wants to throw it off one of these rough-plastered sloping walls. He knows if he does that then Eight will turn its light out and he will be plunged into complete choking black and he'd never find Eight again and he'd never ever find his way out.

'WE'LL FIND YOU CAY-LEB.'

'BAD FRIEND. BAD FRIEND!'

'WE'RE COMING CAY-LEB.'

He's certain those boys don't need light to find him down here, those dead hungry boys. But they can use Eight's light to track him down. He needs to keep moving. But the floor is jittering around in that flashing glare.

Caleb turns Eight, squints into its window, feels like his eyes are getting pushed right back into the sockets. 'Why are...' Finally he sees the message.

GOING

WRONG

WAY

Each word bashes out after the other in rapid succession, an alternating alarm. The words slow, like Eight's realised Caleb has read them at last, like Eight's calming down. It settles on a soft wordless glow.

'I can't go back,' says Caleb, and the hooting of dead boys confirms this.

'CAY-LEB.'

'PULL YOU APART, BAD FRIEND.'

'I can't go back!'

NO SHIT, SHERLOCK

Caleb shakes the ball, frustrated. 'If they get me, they get you as well!'

When the screen settles again, it reads, YOU MUST HIDE.

'Where?' He's in another long tunnel, another after run-stumbling down long tunnel after long tunnel, and he can't burrow into the walls, even though he's so scared he wants to dig-dig-dig until his hands are bloody stumps. 'There's nowhere to go! There's nowhere!'

MUST GO ON

He wanted Eight to come up some magic solution, some secret way back to where he's come from, to the normal world above, a way past the dead boys. Instead it tells him to GO ON. GO ON means further into the tunnels, further into the dark.

'CAY-LEB.'

He runs on. It's easier with a steady light. What if Eight is lying? What if they reach another junction and Eight sends him the wrong way? It can't lie. It's okay, the ball can't lie. But who said it can't lie? The ball? 'I hate you,' he tells it, and listen to the layers of hot panic! So breathless, shaky. He's not far from losing control. And he's too far into these tunnels. How many turns has he taken? Is Pernicious House behind him? To the left? The right?

Eight might not know the way. Eight just wants to run and guess and they'll be lost down here until they're caught—

That's flat wall up ahead. It's a dead end. Dead. End. Caleb hears himself, tears in his words: 'No, no, no, no, no, no...' Still he runs, like he could smash straight on through, like it might be an illusion, a trick of the hard light. 'Please, please, please, please, please, please...'

A junction! Sharp turns in either direction. There's still a chance, whispers his hope, a tiny, tiny chance. 'Which way?' he asks of the eight-ball. 'Hurry up, which way?'

LEFT LEFT LEFT

Caleb goes goes goes.

'BAD CAY-LEB BAAAAAAD.'

The echoes swirl around his head, bounce from ear to ear, and there's laughter in it now, cruel laughter. Dead boys enjoying the game, loving it because they know that in the end they will win, they will seize their prize.

The tunnel is short. Caleb stumbles out of it into a small chamber, half a dozen rectangular columns on either side (he's been here before, he's been here as Gramps, he's been in this bad place, it's a bad bad place) and he doesn't want to stay anywhere near them and sticks as close to the middle as he possibly can; actually draws himself in thin because arms stick out and are grabbable. Archways ahead and either side. 'Eight?'

KEEP ON AHEAD

Caleb doesn't want to keep on anything. He moves into the next chamber; more columns (graves) in here. Seven either side, with seven behind each of those.

Does he hear a thin dragging sound?

'CAY-LEB!'

ON ON ON

He's jogging again. Really really doesn't want to be down here a single second longer. That dragging body-part sound, muffled, like it's inside something. He's passed it; leaving it behind. Let whatever it is (dead thing, it's a dead thing) scrape about all it wants as long as it's behind him. Far behind.

ON KEEP ON

Building to a run because the boys will be catching up, they won't slow for scrapes or fear.

'YOU'RE LOST.'

'STUPID LOST FRIEND.'

'NO ONE WILL EVER FIND YOU.'

'WE WILL, CAY-LEB, WE WILL.'

Caleb almost screams. They're hard to pinpoint amidst echoes and running, but they sound like they're entering the first chamber.

He is screwed.

LEFT RIGHT LEFT

He takes these turns, running hard, running from ghosts, running from the graves that surround him. His feet-slaps are teeth-grindingly loud in the flat silence of underground. Trackable. Findable. Thundering past so many columns, so many graves, so many dead. Weaving one way then the next. Deep in the maze, far past lost.

No one knows he's here. No one living has a clue where he is.

STOP STOP STOP

That can't be right.

STOP NOW NOW and the words turn the thick hot red of fresh blood and the chamber around him turns bloody too and he's in the fat veins of the terrible creature that heaves under the ever-growing graveyard, and that's what stops him.

His heart is about to pop.

HIDE BEHIND COLUMN

'That won't help!' he whispers. 'They'll find me straight away!'

NOT FROM THEM

A thud. Someone (thing) falling. Tripping over. Or tumbling out of something. Out of one of the columns.

He hears it gasp. Caleb creeps into the corner of the chamber, steps light, breathing stopped.

'CAY-LEB.'

The boys haven't stopped to hide in a corner. 'I can't stay here. They're coming. Eight? Eight?'

The ball only says this: WAIT RIGHT HERE.

115

Heavy thumping. Someone wants an answer and isn't going away until they get one. THUMP THUMP THUMP. THUMP THUMP THUMP. Granddad stands within reach of the handle, watching his front door rattle. He knows who's on the other side. It can only be one man. The bastard can't wait. THUMP THUMP THUMP. THUMP THUMP THUMP. A beastly heartbeat, irregular, caught up in anger and panic.

'I hate you,' whispers Granddad.

The banging stops.

Granddad steps lightly to one side. Snakes of light crackle between the knobbles of his fingers. He's tired, but he's not yet out of tricks.

Pressure pulls from outside. He plants his heels. CRUMP the door is sucked away; the welcome mat shoots out with it, and shoes, and umbrellas, and coats and hat stand.

Crosswell takes a single stride in.

The blast from the light-whips blows Crosswell sideways down the hallway, knocking him senseless. Before he can recover, before he can find his feet, Granddad flicks both wrists and shrills an ululating note, wrapping the whips around Crosswell's limbs, binding him. The old man's chest heaves and rasps from the effort.

Granddad peers out where once there was a door, expecting to see more of the Crosswell clan. Chunks of wood are scattered all over the garden. There's nothing else but gravestones. 'You came here alone? I knew you were arrogant, but I didn't think you were stupid as well.' A pain zips up and down his left arm, pinches at his side. He sags a little, forces himself to stand upright before Crosswell can look at him.

He can't, however, completely wipe the grimace off his face.

116

Beams slash around the street, searching. Neuman has stopped bellowing the boy's name. The silence is worse. It indicates total concentration, a single-minded determination to find prey.

Morgan gives Misha a nudge. 'We're out of here. Soon as I tell you, we run and don't stop.'

'I don't belong to you,' snaps Misha. 'You can do what you want.' Misha edges away along the fence, heading for the road. Morgan catches her.

'Do you want to die?'

'What do you care?' Swoosh go the lights. Swoosh, swoosh over their heads. 'Two weeks ago you and Crosswell were saying how much easier your lives would be if I was dead. So I'm doing you a favour, aren't I?' She yanks away from Morgan's grip.

'Oh screw you, you little brat. Why am I even bothering? You can—' The fence shatters as Neuman piles through it, slamming into Morgan and knocking her to the ground, belly-flopping down on top of her. She's face-down in grass, and trying to wiggle loose. Without thinking Misha steps forward to help. Neuman's head snaps round, that head with those twin torches in.

She sees

the world beneath her own, the scorched truth within this street, the burnt-out shells of houses, and the monsters waiting inside them. They're all looking at her, blue fire slavering from their eyes, mouths wide and hungry. Beneath each of them, six feet under, lie piles of the dead, bodies sagging like empty sacks, steaming energy. Between the carcasses of houses, far off in the distance but coming, steadily coming, march an army of revenants, all eyes aglow: raveners, destroyers. And Neuman, pinning Morgan, a taloned overlord of the Underworld, a metallic fog pouring from its skin, reaching down to press on her chest, press, press, push through, and those hands push right on in, sink into the cavity within her ribs, cupping her rabbit-pulsing heart and squeeeeeeeeeeze.

Misha falls to her jellied knees, gasping. The world snaps back to normal, and normal now is Neuman hunched over Morgan's jerking body, torches blazing directly into her head. Misha turns away from the melting eye sockets, tells her legs to behave, she has to move, she has to go far from here.

But she needs to find Caleb first. This street is full of revenants; they might already have him; he might already be one of them. If he is, that will be a shame, and she will need to find Eight and run.

She scrambles away from Neuman, from dying Morgan and her cooked eyeballs (the smell, oh the smell), runs around the back of the cul-de-sac to Caleb's garage, climbs up faster than she can, feet slip-sliding on brickwork, hurry, hurry, imagining hands snatching at her heels. Her nerve-endings flutter. On the garage roof, nothing behind her climbing up. Neuman is still dealing with Morgan. Silly old cow.

Silly dead old cow.

Caleb's bedroom window is shut.

She tries it anyway. Shut, but not locked. Misha prises it open and slips into his bedroom. No boy, and a brief glance around reveals no Eight. That's to be expected. Eight will be with Caleb, wherever that might be (if he's not dead like that silly old cow).

'Shut up,' she tells herself, but it doesn't dispel the idea, doesn't make it definitely wrong. He better not be dead. She wants her ball back.

He better not be dead.

They sat there, together on the floor as he read from his Gramps's journal. She had listened to it all, but she'd been thinking too, thinking and feeling. So close, arms touching. So close to another person. This boy with a dead mother (father too) and little to make him feel part of the world. Sitting there beside the boy outside of the world, she'd believed that she could talk to him, tell him things. Misha had thought that perhaps he would understand, and she recalls the rush that hope gave her. All at once this fired through her head, a hot pulse along the lines of communication, a telegram after a life alone on an island, a text after years of no signal. So close to telling him what Granddad was up to and why she knew he was wrong and why she always resisted the old man. So close.

Then they were interrupted, and there was running, and Vic Sweet dead, and Caleb showed that he could be just as dumb as everyone.

Why did he have to go and steal Eight?

She hates him!

Over goes the mattress as she shouts her wordless hate and frustration. She hates him! Smash goes his keyboard off the wall. She hates him! Games console meets floor in a plume of plastic splinters. She hates how much she loves him!

She's completely trashed his room. Poster pieces flutter. Fluff has prolapsed from the pillows. A crack has stabbed across the TV screen. Gouges in the plaster. How long was she raging? And how loud?

Beams sweep across the windowpane. This is how criminals feel when the police helicopter pins them down.

Out of his bedroom, onto the landing, checking inside each room as she goes. A bathroom. A separate toilet. A grown-up bedroom. A spare room for storage. No Calebs, no Eights.

Down the stairs, down-down quick. An empty ground floor toilet. Living room and dining room where there has been a major struggle. Broken chair, flipped table, battered sofa, broken mirror. It's almost as big a mess as the one she's left upstairs.

Where is that stupid lying boy?

The kitchen has also been a battleground. The fridge is open, its shelves tumbled. A cupboard door off the hinges. Plates smashed across the drainer. A man standing on the back step, staring at her. 'Cay-leb.' It's not said with love; it's a craving, a hunger. 'Cay-leb!' She runs. The boy's not here, and she doesn't want to be either.

Neuman stepping out of the front room, lights sweeping before her. Lashes a crinkled hand out at her. She drops, slides, kicks Neuman in the shins. The legs buckle and Neuman collapses and those lightbeams swing down and blare into her eyes

and she sees

right into Neuman's head, to the brain inside a cracked skull, and there are storms raging, forks of lightning crackling within cloud-bundles, and past this she sees not a ceiling but the remains of a roof, rotten beams barely hanging together, and beyond this lies a roiling blue-grey sky, storms raging, forks of lightning crackling within cloud-bundles, the clashes of a brain inside a broken skull and

Neuman's forehead bashes into the bridge of her nose, and a hot spike of pain accompanies the crunching noise as the bone snaps, and she's agony-blind. She raises a hand to the bloody injury. Smashes an elbow across Neuman's face before she is pinned under the revenant's weight. Neuman falls to her right, and Misha wants to curl in a ball around the searing pain of her nose.

She screams as a hand pulls her up by the hair, strands popping out of her scalp.

'Where's my boy?' bellows Caleb's father in her ear, and through her tears she can blurry-see the tatters of his scorched face and the teeth that can still bite, and he's lifting her higher, higher until her feet are off the floor and it feels as if all her hair is about to rip out of her head in one lump, and Neuman throws herself into Caleb's father. They crash into the wall. Misha falls to the floor. To hands and knees, scrambling away. The battling revenants tumble over the top of her, almost flattening her, but she doesn't stop, she goes goes goes because this is a place gone very bad and she shouldn't have come here, not even for Eight, not even for the boy.

At the front door. Eyes streaming. Face burning. It's not opening, handle's not moving. She screams loud enough to strain her throat. Dead things are fighting behind her and she can't get out! A key on a hook by the door. She snatches at it with sausage fingers. Neuman's beams are slashing around the hallway, and there's shuddering, everything's shuddering as a low pulsation throbs her bones, a tone that lifts through the octaves, an off-key squail that thickens the air like flat mud, and she feels it pressing on her skin, the air, the fat air is pressing on her, pressing hard like palms on her flesh and

her fingers

are really

struggling to

move

to turn the goddamn key, the key that she doesn't have the strength to turn.

The lock clicks.

She hauls the door open.

A thump in the back throws her out onto the doorstep. Arms out to protect her face, paving slabs coming up to meet her. Skin tears from her elbows. A ball of Neuman and Caleb's dad rolls out after her, and they bring that noise, that rib-squeezing, energy-draining, chest-puncture of a racket, and Misha crawls on blood-burning elbows and knees, because she just can't get up, the pressure is everywhere, that noise doesn't pause for anything, not breath or fist

and then it does stop, with a wet splash, and the pressure's gone, and Misha's back on her feet and she can run, and she does, not daring to look back at whatever mess she's leaving behind. There's more to see. Once-alive people, scorch-eyed, marching out into the street, towards her.

Bad, bad place.

Run, run, run.

117

Slither, splat.

The sound ties knots in Caleb's intestines. A dead thing, slid from its grave, crumpled in the dirt. And listen to the susurrations as it shumples up the roughness of wall, and shuffle-feet drag.

Eight's light has gone out. No messages, no taunts, no instructions, true or false. Caleb is alone, trapped with the dead.

And the boys have gone quiet. No shouts, no taunts, true or false. Perhaps they heard the slither-splat, and perhaps they don't like it either.

He hates it. His guts hate it. He wants to scream because the primal part of him says that if he screams then help will come, but what's left of his rational self knows that a single noise will be the end of him.

Ssshhh slide. Ssshhh slide. Feet that struggle to walk properly, coming his way.

Can it see in the dark?

He can't see a damn thing. His eyes are bulging against the blackness. He edges around the corner of the column (*grave*), ajangle with every whispering brush of his skin or clothes, each scrape of his heel over some tiny pebble. Whispers and scrapes. Any of these will kill him.

Ssshhh slide. Ssshhh slide. It's heard him. Or smelled him. Or doesn't matter why, it's coming, and he slips further away from the corner, and every last inch of his skin is screaming, sure that a long, long arm is stretching out in the dark, stretching towards him, to

touch.

He can't see one inch in front of his face, can't see where he's going, where escape might be, he can't, he can't.

A tiny blip on Eight's screen. So small, fractional light. So small he almost misses it. Caleb lifts the ball up close to read the miniscule message: I LEAD YOU.

One bright loud thought in Caleb's mind: *Get Me Out.*

FOLLOW MY INSTRUCTIONS

Okay, Okay. Tell Me, Tell Me.

FIVE STEPS FORWARD

DO IT QUICK

Caleb's lungs are rushing, a flood of air. He treads light, one, two, three, four, five.

ROUND CORNER LEFT

NOW STAY STILL

His legs are crying out to run! Get far from the monsters! Eight's words vanish again. Caleb's back in the black. The dead thing is peering down the short corridor he's just stepped out of. No sound. It's deciding. Choosing. Keep going or turn back.

If it finds me, thinks Caleb, *what will it do?*

Tiniest letters yet. PULL YOU APART.

FACE IN CAVITY

SUCK OUT SOUL

A hungry noise. Shuffling forward. Coming after him.

TURN YOURSELF LEFT

STOP STOP STOP

FORWARD TWENTY PACES

Caleb obeys, and he counts the paces fast, and he's making more noises now but he's totally focused on the instructions. He trusts Eight completely.

TAKE NEXT RIGHT

RUN THIRTY PACES

And Caleb runs. In pitch black, he runs. Not a half-jog or fearful stumble. Headlong into hard nothing. He could run face-first into a wall now. Or now.

Thirty paces. Stop.

TURN LEFT STOP

FORTY PACES RUN

118

Chest burning, she has to stop, can't run another step. There are streets between her and Caleb's horror house, five minutes full-tilt running between her and scorched Morgan. All those revenants, those ex-people. No one left alive. Each fixated on her, the only living thing in the street.

Only Vic Sweet's ever been that scary. Only his hunger was worse.

That's all over because Vic Sweet's dead, dead like those people. People she didn't know, and who were probably as bad as everyone else, so why should she care about them? It was people like them who let Vic Sweet do what he did. They deserve it; that's what she's always said. Hands on knees, hauling down air, Misha's exhausted and wishes she could delay all this for one more night – and that, out of nowhere, brings a genuine laugh. Granddad is the one for delays. Granddad is the scared one, not Misha, not ever Misha. Her blood's rushing, but don't confuse that with being scared.

She's frightened, though. The self-pep talks are failing. All her certainty that this has to happen, that this is what must be, trembles under the sweep of light beams and scorched eyes. She wants to live. She wants all the bastards of the world taken down. She just doesn't want it to happen to her, doesn't want to be Morgan with the cooked eyeballs and burnt-out soul.

Where else would a Caleb go?

She starts jogging again, to his grandfather's house.

119

A gurgle splatters from Vic's crusted throat. He's seen her, finally. Follows.

120

No matter how large a breath he takes they all seem thin, too meagre for his aching lungs. His eyes are wider than they've ever been, even though he can't see a damn thing. Sweat pastes his skin, the eight-ball slippy in his shaky hands. Tiny flashes of the tunnel are all he's given as the endless instructions spit from Eight. TURN this way and RUN that much and WAIT here and RUN now NOW NOW NOW then

STOP RIGHT HERE.

Caleb does, hot feet sliding in dust, waits for the next direction, the next number of paces to take him away from the shuffling corpses and the dead boys sweeping after. But this final direction is different: UP IS OUT. The message flashes three times, large then larger, split seconds of light that briefly expose the dead end he's reached.

Dead. End.

Rivulets of panic turn his voice liquid. 'What do you mean, what do you mean up is out, I'm underground, up's always out, what do you mean...'

UP IS OUT

Eight turns its touchscreen on full blast, so bright that Caleb must squint through dull-adjusted eyes. He pans the ball around.

A ladder. To a hatch. Up is out.

A smile instead of words inside Eight's light. Using the ball as a torch, Caleb doesn't see the smile, the fat slugs of lips, the craggy rock black teeth.

121

These fizzling ropes are hot on his skin. His legs are bound achingly together. His arms sear, won't quite go numb. He is hanging from the ceiling, a table beneath him. On the table are the old idiot's diagrams and maps, one so large of the graveyard that it spills over the edges. It's a map that's grown bigger over several months, pieces of thick A4 stuck along its sides to represent expanding borders, the intricate detail of the original map giving way to haphazard sketchings, and all over the whole thing are scribbles and arrows and box-outs, a forever-shifting code, a rough and fluid strategy.

Crosswell drools watching the saliva string splatter on the west side of Daisy Hill.

'Glad you're awake,' growls the old man, so focused on the dangerous man hanging from his dining room ceiling that he does not hear the faint scree of a hatch eased open.

'Glad I'm not dead.' In such pain as he's suffering, Crosswell struggles to say the words levelly.

'I'm not you,' the old man says through a thin smile. 'I'm nothing like you. Sometimes I wish I was.'

Crosswell watches him rub his left arm. 'How about you let me down then, Mister. Nothing Like Me?'

'After everything you've done? You're staying where you are.'

'I've done nothing.'

'Weeks of nothing! Weeks of leaving me to turn the dead!'

'Because it's time. This is what it's been all about…'

'No!'

'Not no! You got it all twisted up in your head! You've let yourself think it's up to you, that you get to decide. We were here to get them aligned, get them ready to come at the same time. They're aligned! There's nothing else for us to do! We just kiss goodbye to the world as it is, and let them go!'

The boy in the hall, too exhausted to run, listens as the old man snaps, 'What if they're wrong about the time? Why can't we give the *world* more time? These people deserve a chance...'

'A chance to what? Put things right themselves? They don't want to. That would take effort from everyone. What makes you think that could ever happen? You're delaying the very event you're meant to lead. This is the reason you're here.'

'Our reason for being here is to do this at the *right* time, if that time comes! Nnnnnggg...' He leans on the table, scrunches the map as the pain in his chest intensifies.

'Goddamn it, man, even that idiot girl of yours is on our side!'

'No, she isn't...'

'She is. She doesn't want to hear all your science about the Turn because she understands better than you. The world is rotten. It went bad. The girl sees it better than you.' The slap across his face rocks Crosswell hard, so it feels like his arms will pop from their sockets.

'You don't know her.'

'Neither do you.'

Neither does the boy in the hall.

The old man taps a spot on the map, one of thousands of graves. 'This one got out, I know that! You do too! This one got out. So they aren't all aligned, you lazy fat pig! How can they be aligned when they're already out? If they go at all, they're meant to go all at once! People are going to see them now. They'll have time to react!'

'React how? They won't know what to do whether it's one or a thousand. It's excuses with you, always excuses. Tell the truth, old man! You're a coward, you've bottled it. You thought you were tough enough, but you're not.'

'I've got a daughter to think of!' Clutching his arm again.

'A granddaughter. And she hates you.' Crosswell feels good about saying that. It's the knife he's been grasping for. He can wound deeply with this. 'She's never here.'

'Shut up.'

'She spends all of her time running away from you.' Numb fingers are clumsy and make for shoddy work, but he's been humming low and quiet when the old man speaks, low and quiet and deep in his throat, and the old man must be hurting because he's missed it, heard not one note, and Crosswell has two darts now, flimsy and uncertain ammunition. 'She's told us all.' A few more sucker punches to wear him down. Quick punches; Crosswell's shoulders are pouring fire. 'She's said it again and again…' he aims a dart towards his feet which are tied together with a light-whip that frazzles and spits '…how she's tired of the constant unending pressure…' If he hits his own heel it will burn far worse than his arms are. That's if the dart holds together long enough. '…and how she wants you to get the message already…' A very short hum, a directional note, a guide, he hopes.

'Shut up!'

'…and how she hates her parents for dying and leaving her stuck with you.'

All at once: the old man's face greys and pains, a storm-ball gathers in his knot-fingered hands, Crosswell wills the dart to fly.

The dart slices through the light-whip with a burst of shards. Gravity does the rest. His legs swing down fast, pulling the rest of him with them. A jerk at his arm sockets, the whole of his body weight dropping. He cries out louder than he ever has. The bonds around his wrists snap. He's falling. Hits the tabletop in a sitting position. Electric bolts fire across the top of his head, burn a streak through his hair, scorch a trough in his scalp. Two more shots fly too high.

No need for quiet now! Crosswell uses his pain, hollers a note loud and round, throws out his second dart. It shears the air, leaves a wake. The old man is crumbling, the exertion too much. The dart clips his ear, blasts off the lobe with a flesh-scorching flash.

The old man's finished.

Crosswell chooses to finish him anyway.

The third dart hits the centre of his chest. The old man hits the floor behind the table. Crosswell scrambles away even though he's certain it's over. Certain sometimes is not certain enough.

Caleb has heard all of this, and is sure now that Hell never ends.

122

She knocks and knocks and knocks because her guts say that Time is shrinking, and isn't that sick when once she thought there was so, so much?

Misha kneels, shouts through the letterbox, 'Hello? Caleb? You in there? I know you are!' Waits to listen for answers, for telltale shuffles or whispers. 'Damn it, Caleb, you answer this door right now!'

A cardigan and brown corduroy trousers appear in the hall, coming towards her quickly. She bounces up and away from the letterbox. It snaps shut, and she smooths herself upright as if she's been waiting patiently the whole time. The door opens. Her smile is that of a girl who does not ever bellow into people's houses. She needs Caleb, not to have a door slammed in her face by displeased grandparents.

She has time to think *same eyes*, then he grabs the front of her dress and drags her inside. A thousand horror stories shoot through Misha's head, all worse than revenants and haunted streets, all far too real; Vic Sweet's grabbing hands. His thick sweat. Rotting trees.

Too late to punch. Granddad's got her arms. And now they're in the living room. He plumps her down on a sofa, holds a hand up flat in her face before she can spring back up. 'If you care for my boy at all, you must listen. Time is short.' An echo returning to her in someone else's voice. 'Knowing Caleb, he is running towards trouble right now, and he is the only thing left that matters.' He takes hold of her chin, stares into her. Sunny green flecked brown. Like his. 'I might not be able to say any of this again. I'm fading, understand?' His hold is too firm for her to shake her head. 'Caleb, he's a bright boy, and stupid in so many ways. The world has hurt him badly, and it makes him desperate to put things right, makes him certain that misery must be fixable. He's gone up there with a head full of this foolishness.

My stupid boy thinks he can stop it all.'

Misha is all thumping heart. 'Maybe he can.'

'No! I made that mistake once! I thought I could set wrongs right, I thought I could get my revenge and everything would turn out okay. I had no idea what's out there, what's coming!'

'That's great. Is Caleb up Daisy Hill?'

'That's what I'm trying to tell you. He's going to try to talk that lunatic round. He's stupid enough to believe there's an element of humanity in him. That man has been working for years and years bringing every single dead soul up there back. There's not one bit of good left in him. He's warped; he doesn't think the world deserves to carry on.' Misha almost laughs. If Gramps here knew the truth, what would he do to her? 'I've been up there, I've seen it all myself.' He lets go of her chin, picks up the journal. 'I wrote it all in here! I forgot, but now I remember, but it's all going again!'

'Okay, Mister, if I'm going to catch up with Caleb...'

'Go now, yes! Keep him away from your grandfather. Bring him back to me, before I forget him. Please.'

'Don't worry,' she says. 'I won't let that horrible old man get him.' Misha hangs back in the doorway. 'You're sure he's up there?'

'Positive! He was very determined.'

She goes, and he wanders into the kitchen, where the light-map hovers. It shows a house next to Daisy Hill. There are blips inside it. More underneath it. A lot more.

On the wall is a photograph of a younger him with some woman. He does not know who that woman is.

123

Caleb can't hear any movements in there.

It's incredible how much noise his lungs seem to make. It's amazing how every bit of his body wants to twitch and itch and give him away. His nerves are electrified. Someone will step out of that room any second and see him.

124

Running.

She hates it.

She hears screaming as she heads towards the graveyard. To her left, distant, but real. People getting hurt. The Turning, it seemed like such a good way at getting back at them all, before it was actually happening.

Caleb, I need you.

125

Crosswell's plucking at the air. His hums summon particles together. Frantically he pulls them towards each other. Beyond table and chair legs he can see the collapsed old man, unmoving, possibly not even breathing. Possibly.

He's making a shield. He has little capacity left for anything else. He has to hope that one deflection is all he will need.

Ache cannot begin to describe the state of his muscles. A beating would not leave him feeling more bruised than this. He pushes with his feet, slides his back up the wall until he's mostly standing. The old man remains still. 'Didn't think it would end this way, did you?' he growls.

Once he's sure of his feet, he edges out of the room. No prodding the body to see if it will jump up to attack. The dead are coming. It is time for Crosswell to leave. Time to hide for a while. Ride out the tide, re-emerge behind it.

He never turns his back on the old man. Certain is sometimes not certain enough.

And two minutes after he's slunk away, Caleb gradually leans out to check the kitchen, still convinced Crosswell will be waiting for his face to appear.

The skin on Caleb's back won't stay still. The hatch is behind him. The walking corpses are down that hatch. The dead boys. It's a hatch that needs heavy things holding it down.

Foot-slide into the kitchen. There's only Misha's grandfather in here, a broken lump on the floor, light fragments skittering off his chest and dissipating. Caleb kneels beside him, plucks at the tiny dazzling fibres, his God-fingers closing on a field of stars. One crackles along his thumb, metallic blue tendrils tracing the whorls. He wants more but now they're all gone, back in the air.

And he sees that the old man is watching.

126

If she'd been a few seconds faster, Misha would have seen Crosswell stumble-walking down the east slope of Daisy Hill, and perhaps she could have reached a different conclusion. If Crosswell had been a little slower escaping, then she'd have wondered what he'd been doing at her house, and taken her anger out on him instead.

It's these little slices of time that change everything.

Without interruption, without distraction, she heads home. For once it isn't raining.

127

And in that underground labyrinth, from out of those grave-columns, the dead slide out, more of them, and more. And they swarm along the tunnels, and they will find the exits.

128

And Neuman watches, blaze-eyed, as the revenants pour towards fresh doors and garages and back yards, and all are blown open by escalating scales of notes, and in the middle of all these chaotic songs are screams.

129

There's a glimmer left at the farthest end of the forever-black tunnel of his iris, the last sparks of a life about to be shut out for good. Caleb has seen ghosts and walking corpses, but this is a man dying, a life ending, and some fibre deep in his core is reaching out, cannot bear to see this soul drift into the night.

Yet Caleb knows there is nothing he can do. Any help he calls for will be far too late. Even if they came in time, would they know how to fix what's been done? So Caleb lies on his side, and looks into those dying eyes, and holds the grandfather's hand, and tries very hard not to cry because this man should die seeing a smile, not distress. This is Caleb's responsibility.

His own mother lay dying like this, but he wasn't there.

The old man's voice comes from the far distance of his glimmer. 'Can't be stopped. That's why you're here, to stop it. But you can't.'

Caleb pushes worry and doubt away, doesn't want either in his voice. 'It's gonna be okay, I know it. You held them off for so long doing those Turnings, right?'

'Delayed the inevitable. And once they're out...'

'There's always a way! I can get Misha to help. She's powerful, isn't she? She'll stop this.'

'She doesn't want to.' It's said with total defeat.

'She will help. When Misha sees all the dead and what they'll do...'

'This world...it's hurt her too many times. She wants it gone. I know. Tried so long.'

The anger comes in a rush. Caleb's trying to soothe this dying man, this grandfather to the girl he loves, yet he's saying everything he doesn't want to hear. 'No, she'll listen, of course she will...'

'Misha will not listen to you. Just run. Hide if you can.'

'That's bull!' Caleb moves away, up on his knees. 'You're

wrong! I won't let it happen! I won't let it end like this, I'll make her see!'

Her voice is an ice-knife slice. 'What have you done?' Caleb snaps round to see Misha on the other side of the table. She's taken back Eight. 'What have you done to my granddaddy?'

Caleb is all surprise and confusion. 'I didn't...'

'Get away from him!' she screams, and her skirts flare out and her hair bursts wide despite no wind, and her hands whip up in front of her, palms out, fingers splayed with sparks rushing to them, gluing to her skin. The table bursts apart, like a giant foot has kicked it from underneath. Caleb falls away from the chunks of wood, out of the kitchen, lands on the point of his elbow. The pain is a javelin from wrist to armpit. Misha's speaking, probably to her granddad. Caleb can't concentrate on any of it. He curls up around his numb arm, back to the wall, sure the agony won't end. He soon realises that the high-pitched squeal is coming from him.

He also realises that Misha has gone silent.

She's staring at her grandfather. The light has gone from his eyes. Her arms hang at her sides. Eight dangles in her right hand. No, not quite. There's an inch of space and light between palm and Eight. Tiny lightning strikes crackle through this gap.

The crackle. The electric-tension.

Eight rotates to the flex of her fingers. Levitates up to her eye level. 'Did he do this?' she asks and Eight, who cannot lie, answers: BLOOD ON HANDS. And she turns her burning glare onto Caleb, and sees what she's been told to. Caleb's been through blood and dirt and more. He's been through it all.

'Misha, whatever it's said...'

She sets the ball spinning hundreds of revolutions a minute, and Eight has one more message for him: I WARNED YOU.

With thumb and forefinger Misha pinches hold of the very air itself, and there is light everywhere, swirling and surging like water. She pulls and lashes upwards. A whooshing streak blasts across the room, ploughing through floorboards, piling into the wall by Caleb's head. Plaster chunks and sparks tear into his ear, his cheek.

Numb arms are distant memories.

He jumps up, clutching his torn face, diving away from the demon in Misha's dress. She doesn't sing the controlling notes, she screams them as she thrashes up and left, and up go Caleb's feet. Airborne, flipping, upside-down, paintings and maps and wallpaper on fire as chunks are torn from the walls, four long troughs as if ripped through by massive talons.

He lands and rolls, and Eight's words are projected down the hall, spinning. I HATE YOU I HATE YOU I HATE YOU I HATE YOU in nine foot letters, and just as Caleb gets to his feet, he is knocked to the floor again, the air suddenly a solid weight that presses him down, and there's lightning in the house and it blows out all the windows.

'I came for you, Caleb!' Her voice is as loud as the lightning. 'I came to save you!' He's sliding down the hall and the trapdoor flips open. He's sliding to the trapdoor, back towards the underground. He can't grab hold of anything to stop himself. 'You're worse than any of them! I hate you, Caleb!' Hands reaching out of the basement. Grey, dusty hands ready to pull him down and never let go.

Misha wails a double note, layering them, and adds another, and it feels like the whole house tips and Caleb accelerates and

stops, and the notes stop too, and the air thins out, and the crawling electricity falls from the ceiling in shimmering sheets. Caleb looks back. Vic Sweet has Misha pinned by her throat to the doorframe, clawing at her clothing. He squeezes. No voice to make notes with, only rough choking.

Getting to his feet is Caleb's mountain to climb.

Vic will kill her if Caleb doesn't stop him.

Misha was going to kill Caleb.

He can't let her die.

Can't let anyone else die.

Up, and starting to run, every single muscle telling him to stop.

Eight, skittering across the floor, spinning, shooting out letters.

M O T H E R I S D E A D

F A T H E R I S D E A D

C A L E B I S N E X T

Massive letters crawling around the walls.

Misha finger-clicking, hard and loud snaps, fast rhythm.

Vic's huge hand squeezing, arm bulging.

Caleb running; the hall must be stretching; they're so far away. Click click click

Vic's grip slackens. He's pulsating. With each click click click

A wet explosion. A world turned red. A wave splashes over Caleb, thick and hot. The force pushes him backwards, clawing the splatter from his eyes, his mouth. He retreats while Misha, crimson, still gasps for air because

C A L E B I S N E X T

The words spin white-on-red in this hallway of gore.

She's still whooping for breath as he staggers into a room. It's hers, and he leaves bloody handprints on the surfaces, struggling to hold himself up.

She did that, Misha did that.

She could do that to anyone.

C A L E B I S N E X T

She can do anything she thinks of.

She can take the world, the very world itself, and turn it against anyone. She can turn it.

He has to get out, but now the house is *ROARING*

130

Hauling air down her ragged throat, Misha looks up in time to see Caleb stumble into her bedroom and he cannot leave, she's chased him all over this town and he is

NOT LEAVING NOW.

'Not leaving now!'

Her splattered hands are out at her sides, grab bunches of air squeeze and

lift

and it resists and pushes back and doesn't want to move and Misha is all blood and fury and everything *will* go her way.

She grips and twists.

Spark showers pour from her fists and the house ROARS and it starts to tear loose, a tooth from the gum, a tree from its roots. The undead crawling out of the basement fall away as the house and its foundations rip themselves free of the earth, and it rises up and up and up.

131

Caleb slides and tumbles down Daisy Hill, chunks of soil and concrete dropping off the bottom of the levitating building. A huge hole has opened up, a slice taken off the top of the basement labyrinth, letting all the dead out.

Caleb can't care about that. He has to be out of sight before Misha realises he slipped and tore his way out of the window. His arms and side are bleeding from the ragged window frame and that is infinitely better than having her click click click those fingers.

The whole hill shudders and jumbles, crashing him into gravestones, more hard, dark bruises. It feels like a limb being pulled off the planet, like he'll be torn away next. He throws himself in amongst trees and collapses. Flat on his back. Chest heaving. Torn arms burning. The earth rumbling under him as lumps of concrete crash down into the labyrinth.

He looks up at Daisy Hill. At the house in the air above it. At the dead things dragging themselves out of the hole. A graveyard torn open. The guts of the Underworld spilled forth. The plug pulled.

Caleb knows he should run, but he has no run left.

132

Crawl is the last option left, and it brings him here, to this graveside, because where else could he ever go?

He is on hands and knees above her, he is blood and dirt all over, he looks like the corpses stumbling down Daisy Hill. 'Why won't you come back?' he asks, heart aching like it did the day she left. 'Why didn't you ever come back? I need you! I've always needed you!' He thumps the ground, both fists. 'Even Dad came back! Where are you? People who hate me are coming back, so where are you, Mum?' Through all of this he has needed her, and she hasn't returned. The only ones that have, in his street, underground, in the gardens, are murderous, deadly. Mum could not be one of them. His own mum couldn't. His own mum won't come back to him.

Caleb, the hated boy.

He screams, a note all his own. It is everything he cannot say, everything he wanted to tell Misha, everything he's never been able to tell anyone. Mum said she'd stay forever but now she's nowhere at all, and he screams on her grave as the dead descend Daisy Hill.

133

I waited in that house for three days, listening to the scratchings in the tunnels beneath me, knowing she was outside amongst the gravestones, biding her time. I waited for her to come to me, no sleep and no need of it. I waited while her dark shape shuddered across the hill.

I waited, until at last my Evelyn came to the door, and we met that final time.

Lodestone Books

YOUNG ADULT FICTION

Lodestone Books offers a new imprint, which offers a broad spectrum of subjects in YA/NA literature. Compelling reading, the Teen/Young/New Adult reader is sure to find something edgy, enticing and innovative. From dystopian societies, through a whole range of fantasy, horror, science fiction and paranormal fiction, all the way to the other end of the sphere, historical drama, steampunk adventure, and everything in between (including crime, coming of age and contemporary romance). Whatever your preference you will discover it here.

If you have enjoyed this book, why not tell other readers by posting a review on your preferred book site. Recent bestsellers from Lodestone Books are:

AlphaNumeric

Nicolas Forzy

When dyslexic teenager Stu accidentally transports himself into a world populated by living numbers and letters, his arrival triggers a prophecy that pulls two rival communities into war.

Paperback: 978-1-78279-506-3 ebook: 978-1-78279-505-6

Shanti and the Magic Mandala
F.T. Camargo
In this award-winning YA novel, six teenagers from around the world gather for a frantic chase across Peru, in search of a sacred object that can stop The Black Magicians' final plan.
Paperback: 978-1-78279-500-1 ebook: 978-1-78279-499-8

Time Sphere
A timepathway book
M.C. Morison
When a teenage priestess in Ancient Egypt connects with a school-boy on a visit to the British Museum, they each come under threat as they search for Time's Key.
Paperback: 978-1-78279-330-4 ebook: 978-1-78279-329-8

Bird Without Wings
FAEBLES
Cally Pepper
Sixteen-year-old Scarlett has had more than her fair share of problems, but nothing prepares her for the day she discovers she's growing wings…
Paperback: 978-1-78099-902-9 ebook: 978-1-78099-901-2

Briar Blackwood's Grimmest of Fairytales
Timothy Roderick
After discovering she is the fabled Sleeping Beauty, a brooding goth-girl races against time to undo her deadly fate.
Paperback: 978-1-78279-922-1 ebook: 978-1-78279-923-8

Escape from the Past
The Duke's Wrath
Annette Oppenlander
Trying out an experimental computer game, a fifteen-year-old boy unwittingly time-travels to medieval Germany where he must not

only survive but figure out a way home.
Paperback: 978-1-84694-973-9 ebook: 978-1-78535-002-3

Holding On and Letting Go
K.A. Coleman
When her little brother died, Emerson's life came crashing down around her. Now she's back home and her friends want to help, but can Emerson fight to re-enter the world she abandoned?
Paperback: 978-1-78279-577-3 ebook: 978-1-78279-576-6

Midnight Meanders
Annika Jensen
As William journeys through his own mind, revelations are made, relationships are broken and restored, and a faith that once seemed extinct is renewed.
Paperback: 978-1-78279-412-7 ebook: 978-1-78279-411-0

Reggie & Me
The First Book in the Dani Moore Trilogy
Marie Yates
The first book in the Dani Moore Trilogy, Reggie & Me explores a teenager's search for normalcy in the aftermath of rape.
Paperback: 978-1-78279-723-4 ebook: 978-1-78279-722-7

Unconditional
Kelly Lawrence
She's in love with a boy from the wrong side of town...
Paperback: 978-1-78279-394-6 ebook: 978-1-78279-393-9

Readers of ebooks can buy or view any of these bestsellers by clicking on the live link in the title. Most titles are published in paperback and as an ebook. Paperbacks are available in traditional bookshops. Both print and ebook formats are available online.

Find more titles and sign up to our readers' newsletter at http://www.johnhuntpublishing.com/children-and-young-adult Follow us on Facebook at https://www.facebook.com/JHPChildren and Twitter at https://twitter.com/JHPChildren